A Criminal Affair

By the same author

The Unaccomplished Lady Eleanor
The Meticulous Messenger

A Criminal Affair

Wendy Burdess

ROBERT HALE · LONDON

First published in Great Britain 2008

ISBN 978-0-7090-8724-3

Robert Hale Limited
Clerkenwell House
Clerkenwell Green
London EC1R 0HT

www.halebooks.com

2 4 6 8 10 9 7 5 3 1

Typeset in 11/14½pt Garamond
Printed and bound in Great Britain by
MPG Biddles Limited, King's Lynn

For my wonderful parents

Chapter One

ALTHOUGH it is said that patience is an admirable virtue, it was not one that was featuring strongly amongst the Hamilton sisters that particular day.

'For goodness sake, Charlotte, if you do not come out soon, I shall die on this very spot of a severe case of anticipation,' declared 17-year-old Harriet Hamilton stoutly.

In the plush blue dressing-room of the London mantuamaker, Charlotte Hamilton, her sister's elder by some four years, made a futile effort to conceal her own impatience. Raising her eyes to the ceiling, she attempted a calming breath, before retorting, 'Do be quiet, Harriet. I have just told you that I shall be out in five minutes.'

'But that *was* five minutes ago,' countered Harriet. 'And you said exactly the same thing five minutes before that.'

'Then by the mere passing of time, you should assume that it will be any moment now,' expostulated Charlotte, who was feeling every bit as irritated as her sister by the protracted session. She had been standing still for what seemed like an age while the wretched woman stuck pins into her dress. Suppressing a sigh, she looked down at the mantuamaker who had finally moved her concentration from the bodice of the gown to the hem and was, quite literally, kneeling at Charlotte's feet. Charlotte studied the top of the woman's head – her obviously once red hair, now dull and streaked with grey, was gathered in a bun from which several wispy tendrils had escaped. She had come highly recommended and Charlotte could tell that she was taking a great deal of pride in her work.

Work that, she chided herself silently, she should be appreciating. But the mantuamaker, as Charlotte was well aware, was not to blame for her irritation. The problem was that she was tired; so very, very tired. Sleep over the last few weeks had done a successful job of evading her and last night had been no exception. As she lay in her bed, thoughts had once again relentlessly bombarded her mind like a torrent of heavy lead cannon balls.

She started as she realized the woman had vacated her position on the floor and was now standing opposite her, alongside a full-length gilded mirror.

'My,' she exclaimed, through a grin of crooked teeth, 'if I'm not mistaken, you are going to look a relative little peacock when you walk down that aisle.'

The notion of resembling a bird on her wedding day paled into insignificance as the dread enveloped Charlotte at the mere thought of walking down the aisle. She managed a weak smile in response to the woman's compliment before turning her attention to the mirror. The sight before her did little to improve her mood. Her normally creamy skin had adopted a distinctly grey pallor; her mane of black hair was lacking its usual lustre and there were dark shadows under each of her large hazel eyes. Perhaps it would not be so bad looking like a peacock after all, she pondered, for she was certain they did not demonstrate such unattractive features when they were tired. Moving on to examine the dress, she was relieved to see that it appeared to be faring much better. This was only her second fitting, but it was clear that the mantuamaker was making impressive progress.

'*That* is another five minutes. Surely you are ready now, Charlotte,' called an indignant Harriet, bringing an abrupt end to her sister's musings.

Taking a step to the side, the mantuamaker drew back the blue velvet curtain, which separated the dressing-room from the main body of the shop, and gestured to Charlotte to step through. She did as the woman bid, walking over to the red velvet *chaise-longue* on which her sister had made herself comfortable.

'Really, Harriet,' she scolded, 'I do wish you would learn a little more restraint. It really does not do at all to be so impatient.'

Harriet opened her mouth to protest at the rebuke. But, as her older sibling came to stand before her, she suddenly found herself in the unfamiliar predicament of being lost for words.

Charlotte widened her eyes and placed her hands on her slender hips. '*Well?*' she demanded in mock exasperation. 'Don't tell me you have nothing to say after creating such a fuss.'

Harriet gulped. 'Goodness,' she uttered. 'I can scarce believe that my own sister is to look as fine as a princess on her wedding day.'

Despite her low spirits, Charlotte could not resist a smile at the look of amazement on her sister's pretty round face, framed with chestnut curls. 'Well, I doubt very much that I shall look anywhere near as grand as a princess, but the gown is certainly going to be beautiful. Now come along and help me out of it, Harriet. It is time we were making our way home. Poor Albert will be worrying about us, we have been gone so long.'

With the aid of both her sister and the mantuamaker, Charlotte managed to escape the confines of the dress with surprisingly few pricks and scratches from the profusion of pins. Donning her pale blue carriage gown, she and Harriet then bid their farewells and, accompanied by their footman, made their way to their carriage, which was awaiting them at the end of the cobbled street.

It was mid-September and, for all it had been a bright day, there was little doubt that autumn was making a concerted effort to exert its presence, the days rapidly becoming shorter and the evenings distinctly cooler.

'Gosh,' shivered Harriet, as they marched briskly towards their destination. 'I didn't realize it was quite so late or so cold. Poor Albert must be freezing by now.'

'I know,' agreed Charlotte, pulling a rueful face. 'I had no idea the woman was going to take so long. It will be quite dark before we arrive home.'

As they neared the end of the street, Charlotte spotted Albert amongst the half-dozen other carriage drivers, who were waiting in the small square. She was relieved to see that he had wrapped up well against the fresh evening air.

'Albert, I'm sorry we are so late,' she said, as they approached the carriage. 'I was hoping we would have been home by now, but the mantuamaker took an interminable amount of time sorting out the bodice of the dress and I—'

'Now you know it don't normally matter to me how late you are, miss,' cut in Albert, from his driver's seat, 'but I reckon we'd best be making haste this evening. Not only will your father be worrying about you, as he does, but Mrs Tomms is making one of her beef stews and if I'm not back in time, our William'll be helping himself to the lot.'

Charlotte and Harriet exchanged a furtive look, each daring the other not to laugh. Not, of course, that Albert would have found anything at all amusing in his observation. Food for Albert Tomms was a very serious business indeed and one which was constantly at the forefront of his mind.

'Well, in that case, Albert,' said Charlotte, in as serious a tone as she could muster, 'we should indeed make haste. Come along now, Harriet. Albert's supper is at stake here.'

With the two girls ensconced within and their footman in his rumble seat at the back, the carriage rattled along the cobbled streets of the capital. Darkness was beginning to wind its way around the city giving it a ghostly air. Charlotte tried to relax against the green velvet squabs. She closed her eyes and tucked the travelling rug under her chin in an attempt to stop the shivers flitting up and down her spine. The soft wool did nothing to warm her though, for it was not the cold that was making her shiver, but the same thoughts that kept her awake at night. Strange, she pondered, that these thoughts caused her body to shiver during daylight hours and yet, in the still of the night, the brief snatches of sleep she did manage, ended abruptly and she found herself lying in a pool of sweat. Her hand crept up to the pearl necklace hanging around her neck – her late mother's necklace – without which she was rarely seen. She closed her fingers around it. Her mother would know what to do; her mother had always known what to do. But, if her mother had still been alive, Charlotte had no doubt that the dreadful situation in which she now found herself would not exist. Her musings were interrupted as Harriet turned to her, the whites of her eyes shining brightly in the dim light of the carriage.

'Have you heard, Charlotte, about the dashing highwayman they are calling the Courteous Criminal?'

Charlotte's level tone belied the fact that she gratefully welcomed the distraction. 'I should think, Harriet,' she replied, 'that there is not a person in the whole of the south of England who has not heard of the man.'

A wave of excitement washed over Harriet's face. 'He is, they say, extremely handsome and positively charming.'

Charlotte tutted. 'How on earth can a man be described as "positively charming" when he is holding a pistol to your head?'

'That I cannot say for certain, of course,' sighed Harriet dreamily. 'But imagine being held up by a dashing, handsome stranger. I think it should be quite the most thrilling thing.'

Charlotte rolled her eyes. 'My dear Harriet, you are obviously spending far too much time reading those romantic novels of yours. Personally, I cannot think of anything worse than to be staring down the barrel of a pistol whilst some criminal demands your jewels.'

Harriet appeared not to hear as she gazed pensively out of the window. Then, turning her eyes to her sister once more, she said, 'Oh, I do hope that *I* meet a dashing, handsome gentleman during my come-out next Season, Charlotte. I do *so* want a husband who is handsome.'

'A handsome husband is all very well, Harriet,' pointed out Charlotte, with more than a hint of exasperation, 'but what of his other qualities? Do you not wish for a man who loves you, who treats you kindly and respects your opinions? A man who will make you happy?'

'Oh, of course,' replied Harriet, waving her hand in dismissal. 'All of that, too. But I am certain I could not even begin to love a man who was not handsome.'

Charlotte shook her head, incredulity sweeping through her at her sister's naive view of the world.

'Of course Mirabelle says,' continued the younger girl earnestly, 'that one should not be distracted by such minor diversions as good looks. Mirabelle says that the most important thing is that one's husband is rich. Mirabelle says she would not even consider a man with less than twenty thousand a year.'

'Does she indeed?' remarked Charlotte, feeling the familiar prickling of irritation at Harriet's mention of her best friend.

Harriet nodded. 'And Mirabelle also says that, due to his large fortune, your Lord Farrell is one of the most sought-after gentlemen in the whole of England. Mirabelle has heard that he is in receipt of ...' – she paused, as if to divulge the very greatest of secrets – 'at least *thirty thousand* a year.'

If Harriet was expecting her sister to demonstrate a favourable reaction to this apparently extraordinary revelation, she was sorely disappointed.

'Really?' uttered Charlotte, her voice betraying nothing of the contempt she felt for Mirabelle McGregor who, at little more than eight-and-ten was far too worldly for her years and an indisputably bad influence on Harriet.

But, oblivious to her sister's scornful tone and low opinion of her friend, Harriet was blithely continuing with her speech. 'And Mirabelle also says, Charlotte, that you should consider yourself very lucky to have snared such a catch. During the Season, Mirabelle says that London was positively swarming with young ladies who had set their caps at Lord Farrell.'

Charlotte stiffened. 'You may tell Mirabelle,' she retorted angrily, 'that I did not *snare* Lord Farrell. Indeed I was scarcely aware of the man's existence before he offered for me.'

At that moment the carriage met an unexpected pothole, causing it to jolt sharply. As both girls braced themselves against the seat cushions, Charlotte drew in a calming breath, grateful that the uncomfortable conversation had been brought to an end. Biting her lower lip, she turned her head towards the window, burning with a combination of anger and self-contempt.

Of course, she knew what the odious Mirabelle McGregor said was true: there were indeed many young ladies who would be more than delighted to be marrying into the prestigious Farrell family and there was good reason why: the family was one of England's finest, their ancestral roots being traced back as far as William the Conqueror. Having been held in great favour by King William, and the majority of his successors, the Farrells were now one of the largest landowners in England, residing in the imposing Wetherington Hall. But, unlike most young ladies, such affluence did little to impress Charlotte. During her one-and-twenty years, she had discovered a strong correlation between persons with an abundance of wealth and those with a deficit of personality. The larger the fortune, she had long ago concluded, the more self-obsessed, pompous and egotistical the person. She therefore did her utmost to avoid the grandiose gatherings where such unsavoury personalities were generally to be found. Very occasionally, though, she was forced to succumb to social pressure and it was on one such occasion, having reluctantly agreed to accompany her father to a predictably dull engagement, that she had first found herself in the company of Frederick Farrell.

Having exchanged nothing more than polite greetings with Lord Farrell during the dreary evening, Charlotte was more than a little amazed when the man had called upon her and her father the following day and had, thereafter, continued to make regular calls to Hamilton Manor. Demonstrating no more than the same degree of acceptable courtesy she would extend to any visitor in which she had little or no interest, Charlotte was completely dumbfounded when, after three weeks of such visits, her father had taken her to one side and informed her that Lord Farrell had asked for her hand in marriage.

Lord Hamilton, naturally, had been as stunned as Charlotte herself and had urged her to think over the proposal carefully. Charlotte had thought of little else for a full week before she eventually confided her decision to her father. She had done an admirable job of convincing him that, in time, she did believe she could love Lord Farrell and that she was certain he would prove a worthy husband. That was a little over two weeks ago and the wedding date had been set for the beginning of November – less than two months away. Of course, Charlotte was aware that, under normal circumstances, she would not have given the proposal a second thought. Lord Farrell was a pompous, whingeing popinjay whom she knew she could *never* love and who would definitely *not* make a worthy husband. But circumstances were far from normal; they were in fact desperate, and the only way Charlotte could see to salvage the situation had been – with a heavy heart – to accept Lord Farrell's offer.

Chapter Two

AS their carriage swung through the gates of Hamilton Manor, some forty minutes later, and the beautiful house came into view, Charlotte experienced a rush of reassuring warmth. Her grandfather had commissioned the building some fifty years before. Built of stone the colour of golden butter, the house was entirely symmetrical, with three rows of floor-to-ceiling windows. Entry was gained by climbing the four wide steps to the imposing oak door, guarded by two stone pillars and a triangular portico bearing the Hamilton family crest. A long, gravelled driveway wound its way up to the house, fanning into a semi-circular courtyard at the front and leading around to a stable block at the rear. The building was one of the most fashionable and elegant examples of architecture in the south of England. Enveloped now, in a blanket of velvety darkness, its windows filled with orange candlelight, it glowed warmly like a precious, glistening jewel.

Albert drew a halt in front of the entrance and the footman immediately sprang to his duties, opening the carriage door and pulling down the steps.

'Thank you, Jenkins,' said Harriet, as she alighted from the conveyance. 'And you too, Albert. I do hope we are in time for your stew.'

'At this hour it's touch 'n' go, miss,' sighed Albert, still perched in the driving seat. 'But never you be minding about me.' He indicated a small curricle tethered to the rail at the side of the house. 'It looks like you've got a visitor.'

Harriet turned to peer at the gig. 'Oh my,' she gushed. 'I do so love it when we have visitors. Who do you think it could be, Charlotte?'

Charlotte, gathering up her skirts in preparation for her descent, popped her head out of the carriage and squinted at the outline of the unfamiliar conveyance. 'I have no idea,' she confessed. 'But I am sure we shall find out soon enough.'

With both girls safely deposited on the ground, Albert drove the carriage around to the stables at the back of the house. The weighty front door, meanwhile, was slowly heaved open by another member of the household staff. Adams, the butler, was a thin man of some fifty-plus years. He sported sharp, hollow features, a distinctly grey pallor, thinning grey hair and a rather perturbing ghost-like presence. He wandered about the house so silently, popping up when one least expected him, that Charlotte would not have been at all surprised to learn that he had come from a different world to that which he currently inhabited.

'Good evening, my ladies,' he declared solemnly, holding open the door and bowing his head to them.

'Good evening, Adams,' chorused the girls, as they glided past him into the large, square, wood-panelled entrance hall. The warmth from the enormous fire crackling in the grate instantly enveloped their slender frames.

'Your father asked that you join him upstairs the minute you arrive, my lady,' announced the servant, as Charlotte untied her bonnet strings.

Charlotte wrinkled her brow. 'Upstairs?' she repeated. 'What on earth is he doing upstairs at this early hour?'

The butler released a heavy sigh. 'He is with Master Edward, ma'am. The young master was attempting another of his experiments this afternoon – relating, I believe, to the theory of gravity. The experiment involved him climbing a tree.'

Charlotte grimaced. 'Oh no. Not again, Adams.'

'I am afraid so, ma'am,' said the butler gravely.

'Ugh. That boy really is the most tiresome of brothers,' declared Harriet, with more than a hint of vexation. 'Well, what has he broken this time, Adams?' she demanded, as she shrugged her arms from her pelisse. 'It's not his wrist again, is it? That would be the third time in two years.'

'I believe there are no broken bones, my lady,' informed the servant. 'Although both of his legs, so I have been reliably informed, have been damaged.'

'Oh,' groaned Harriet, screwing up her features. 'Well, if he is unable to walk, he will be positively unbearable. The last time he was confined to his chamber, he made me run up and down the stairs to him at least twenty times a day. I shall go to him at once, the wretched boy.' And with that, she tossed her pelisse and bonnet to Adams, sprinted to the branching marble staircase and bounded up the stairs two at a time. Charlotte, having rid herself of her outdoor garments, followed, albeit at a much more sedate pace.

Edward's bedchamber was a large, light, square room situated at the front of the manor with uninterrupted views of the drive and the surrounding countryside. A door to the right of the bedchamber led to a drawing-room and a door to the left, to a dressing area and one of the more recent additions to the house, a private bathroom. All the rooms were decorated in Edward's favourite shade of peacock-blue which, in Charlotte's opinion, suited her 13-year-old brother perfectly, combining both masculinity and elegance.

Edward was laid atop the embroidered counterpane of his four-poster bed. Despite the fact that his mop of light-brown hair was somewhat tousled and there was not a trace of colour in his usual rosy cheeks, he still looked as handsome as ever. His knee breeches left his audience in little doubt as to the extent of his injuries. The area around his right knee, upon which a poultice was resting, had swollen to almost twice its normal proportions, while part of his left calf was heavily bandaged.

Having made her ascent with unprecedented haste, Harriet was already in the room when Charlotte arrived. Perched on the side of Edward's bed, she was mid-flow, telling her brother, in no uncertain terms, exactly what she thought of his latest calamity.

'Hello, Charlotte,' sighed Edward wearily, interrupting his sister's ranting. 'How good of you to come and see me. Harriet was just telling me how I do not deserve any visitors. I am, apparently, nothing but a constant source of anguish to you all.'

'Well, that I certainly cannot deny, Edward,' proclaimed Charlotte, as she walked over to him. 'How are you feeling?'

'A little sore,' he replied with a grimace. 'But it could have been worse.'

'Indeed it could,' agreed Harriet stoutly. 'I do wish you would stop all these daredevil experiments of yours, Edward. Goodness only knows what you will do to yourself next.'

'But I couldn't possibly stop, Harriet,' informed Edward, with mock solemnity. 'What on earth would happen to the world of science if I brought an end to my experiments? And besides, how else am I ever to become famous and have my name recorded in the history books if I do not discover some exciting new phenomenon?'

'If you wish to be recorded in the history books, Brother dear,' pointed out Charlotte, 'I should think you will be required to live a little longer. Why do you not engage in something a little less life threatening? Something more sedate like … like writing? That is an altogether more *normal* activity.'

'Ah, but therein lies the problem you see,' giggled Edward, the accident having evidently quashed none of his mischievous spirit. 'I'm afraid there is nothing at all *normal* about me.'

'That,' agreed Charlotte, as she lowered herself into the chair at the side of her brother's bed, 'is perfectly obvious to us all, Edward.'

'A fact which I entirely endorse, ma'am,' concurred a deep, masculine voice.

Startled by the unexpected presence of a stranger, Charlotte whipped her head around to find a tall, broad-shouldered gentleman approaching from the bathroom. Contrary to the polished, contrived appearance of most gentlemen of her acquaintance, Charlotte's initial thought was that this man was somewhat unkempt. He was wearing a crumpled white linen shirt, which was open at the neck, and a black unbuttoned waistcoat. His tight yellow pantaloons were tucked into dusty hessian boots and his thick dark hair hung in loose waves to his shoulders. His eyes were so dark they were almost black and were observing Charlotte's obvious appraisal of him with a twinkle of humour. Colour swept over her cheeks as her second thought, rapidly replacing the first, was that, shoddy appearance notwithstanding, this was quite the most handsome man she had ever encountered. He came to a standstill alongside her chair.

'With a *normal* patient,' he continued, his tone lilting with amusement, 'I would not have to threaten them with amputation in order to have them lie still long enough for me to bandage their leg.'

Harriet and Edward giggled, whilst Charlotte could not help but smile.

'Charlotte. Harriet. I believe you have not yet made the acquaintance of Dr Daniel Leigh,' said Edward, ever mindful of his excellent manners. 'Doctor, these are my two sisters, Lady Charlotte Hamilton and Lady Harriet Hamilton.'

The doctor flashed both girls a dazzling smile and inclined his head. 'Delighted to meet you, my ladies.'

Charlotte gulped. Wholly disconcerted by the man's good looks, it was all she could do to offer a croaky, 'And, er, we you, Doctor,' in reply.

'Although I must say I do not envy you your task, Dr Leigh,' piped up Harriet, her vocal skills clearly not affected at all by the man's presence. 'Edward is quite the most tiresome of patients, despite all the practice he has had.'

The doctor grinned at his young charge. 'Oh, I can assure you I have had much worse, ma'am.'

Before the physician had a chance to elaborate on his remark, the bedchamber door was thrust open and in marched the rotund figure of Lord Hamilton. His head of thick grey curls was in its usual state of disarray, with a particularly wayward tuft jutting out at a right-angle directly above his left ear. 'Now then, now then,' he boomed. 'What's the diagnosis? Will the boy live, Doctor?'

'I believe so, sir,' replied Dr Leigh, continuing to smile. 'However, because he landed with his right leg bent, it has caused serious damage to the ligaments around the knee. The cut on the left leg, meanwhile, although it does not require stitches, is still relatively deep and must be kept scrupulously clean. I recommend the dressing be changed daily. All in all, my lord, this young man has been extremely lucky to have escaped without any broken bones. But, I am afraid that, despite that fact, it will still be quite some time before he is up on his feet again. The best cure I can recommend for the ligaments is a few weeks' complete rest.'

Edward groaned loudly. 'Complete rest! But what of my experiments, Doctor? The world of science may well collapse without my input.'

'Never mind about the blasted world of science,' declared Lord Hamilton. 'At least the rest of us won't have to concern ourselves with being blown up or having flying bricks falling on our heads for the next few weeks.'

At this observation, all five of the room's occupants began laughing, but the smile on Charlotte's face did not last long, as her father turned his attention to her.

'Now, Charlotte, I bumped into Lord Farrell earlier today and invited him and his family to dinner this evening. They will be arriving shortly so I suggest you two girls run off and carry out those preparations you young ladies always deem so necessary.'

Charlotte's stomach began to churn. 'Th–the Farrells, Father? Coming to dinner? Here? This evening? But-but why?'

'Why?' boomed the old man jovially. 'Because we shall shortly all be family, that's why. And I thought it a marvellous opportunity for us to become better acquainted.'

'B-but don't you think it best to cancel, Father?' blustered Charlotte. 'After all, none of us has yet made the acquaintance of Frederick's sister, Perdita. And what with Edward's accident. We could put them off until another evening. One when it is more convenient. When Harriet and I do not have to rush to—'

'Poppycock,' interjected Lord Hamilton. 'If we all cancelled our social engagements because of Edward's misdemeanours, then none of us would ever go anywhere. Besides, I thought you would be delighted to be presented with the opportunity to spend an evening in the company of your fiancé.'

Charlotte bit her tongue, resisting the urge to say that she should prefer to remove one of her own toes than spend the evening in the company of Frederick Farrell. But, as she gaped haplessly at her father, the old man evidently noted nothing of her despair, directing his next comment to the doctor.

'You will, I hope, do us the honour of joining us for dinner, Dr Leigh?'

The physician, who, Charlotte noticed, had been regarding her with a questioning expression, diverted his eyes to the timepiece on the mantel. Upon noting the hour his features twisted into a rueful expression. 'That is exceedingly kind of you, my lord, but I'm afraid I shall have to decline. I have a long ride back to my lodging, you see and it is already—'

'Nonsense,' cut in the older man. 'You shall stay for dinner and I will have a room made up in order that you may spend the night. No need to be gadding about the countryside when we shall only require you to come all the way back in the morning to check on the rascal.'

'Ah-hem,' piped up Edward. 'I assume by "rascal" you are referring to your one and only beloved son, Father?'

'I am referring to the one and only rascal in the family,' rejoined Lord Hamilton, in equally good humour. 'Now come along everyone – up and at it. We don't want the Farrells thinking we are a load of disorganized nodcocks.'

'But we are, Father,' remarked Harriet playfully.

'Yes, well, it's all very good us knowing that,' chuckled Lord Hamilton, 'but best not let the Farrells in on it, eh?'

Chapter Three

THE door to the crimson drawing-room creaked open slowly. The party seated round the fireplace swivelled their heads around to observe it. The doctor's dark eyes grew wide as the door's opening appeared to completely lack human intervention. Growing a shade paler, the physician gulped and seemed to be on the verge of voicing some supernatural concerns when in trooped a very grim-looking Adams.

'Lord Frederick Farrell, my lord,' he announced, in such a depressed tone that Charlotte should not have been at all surprised if he had then proceeded to burst into tears – a state from which she herself felt not a million miles removed. Fortunately, her father was demonstrating a good deal more fervour as Adams stepped aside to allow their dinner guest entry.

'Farrell, my dear boy,' he bellowed, thrusting to his feet and striding over to greet the bony figure hovering on the threshold. 'Delighted you could come.'

Flamboyantly attired in a high-collared shirt, silver breeches, striped waistcoat and blue tail-coat, the look on Frederick Farrell's cadaverous face was markedly less excited. 'My lord,' he replied, unsmilingly, as he inclined his head of perfectly coiffed, pale-red hair.

'But where are your mother and your sister? We are all so looking forward to making Perdita's acquaintance this evening,' enthused Lord Hamilton, peering behind their guest's gawky frame.

Frederick emitted a weary sigh. 'I have been forced to come alone, sir. My mother and my sister are somewhat indisposed. They wish me to convey their sincerest apologies.'

'Oh,' remarked Lord Hamilton dejectedly, then, injecting his tone with a large dose of enthusiasm, 'Well, that is indeed a great pity, but no matter. No matter at all. I am sure we shall all still have a marvellous evening. Now do come in, man.' He placed his arm around their astounded visitor's bony shoulders and led him into the room, steering him first in the direction of Dr Leigh.

'Now, let me introduce you to our other guest. Farrell, this is Dr Daniel Leigh, who is here to attend to young Edward. Doctor, this is Charlotte's fiancé, Lord Frederick Farrell.'

The two men exchanged the usual courtesies before Frederick lowered himself, with a grimace, into the chair next to that of his betrothed. 'Charlotte,' he muttered, tossing a cool glance in the girl's general direction.

'Lord Farrell,' mumbled Charlotte, with the small degree of zeal she could muster.

'Well,' chuckled Lord Hamilton, as he settled himself back into his armchair. 'Do you know, Farrell, that Edward has only gone and met with yet another accident this afternoon trying some experiment or other? I own, that boy is enough to try the patience of a saint.'

'Indeed,' sniffed Frederick, flicking a speck of imaginary dust from his sleeve. 'Then may I suggest a little more discipline, sir? It is my opinion that children should be neither seen nor heard.'

Whilst Charlotte emitted an audible gasp at this declaration, Frederick Farrell paid her no heed, turning his attention to Dr Leigh. 'I don't suppose, Doctor, that you have anything for the headache? I have had the most dreadfully taxing day and my head is positively pounding.' He closed his eyes, pressing two fingers to his right temple.

'Taxing day, my boy?' echoed Lord Hamilton. 'Nothing too disastrous, I hope?'

Frederick remained quite still with his eyes closed. 'Staff, sir,' he huffed. 'They really can be such a tiresome burden at times.'

'Not been caught pilfering, have they?' enquired Lord Hamilton, as he accepted a glass of claret from the footman.

This time Frederick deigned to open his eyes. His fingers remained pressed to his temple. 'I am having the most ghastly problems with my valet, sir. Not only did the man cut my face whilst shaving me this morning, but he prepared completely the wrong outfit. Who on earth wishes to be seen in black silk on a Tuesday, I ask you?' He flashed the look of a wronged victim around the group before closing his eyes again and resting his head on the back of the chair.

Charlotte glanced at the other members of the room and found every one of them regarding her fiancé with an unfathomable look upon their face. It was Harriet who eventually broke the silence.

'Oh, er, dear,' she muttered. 'How very, er, tiresome for you, Lord Farrell.'

'That it is,' sniffed Frederick, regarding Harriet through half-opened, watery-blue eyes. 'It is my considered opinion that people greatly underestimate the responsibility placed upon us members of the aristocracy. Sometimes, I confess, I find it a great deal to bear. So, Doctor, do you have anything?'

All eyes shifted to the doctor who was regarding Lord Farrell in exactly the same manner one might regard a three-headed elephant in a travelling fair.

'Wh-what?'

'Something for my headache, man?'

'Oh,' floundered the doctor, regaining something of his composure. 'Of course. Please excuse me for a moment. I shall make up a draught.'

Some minutes later, with the draught administered and Lord Farrell declaring that he was feeling a little revived, the party made their way into the dining-room. The rectangular room, decorated in shades of cream and apple-green, was one of the most charming in the house. In the middle stood a round, mahogany table, set with exquisite white china, heavy silver cutlery, two glittering candelabras, and a large crystal vase crammed with cream and orange roses. No sooner had the party taken their seats around the table, with Charlotte between her sister and her fiancé, than the footmen began serving the first course.

'Good lord,' declared Frederick, wrinkling his nose as the servant presented him with a bowl of tomato soup. 'I cannot eat this. Tomatoes have the most unpleasant effect on my constitution. Take it away at once, man.'

As the bewildered lackey did as he was bid, a look of confusion flittered over Lord Hamilton's countenance. 'Oh. Well, er, not to worry.

You'll have some of the baked carp though, I hope, Farrell? It is cook's speciality and the best I've ever tasted, even if I do say so myself.'

Frederick shuddered. 'Baked carp? Heavens, no! I cannot abide the stuff. No, a little cheese and some ham perhaps.'

'Oh. Of … course,' said Lord Hamilton, with a strained smile. 'Walters. Some cheese and ham for Lord Farrell.'

As the footman took his leave in order to carry out his instruction, another awkward silence descended over the party.

'Um, so,' began Lord Hamilton, 'how are your dear mother and sister, Farrell? I hope it is nothing serious that ails them this evening.'

Frederick shook his head before emitting a mournful sigh. 'Unfortunately, they are both, like myself, sir, of an extremely delicate disposition. Suffice to say that they are coping as well as can be expected in the circumstances.'

'Circumstances?' repeated Lord Hamilton, a network of deep lines decorating his furrowed forehead. 'Nothing untoward going on at Wetherington, I hope?'

'I am referring to the wedding, sir,' replied Frederick, somewhat tetchily. 'The huge task of planning such an event is causing them both a great deal of anxiety. Needless to say, my poor mother is on the verge of her palpitations.'

Lord Hamilton's spoonful of soup stopped mid-way to his mouth as he regarded their guest in astonishment. 'Palpitations, eh? Well, well. That is a great, um, pity.'

As no other contributions to the conversation were forthcoming, Charlotte flicked a glance around the table and found that everyone, apart from Lord Farrell, appeared to be utterly engrossed in their food. It had to be said that even a bowl of under-seasoned tomato soup was infinitely more interesting than her fiancé. But, unfortunately for them all, he appeared to have not yet completed his dismal dialogue.

'In spite of her unfortunate disposition,' he sniffed, 'my mother has requested that Charlotte attend Wetherington at three o'clock on the morrow in order to discuss the wedding preparations.'

At this unwelcome announcement, the spoonful of soup which Charlotte was in the process of swallowing, caught in her throat. Frantically gasping for breath, tears began streaming down her cheeks.

But, whilst the three other diners regarded her aghast, Lord Farrell carried on with his speech, completely ignoring her.

'I'm sure you will agree, sir, that my mother is an extremely admirable woman to carry on amid such adversity,' he continued, directing his comments to Lord Hamilton.

Lord Hamilton, however, did not appear to hear. He gawped anxiously at his daughter as she reached for her glass of lemonade and took a few tentative sips. Fortunately, the tactic was successful and, several seconds later, Charlotte's choking abated. Lord Hamilton, satisfied that his daughter was not about to drop down dead at the dinner table, then considered it safe to turn his attention back to their guest.

'Sorry, didn't quite catch that, Farrell. What was that you were saying, man?'

Unimpressed that his host had had the audacity to divert his attention, Frederick glared at the older man. 'I was remarking, sir, on what an admirable woman I consider my mother to be. And I am in no doubt that you will agree with me.'

Scrabbling to pick up the thread of the conversation, Lord Hamilton stared nonplussed for several seconds before blurting out, 'Oh. Yes. Indeed she, er, is. That is, she, er, must be. No doubt about it.' His attempt at fervour was not matched by his fellow diners. In fact, it was quite some time before another word was uttered, once again by Lord Hamilton.

'Well,' he declared, his tone dripping with forced cheer, 'I am sure Charlotte will look forward to talking weddings tomorrow, eh?' He flashed his eldest daughter an imploring smile. 'After all what young lady does not like talking weddings?'

'Quite, Father,' agreed Harriet, making an obvious effort to aid the older man in lifting the mood of the proceedings. 'Mirabelle says that on her wedding day the bride should be the envy of all those around her.'

Charlotte put down her spoon and regarded her sister incredulously. 'I hardly think that is the point of a wedding, Harriet.'

'Perhaps not,' murmured Harriet sheepishly. 'But that's what Mirabelle says.'

'Yes, well, believe it or nor, what Mirabelle *says* is not always correct,' retorted the older girl, picking up her napkin and dabbing furiously at her mouth with it.

Suitably chastened, a wave of gloom crept over Harriet's features. She reverted her attention back to tearing apart a bread roll.

For some time, the only sound in the room was the clinking of the spoons against the china bowls, accompanied, very briefly, by the footman padding across the carpet with Lord Farrell's plate of ham and cheese.

'So,' pronounced Lord Hamilton after several minutes. 'This is all very pleasant, isn't it?' He threw a strained smile around the table.

The predominant spoon clinking was broken by a strange noise being emitted from the doctor. Despite the serious look on the man's face as he pressed his napkin to his mouth, it sounded to Charlotte like an ironic snort of laughter.

Following the baked carp and a dessert of rice pudding – which Frederick had refused to have anywhere near him – he announced, much to everyone's ill-disguised relief, that he had need to take his leave. His headache, so he informed, had returned with a vengeance.

'Oh, what a pity,' pronounced Lord Hamilton. 'Particularly when we were all having such an agreeable evening.'

'Quite,' sniffed Frederick. 'Although I confess, my headache notwithstanding, I have no desire to be out on the road too late with this bridle cull they are calling the Courteous Criminal running amok. Only last week the man had the audacity to claim the poor Duchess of Lonsdale as one of his victims.'

'So I believe,' remarked Lord Hamilton, shaking his head. 'What a dreadful business. Why, if the man persists with his campaign, people will be too terrified to leave their houses at all.'

'Oh, but I have heard that he is perfectly charming,' piped up Harriet.

Lord Farrell fixed her with a contemptuous glare. 'Charming? Don't be ridiculous, madam. The man is a criminal and should be strung up as an example to all the other blackguards out there. The very idea of describing such an unsavoury character as "charming" is a perfect example of how standards are slipping to a ludicrously low level in this country. Now, if you will excuse me, I must be on my way. My head is fit to burst with such talk.' As he stood up from the table, he turned to the doctor. 'I wonder, Dr Leigh, if you would be so good as to pass by Wetherington tomorrow and examine us all. Our health does cause my family a great deal of concern.'

The doctor raised a doubtful eyebrow. 'Really, Lord Farrell?' he observed, with only the slightest hint of sarcasm. 'You do surprise me.'

Despite her relief at Lord Farrell's early departure and the welcome opportunity to retire to her chamber shortly thereafter, Charlotte spent another restless night tossing and turning in her bed. As she did so, she attempted to conjure up some redeeming feature about her fiancé, but, to her despair, she failed miserably. What was preying most upon her mind was a fact which did not appear to have occurred to anyone else; a fact which was causing her a great deal of consternation. It did not take a genius to work out why she was marrying Frederick Farrell, but the question which was persisting in causing her so much anguish, was why on earth Frederick Farrell should wish to marry her.

Chapter Four

WITH the afternoon's appointment at Wetherington hanging over her like a dark, oppressive cloud, Charlotte would not have thought that her spirits could have sunk any lower. But, as she sat in the morning-room preparing the menus for the forthcoming week, she soon discovered that she had been grossly mistaken in her assumption. She started as Adams's eerie figure appeared in the doorway, looking even more grey and depressed than usual.

'Miss Mirabelle McGregor,' he droned, in a tone so sombre that it would not have been inappropriate had he been informing them of a sudden family bereavement.

'Oh, Mirabelle. How lovely,' squealed Harriet, who was sitting reading in a chair by the fire. Throwing down her book, she sprang to her feet and rushed over to greet her friend who swam into the room in her usual imperious fashion. Dressed in a burgundy carriage gown and matching high-crowned bonnet, Mirabelle McGregor, with her wide nose, stout frame and unenviable problem with facial hair, was certainly no beauty. But this fact did not deter her in the least from criticizing the appearance of others.

'Goodness, Harriet,' she declared, holding her friend at arm's length. 'You really should refrain from wearing that shade of pink, my dear. It does not aid your colouring in the slightest.'

Disappointment washed over Harriet's face. 'Oh,' she muttered, running her hands over the ruched bodice of the pretty gown. 'But it has always been one of my favourites, Mirabelle.'

'Then may I suggest an urgent review of your tastes, Harriet,' observed Mirabelle haughtily, as she swaggered over to the white and yellow-striped sofa and sank down upon it. 'Now, I am positively dying of thirst. Do order me some tea, my dear. Oh, and perhaps a little cake.'

'Of course, Mirabelle,' murmured Harriet, heading to the bell-pull beside the mantel.

Charlotte, who had not seen Mirabelle since the announcement of her betrothal to Lord Farrell, could feel her blood beginning to bubble at the girl's usual overbearing manner. Making the most of the time before Mirabelle turned her acerbic comments to her, she continued to feign absorption in her menus. But the delay, just as she had feared, was short, lasting only as long as it took Mirabelle to remove her bonnet.

'Ah, Charlotte,' she declared, upon spotting the older girl, 'I was hoping to see you today. I believe I have not yet passed on my felicitations regarding the good fortune of your betrothal.'

Charlotte raised her head and returned the younger girl's scornful smile. 'Thank you, Mirabelle.'

Mirabelle tossed her head of tight ringlets, exactly the colour of muddied water. 'And what, if I may say so, good fortune you have had,' she pronounced. 'Rumour has it that Frederick Farrell is worth in excess of thirty thousand a year.'

Charlotte raised her eyebrows. 'Is he really? I confess I have not the slightest idea of Lord Farrell's income.'

The expression on Mirabelle's face told her opponent that she was not convinced. 'Of course you don't,' she rejoined, her tone ripe with sarcasm. 'How perfectly silly of me. Why, I should have known that *you* would have little interest in such matters.'

Charlotte cursed herself as a flood of hot colour rushed to her cheeks. But Mirabelle, it seemed, was only just beginning.

'I only hope that you find it within yourself to enjoy the Farrell fortune once you are Countess of Wetherington, Charlotte. Despite *obviously* having not the slightest interest in such matters.'

Charlotte searched desperately for a caustic reply, which, to her frustration, obstinately refused to materialize. She shifted in her seat, aware that Mirabelle was enjoying making her squirm.

'Of course, I myself am hoping for nothing less than a marquis,' continued Mirabelle, as she examined her pale, podgy fingers. 'However, for thirty thousand a year, I would naturally consider lowering my standards and settling for an earl. Indeed for thirty thousand a year,' she added with a hollow laugh, 'there is very little I would not lower. Much like yourself, Charlotte.'

Aware of the colour in her cheeks intensifying, Charlotte fought the urge to leap out of her seat and throttle the girl. Fortunately, before their visitor could continue with her malicious diatribe, the door opened and Dr Leigh stepped into the room. All three girls turned to observe him.

'Please do forgive the intrusion, ladies,' he announced, with a courteous bow, 'but I was looking for Lord Hamilton. Do you have any idea where he might be?'

'I believe he is taking a stroll around the garden, Doctor,' informed Harriet brightly.

The doctor flashed her a charming smile. 'Thank you, Lady Harriet. I shall go and seek him there.' And with that, he inclined his head and disappeared from the room, closing the door behind him.

'Hmm,' mused Mirabelle, the moment the door clicked shut. 'What a handsome man. In fact, I would go as far as to say an *extremely* handsome man. Nevertheless, you must remember what I told you, Harriet. Looks are of little import when taking a husband. It is the size of a man's fortune that matters most. One can always amuse oneself with handsome men once one has procured the ring and the title. Am I not correct, Charlotte?'

Charlotte opened her mouth only to find that words, yet again, failed her. But what, after all, could she say? Was not the only reason she had even given Frederick Farrell's proposal a moment's consideration because of his thirty thousand a year? Was she, therefore, not every bit as callous as Mirabelle McGregor was insinuating?

She contributed nothing else to the conversation as Mirabelle, obviously having tired of the subject, turned her attention back to Harriet, and began spouting forth the latest gossip in her own inimitably vicious style.

It was some long thirty minutes later, following two cups of sugared tea, and a slice of Madeira cake, that Mirabelle McGregor eventually took her leave of Hamilton Manor and Charlotte could heave a huge sigh of relief.

Desperate to clear her head following the miserable and humiliating half-hour she had endured in Mirabelle's company, Charlotte finished the menus and flew upstairs to change her attire. The one thing which never failed to lift her spirits, even from the lowly depths at which they were currently languishing, was an outing on her beloved black stallion, Victor. Having ridden almost daily since her fourth birthday, when she had first been presented with her own pony, Charlotte had long ago shunned the conventional, cumbersome female riding-habit, in favour of a pair of much more practical boy's riding breeches. And it was thus, completely unhindered by her clothing, that she had managed to hone her talent to a standard way above that of most gentlemen. In fact, so proficient were her riding skills that, for many years now, her father had agreed to her riding out without the accompaniment of a groom. The rare feeling of peaceful solitude added greatly to her pleasure.

Approaching the back of the house and the cobbled courtyard around which the stables were arranged, the smell of fresh hay, intermingled with polished brass and waxed leather, tickled her nostrils, setting afloat the familiar bubble of excitement she always experienced before such an outing. Having saddled up the animal herself, much to the never-ceasing bemusement and admiration of the grooms, she mounted her steed and trotted him down the drive and out into the rolling countryside.

The day could not have been more perfect for riding. The brilliant blue of the sky was broken, very intermittently, by smudges of lacy white clouds. Autumn, meanwhile, to confirm its seamless arrival, had been hard at work, painting the landscape from its palette of warm, rich colours. Rusty, golden leaves clung tenaciously to their branches in an effort not to join the colourful blanket on the ground, whilst those fields not occupied by ambling cows or baying sheep, were crammed with neat furrowed lines of winter crops.

Having ridden until her cheeks and ears were numb from the surreptitious nip in the air, Charlotte had just slowed Victor to a trot as they passed the small derelict building known ironically as Murphy's Mansion, when she heard a noise which sounded exactly like that of a crying babe. Puzzled, she drew the animal to a halt and listened again. No sooner had she done so, than there came another wail, leaving her in no doubt that there was indeed a child inside. She slid down from the saddle and tethered Victor to a tree at the side of the property.

Murphy's Mansion took its name from the old Irish recluse who had lived in the two-storey building for many years. Since Old Murphy's demise, almost a decade ago, the house had remained deserted and, at the mercy of time and the elements, had fallen into a state of disrepair. Much of the paint on its previously whitewashed walls had long since peeled away and part of the thatched-roof had collapsed, making the upstairs uninhabitable. On the ground floor, several planks of wood had been haphazardly nailed across each of the four front windows. Situated some two miles from Hamilton Manor, the house was surrounded by fields with a wide country lane directly outside it.

Charlotte slowly pushed open the front door, which marked its protest at being disturbed with a loud, creaking groan. Stepping into the house, the door swung defiantly shut behind her, causing her to jump. Inside, the building was cold and gloomy with a strong smell of damp. The only light was provided by the shafts of autumn sunshine filtering through the gaps between the pieces of wood over the windows. Contrary to the child's cries which had caught her attention outside, an eerie silence seemed now to have settled over the building.

Charlotte shivered. 'Hello,' she called tentatively. 'Is anyone there?'

Silence.

She gulped. 'Is anybody there?'

A shuffling sound came from behind her. Charlotte spun around, her heart skipping a beat. She could make out two sets of anxious blue eyes gazing at her from the corner of the room. As her own eyes adjusted to the gloom, she discerned that her frightened audience consisted of two small, raggedy, blonde girls.

She took a step towards them. 'Hello,' she said softly. 'What are you two doing here?'

'Nothing. Honest, miss,' pronounced the younger of the two. Dressed in a brown cotton dress, far too small for her frail body, she looked to be around eight years old. 'Please don't throw us out, miss,' she pleaded. 'We're not doing no harm and we've nowhere else to go.'

Charlotte's mouth dropped open. 'You mean you're – you're living here?'

The little blonde head nodded. 'Two days we've been here, miss.'

'But I-I heard a small child crying,' said Charlotte. 'Is there a baby here too?'

The girl nodded. 'Our Harry, miss. He's nearly one. He don't cry much though, miss. In fact hardly at all really.'

Stunned at these revelations, Charlotte experienced a momentary loss of words as she stared at the huddled pair in bewilderment. Gathering her senses, she stammered, 'Well, er, what are your names?'

'Becky, miss,' announced the girl, thrusting to her feet and bobbing a curtsy. 'And this here is our older sister, Emmy. She looks after us all.'

Charlotte raised a doubtful eyebrow at Emmy, who remained crouched on the floor. The girl looked to be all of two years older than her grubby sibling. 'And is anyone else here with you?' she ventured.

'Three other brothers, as well as our Harry, miss,' informed Becky, with a hint of pride.

'And your – your parents?' asked Charlotte, already fearing the answer.

'Both dead, miss. Our pa died of the pox last year. Then our ma got herself a job as a seamstress in London. When she caught the pox and died a few weeks ago, we were thrown out on to the streets. But them's dangerous them streets, miss. Frightened the life out of us all, they did. So we started walking and kept on walking. For days and days. 'Til we found this place.'

'And so now you – you intend to stay here, do you?' Charlotte attempted to quell the dismay in her tone.

'We'll be no trouble. I swear, miss.'

Charlotte stared at the two girls for several seconds, as the stark, depressing reality of their situation seeped through her. But, concluding that pity was useless to their cause, her sense of the practical swung to the fore.

She forced her lips into a smile before pronouncing, 'Well, my name is Charlotte Hamilton and you must allow me to help you all I can. Tomorrow, if I may, I shall return with some provisions.'

Now Emmy sprang to her feet, a wave of amazement, tinged with suspicion creeping over her pretty features. She raised her chin to

Charlotte. 'There's no need for that, miss. We've got a bit of money our ma left us. We can cope just fine.'

Charlotte smiled at the child, feeling both respect and admiration for her fierce pride in protecting and caring for her younger siblings. As well as losing their parents, she dared not even contemplate what other horrors the young family had been forced to endure during their short lifetimes.

'Oh, I've no doubt at all that you can cope, Emmy, but I should like to help all the same. If you will permit me.'

'There's really no need to trouble yourself, miss.'

'I can assure you that it's no trouble at all,' insisted Charlotte. 'In fact, it will be a pleasure. I live very near here, at Hamilton Manor – just over there.' She indicated the direction of the house. 'I ride by here most days as it is.'

Emmy still did not look convinced. Becky, on the other hand, appeared delighted.

'That's mighty kind of you, miss,' she piped up, giving her sister an indiscreet nudge in the ribs. 'We'll be waiting for you on the morrow. Won't we, Emmy?'

Emmy gave a begrudging nod.

'Very well then,' announced Charlotte, flashing them her warmest smile. 'Until tomorrow.'

Chapter Five

DUE to her unexpected encounter with the two girls, Charlotte galloped all the way back to Hamilton Manor to change out of her riding breeches and into more suitable attire of a sea-green round gown. Despite her haste, she arrived at her appointment some ten minutes later than the three o'clock at which she had been expected. This fact served only to increase her trepidation as she alighted the carriage at the imposing and, in her opinion, extremely ugly Wetherington Hall. Contrary to the warm golden stone of Hamilton Manor, previous generations of Farrells had opted to construct their ancestral seat in materials of the very darkest grey. This alone was enough to render the building forbidding, but, combined with its collection of menacing towers and a façade dotted with the stone heads of leering gargoyles and snarling monsters, the overall effect could most aptly be described as sinister.

The inside of the building fared no better. This was equally as distasteful, albeit for a different set of reasons. This was only Charlotte's second visit to Wetherington and, exactly as she had done during the first, as she followed the butler through the maze of corridors, she could not help but compare the ostentatious interior with its ostentatious residents. Just like its owners, the inside of the house was overpowering and stifling: every surface covered in gold rococo; every cabinet stuffed with priceless collections of china, silver or crystal; every room bursting with the latest in fashionable French furniture and every wall crammed with an array of ugly family portraits all bearing a striking similarity and a supercilious expression. Even the ceilings were richly decorated, depicting colourful scenes of cherubic angels, heroic knights and beatific, smiling virgins. Despite its overwhelming size, Charlotte did not doubt that there remained not a corner of the house where one was not surrounded by some opulent display of the Farrells' wealth – the same wealth that was about to become her prisoner, tying her for the rest of her days to its despicable owners.

The butler stopped in front of one of the doors and pushed it open with an air of aplomb.

'Lady Charlotte Hamilton,' he announced.

Ignoring the bile in her throat, Charlotte attempted to raise the corners of her lips into some semblance of a smile as she absorbed her surroundings. Regardless of the glorious autumn day outside, the room was disconcertingly dark. Heavy crimson curtains had been drawn across each of its six windows which meant that the only light was that provided by the blazing fire. But even the overpowering heat of the flames could not melt the chilling, unwelcoming aura emanating from the three occupants. Lady Farrell, Countess of Wetherington, seated in a high-backed burgundy damask armchair at the fireside, was bearing her usual glacial expression. Her thin pale lips were set in a straight, disapproving line and the same watery-blue eyes as those of her son stared insipidly from the deep sockets of her long face. Her hair, as white as snow, had been coiffed to such an extent that it was devoid of all movement. Around the neck of her charcoal-grey gown, hung several layers of Belgian lace while, from her ears, dangled two large glittering diamonds. In a matching chair on the opposite side of the fireplace was her son, Frederick Farrell. Upon setting eyes upon his fiancée, his expression remained as bland as ever. Between the two, seated on a crimson sofa and propped up by a mountain of cushions, was a thin woman of some eight-and-twenty years. She was dressed in a high-waisted gown of yellow silk, which accentuated her complete lack of bosom. The matching bandeau holding back her pale-red hair was equally as unflattering, sapping her complexion of every bit of colour. Despite being some years older, the girl's similarity to Frederick left Charlotte in little doubt as to her identity: this could only be Frederick's sister, Lady Perdita Farrell.

Although she had never voiced her sentiments on the matter, Charlotte had dared to harbour a faint ray of hope that perhaps life at

Wetherington would be a little more bearable if she could strike up a friendship with her future sister-in-law. But, noting the strange and disturbing manner in which the girl was now staring at her, that solitary ray was swiftly obscured by an enormous, black cloud.

'Charlotte,' intoned Lady Farrell, throwing her a cursory glance. 'Don't lurk, girl. Come in and sit down at once.' This instruction was accompanied by a perfunctory wave of the woman's bony, diamond-adorned hand to one of the other armchairs clustered around the fireplace.

Struggling with a compelling urge to pick up her skirts and flee from the gloomy room's even gloomier inhabitants, Charlotte dipped a curtsy before apprehensively gliding over to a chair between the countess and Perdita. As she settled herself into it, she could scarcely bring herself to look at Frederick who had pulled a handkerchief from his breeches' pocket and was busy mopping at his brow.

'Pills, Roberts,' commanded the countess of the footman in attendance. The servant bowed his acquiescence, before opening the door and slipping through it. Charlotte experienced a pang of envy as she watched him disappear.

No one said a word but, as Frederick continued with his mopping and the countess rested her head against the back of her chair and closed her eyes, evidently awaiting the arrival of her medication, Perdita's cold, colourless gaze remained fixed on Charlotte. At a loss as to what to do or say in the perturbing circumstances, Charlotte emitted a self-conscious little cough.

'So,' huffed Perdita at length, 'you are the chit my brother is to wed?'

'Er, yes, my lady,' was all Charlotte could stammer in response.

Another awkward silence ensued before Perdita picked up one of her surrounding cushions, placed it on her bony knees and slammed a fist into it. An astonished Charlotte jumped several inches from her seat.

'Oh, it is so unfair, Mama,' wailed Perdita, in a piercing tone. 'Everyone is to be wed but me. I shall be the first Farrell to ever die a spinster; the pitiful laughing stock of the family; the butt of all jokes for generations to come. It is too much to bear, Mama. Much too much.' She followed this declaration by jutting out her thin bottom lip, the overall effect making her resemble something akin to a disgruntled fish.

With her eyes still closed, Lady Farrell sighed wearily. 'It is not through my lack of trying, Perdita dear. Although, I own that even *I* am now finding the whole business somewhat wearing. Circumstances, it would appear, are conspiring to work against us in the matter of finding you a husband.'

Perdita slumped back against her pile of cushions, fiddling with the tassels of the one which remained on her lap. Then, swapping her whinging tone to one of haughtiness, she addressed Charlotte once more. 'Of course I was once almost wed, you know. To the Duke of Wittingsall. Mama worked so hard to arrange it all. Did you not, Mama?'

Lady Farrell half-opened her eyes and nodded her head dolefully. 'Such a pity that the man was forced to remove overseas the week before the wedding.'

Charlotte said nothing, but contemplated the fact that if Perdita had made the Duke of Wittingsall feel half as uncomfortable as she did at that particular moment, then it was little wonder the man had removed overseas.

'And then, of course, I was almost betrothed to the Earl of Sly,' sniffed Perdita. 'Mama undertook all of the arrangements there too. Did you not, Mama?'

Her mother, not even bothering to open her eyes this time, shook her head. 'Incomprehensible that the man disappeared like that. And in Scotland of all places. How people can simply *disappear* is quite beyond me.'

'He disappeared?' repeated Charlotte, feeling obliged to pass some remark. 'How very strange. But surely someone must know what happened to him.'

Perdita shrugged her angular shoulders, an unsettling smile tugging at her lips. 'No one whom Mama questioned. I, however, have my own theory. I believe the man was ravaged to death by a wild animal – a bear in fact. They are quite common in Scotland, so I have heard. I had a dream about it. The whole scene played out before me. It was most fascinating. The bear began by—'

Charlotte could think of a great many things that she found fascinating but imagining a bear devouring the poor Earl of Sly was definitely not amongst them. She recoiled in horror, not only at the nature of Perdita's dream, but also at the glee which was emanating from the girl's ugly face as she recalled it in all its gory detail. For the first time since Charlotte had made his acquaintance, she was relieved to hear Frederick's voice as he cut short his sister's gruesome speech.

'Must you really, Perdita?' he broke in with a groan. 'My stomach is feeling somewhat delicate this morning. I have obviously eaten something that has not agreed with me. Most likely yesterday evening.' He slanted an accusing look at Charlotte who, taken aback by the bizarre conversation, could do nothing more than gawp at him askance.

'No bickering, children,' commanded Lady Farrell, fluttering her eyelids. 'My nerves cannot bear another recounting of those dreadful – and, I hasten to add, costly – failed attempts at marriage.' She turned to Charlotte. 'Now,' she began, 'I believe that Frederick has already told you I am finding this wedding business a source of extreme agitation. Indeed, if I am not mistaken, I am poised on the cliff edge of my palpitations.'

'So I believe, ma'am,' mumbled Charlotte, as Perdita's gaze continued to spear her.

'Therefore,' she continued, 'I think it best for all concerned if you simply agree with everything I suggest. Any disagreements may, I fear, tip me over.'

Charlotte opened her mouth to protest but instantly closed it again. For all the thought of tipping Lady Farrell over the edge of a cliff was extremely tempting, she wasn't sure she would be able to cope with the woman's grisly demise on her conscience.

'What I am suggesting is this,' she continued. She reached over to a small side table upon which sat a pile of white paper covered in lines of neat black handwriting. 'Firstly, the flowers. I am proposing my favourite hydrangea.'

'Oh, but I did so hope to have roses,' piped up Charlotte. 'They were my mother's favourites.'

Perdita drew in a disapproving breath. Through narrowed eyes, Lady Farrell, meanwhile, glared at Charlotte, before placing the palm of her hand over the general area of her heart and sighing heavily.

Charlotte felt a stab of panic as an image of a steep cliff flashed before her. 'But I am sure hydrangea will serve well enough,' she added.

Perdita snorted victoriously whilst the countess flashed a triumphant smile and removed her hand. 'Now to the second matter. I have instructed Father Bartholomew that we shall require him to carry out the service. I cannot abide that outspoken little man, Father Jameson.'

'Oh, but Father Jameson baptized me,' protested Charlotte. 'And he is a very dear friend of my family – one of my father's closest friends, in fact. I'm sure he would be greatly upset were he not allowed to marry me, as, indeed, would my father.'

No sooner had she voiced her concerns, than Perdita began tutting censoriously. But it was Lady Farrell's reaction that caused Charlotte the greatest distress. Flinging her sheets of paper to the floor, the woman clasped both hands to her chest. 'Find that wretched footman and my pills, Frederick,' she bellowed. 'And quickly.'

Frederick thrust to his feet, glowering at Charlotte. 'Now look what you've done,' he exclaimed, before striding towards the door. An astounded Charlotte stared helplessly after him. But, before he could reach his target, the door was thrown open by the butler.

'There is a Dr Daniel Leigh here, sir. He says you requested that he call today.'

Frederick stopped in his tracks. 'Thank the Lord,' he declared, raising his insipid blue eyes heavenwards. 'Show him in at once, Higgins. And tell him to hurry.'

The butler bowed his head and had no sooner vacated his spot than it was filled by Dr Leigh, carrying a black-leather medicine bag. Charlotte was aware of an odd fluttering sensation in the pit of her stomach as their eyes met briefly and he offered her another of his enchanting smiles. The moment, however, was swiftly broken.

'Thank goodness you are come, Doctor,' exulted Frederick, allowing the man no time for formalities. 'I do believe my mother's palpitations are about to start.'

'Really?' intoned Dr Leigh calmly, averting his gaze from Charlotte. 'Then we had best take a look at her.'

Lady Farrell was now reposing in her chair in a near-catatonic state. Her eyes were closed and she was breathing heavily, her bony chest rising up and down in the most theatrical of fashions. The doctor picked up a limp wrist and sought her pulse.

'Hmm,' he murmured.

The countess's eyes snapped open. 'Is it serious, Doctor?'

The doctor said nothing but lifted each of her eyelids in turn. 'Hmm,' he muttered again.

A look of consternation was spreading over Lady Farrell's lined face. She watched agog, as the doctor reached into his battered old case and pulled out a wooden stethoscope. Placing it to the woman's chest, he listened for several minutes. As he did so, he caught Charlotte's eye. Her already befuddled mind grew a shade more perplexed. Had Dr Leigh just winked at her?

'Hmm,' mused the doctor, removing the stethoscope and replacing it in his bag.

'It is just my palpitations, is it not, Doctor?' implored Lady Farrell.

The doctor furrowed his brow. 'I'm not sure, my lady. It could be something much more serious.'

Frederick, now back in his armchair, sucked in a rattling breath.

'More serious?' spat the countess, panic oozing from every one of her pores. 'How much more serious?'

The doctor shrugged his broad shoulders. 'I'm afraid it's difficult to say at this stage, ma'am.'

'Then at what stage can you say, man?' demanded Frederick.

'I'm not yet certain, my lord.'

'Not certain? Not certain?' echoed a flustered Frederick. 'What sort of damned doctor are you?'

'Oh, a very good one, I can assure you,' replied the doctor.

'Is Mama going to die, Doctor?' piped up Perdita.

'Perdita!' exclaimed her mother. 'Pray, do not ask such shocking questions, child. I am at my wits' end already with all my wretched health problems.'

'But you could die, Mama. And this girl would be to blame. She has, after all, caused nothing but a fuss about the wedding arrangements.'

Charlotte gulped. 'I have not made a fuss at all,' she protested. 'I simply—'

'Enough!' roared the countess, holding out her hand. 'My nerves cannot bear it.'

Dutifully silenced, Charlotte breathed a sigh of relief as she observed

Perdita's disturbing attentions move away from her and settle on Dr Leigh. She watched as the girl studied him, a coy smile playing about her mouth.

'Oh,' she declared suddenly. 'I do believe I have just had the most marvellous idea, Mama.'

Lady Farrell cast her daughter a doubtful look. 'What is it now, Perdita?'

'Why, it is perfectly obvious, Mama,' exulted Perdita, her colourless eyes glinting. 'With our health suffering as it is, Dr Leigh must remove to Wetherington.'

Taking a few seconds to consider this proposal, the countess flashed her daughter an approving smile. 'That is indeed a marvellous idea, child. Doctor Leigh, you shall remove to Wetherington at once and attend to us all until this wretched wedding business is behind us. With so much agitation, goodness only knows what ailments may befall us between now and then.'

The doctor's mouth dropped open. 'Remove to Wetherington? But I couldn't possibly, my lady. I'm afraid I have other—'

'We shall pay you well for your attentions, Doctor,' said Perdita, fluttering her barely noticeable eyelashes. 'Shall we not, Mama?'

'Indeed we shall,' confirmed her mother. 'We shall pay you three times your usual fee.'

'Three times?' echoed the doctor. 'But I really don't think I—'

'Very well then. Five times.'

'But I already have other obligations, ma'am. I—'

'I shall permit you to honour those obligations, Doctor,' rejoined Lady Farrell, 'providing you are away from Wetherington for no more than two hours each day. Now, I am so exhausted I do not wish to hear another word on the subject. You may send one of my men to collect your things, Dr Leigh. I do not wish to be left without medical assistance for a single moment today. Charlotte, you are dismissed. I have had quite enough excitement for one day. I shall send for you again when I am fit enough to receive visitors which may, I fear, be quite some time.'

Taken aback by the events of the last half-hour, it was all Charlotte could do to summon a comprehending nod of her head as she rose from her chair.

Chapter Six

WITH her heart racing and her body dripping with perspiration, Charlotte awoke from her nightmare with a start. Now accustomed to disturbing dreams, these had been by far the worst yet: shocking images of herself pushing Lady Farrell over a steep cliff and wild bears tearing apart Frederick Farrell – limb by scrawny limb. Too scared to even try to attempt sleep again, lest the nightmares reoccur, she lay staring at the ceiling until the first rays of daylight began shyly peeping around the edges of the plum velvet curtains.

Washed, dressed and breakfasted some hours later, Charlotte began organizing items to take to Murphy's Mansion. Having lain awake for so long the night before, she had succeeded in compiling quite a comprehensive list by the time she arose. First, she visited the kitchens, where she asked a scullery maid to pack two picnic-baskets with food and gather together any unwanted pots, pans and utensils. Secondly, she instructed one of the maids to sort out a pile of blankets. And finally, she requested that a footman go up into the attic and bring down a selection of their old children's clothes. With the bounty duly gathered and ignoring the questioning looks from the servants, she then ordered it all to be loaded on to the gig.

Due to her competent driving skills, Charlotte encountered few problems in negotiating the rattling, laden conveyance through the country lanes to the dilapidated dwelling. She was, nevertheless, grateful that the day had once again fared dry and pleasant as she had the distinct feeling that she may not have coped quite so well had it been pouring with rain.

Some thirty minutes later, with all her gifts intact – albeit a little shaken – Charlotte turned a corner and Murphy's Mansion came into view. The children were outside and, upon spotting the gig, Becky and the three boys – all with the same wispy blond hair as that of their sisters – bounded towards her, shouting their greetings. In contrast to the high spirits of her younger siblings, Emmy, holding a gurgling babe in her arms, stood quietly watching in the doorway.

Charlotte brought the gig to a halt alongside Emmy and, grinning at the enthusiasm of the younger children, began unloading the various baskets and bundles. As Becky removed the muslin cloths covering the food, even Emmy could not disguise the look of amazement on her face at the sight of the delights within.

'Lord,' exclaimed a wide-eyed Becky, pulling out a loaf of soft, floury bread and ripping a hunk from it. 'I ain't never seen so much food in all me living days. Here, Tommy, you have some.' She handed the loaf to one of her brothers, who copied his sister and passed it to the next in line.

Charlotte experienced a surge of warmth at their excitement and their obvious devotion to one another. 'I brought some clothes too,' she said, proffering a bundle to Emmy.

Still hovering on the periphery with the baby, Emmy regarded her earnestly. 'Like I said yesterday, miss, there really ain't no need.'

'And like I said yesterday, Emmy, I want to help. Now please, take the clothes. I certainly have no need of them.'

Emmy managed a fleeting smile. 'If you're sure, miss.'

'But what about your own children, miss?' piped up Becky. 'Don't they need them?'

Charlotte smiled at the child's directness. 'I don't have any children, Becky. I'm not yet married.'

Becky screwed up her little button nose. 'Not married? But you's too pretty not to be married, miss. Do you have a young man?'

'Becky!' chided Emmy. 'What have I told you about being so nosy!'

Becky's expression grew indignant. 'I'm not being nosy. I'm just being in – er, inq— Oh, what's that word again, Emmy?'

'Inquisitive,' said Emmy, shooting a look of amused despair at Charlotte.

'That's it,' declared Becky triumphantly. 'I'm just being inquisitive.'

Charlotte laughed. 'Well, you can be as inquisitive as you like, Becky. In answer to your question, I am shortly to be married to Lord Frederick Farrell.'

Becky's blue eyes grew wide. 'Lord, he sounds grand, miss. Is he handsome?'

As a picture of Frederick's pale bland face flashed across Charlotte's mind, she suppressed a shudder. 'Well, he's, er—'

But Becky appeared not to have noticed Charlotte's lack of enthusiasm as she carried on with her questioning.

'Is he rich, miss?'

'Becky!' remonstrated Emmy again.

Charlotte laughed. 'It's quite all right, really, Emmy. Yes, Becky, he is. Very rich, so I believe.'

'Lord,' puffed Becky, 'I wouldn't mind a handsome, rich husband when I'm ready to wed; one who will give me lots of pretty dresses and jewels. Did he give you that necklace, Miss Charlotte?'

A pang of sadness shot through Charlotte as her hand moved to the string of pearls. 'No, Becky, he didn't. The necklace belonged to my mother.'

'Is she dead, miss?'

Tears pricked at Charlotte's eyes. 'Yes. She is.'

'Just like ours then,' remarked Becky, producing a piece of cheese from her pocket and beginning to nibble it.

'Yes, Becky, just like yours,' whispered Charlotte.

As Charlotte drove the gig home later that afternoon, she could not help but recall Becky's comment regarding their two late mothers and make the comparison between her own plight and that of the children. How could she ever have thought her own situation so desperate just because she was about to marry a man she didn't love? Did not, after all, dozens of women wed men they did not love? The most important thing, she realized, was that she and her family would always have the basic necessities of a decent roof over their heads and food in their bellies. Although, she realized with a shiver, had she refused Frederick Farrell's offer, then that may well not have been the case.

It was at a meeting between Lord Hamilton and his solicitor at the manor a few weeks before, when the stark reality of her family's situation was brought, quite by accident, to Charlotte's attention. She had been aware that her father had not been himself for quite some time: his usual happy, easy-going demeanour replaced by short-temperedness, irritability and a deep-rooted air of anxiety. Charlotte had attempted, on numerous occasions, to coax the old man into discussing his worries with her, each time to no avail. But all had become clear that fateful day.

Discussing the matter at a small table in front of the morning-room window, partaking of a cup of tea and some late summer air, the two men, intent on their business, had failed to notice Charlotte snipping roses from the bush beneath the open window. As the pair had chatted candidly, their words had flowed effortlessly from the room. But, each one heavy with significance, it was some time before Charlotte was able to absorb their meaning. Rooted to the spot, she had been unable to move a muscle as the full, horrific picture was painted before her eyes.

Having a reputation as a shrewd financier, her father had, during his time as Earl Hamilton, succeeded in building his shamefully small inheritance into an enviable sum. Three years before, he had apparently opted to invest a significant amount of money in an exciting new venture in America. Had it been successful, the family would have been rich beyond their wildest dreams and the Hamilton fortune, frittered away by past dissipating generations, would have been restored to its former glory. But the venture had not been successful. It had been an unmitigated disaster and Lord Hamilton had lost every single penny.

During the conversation with his trusted solicitor, it became obvious to Charlotte that her father had been doing his best to rectify the situation. Using the few spare funds he had left to his name, he had been searching for investments with high, short-term returns but these, too, were inherent with risk and had failed to deliver, resulting in more losses. The two men had gone on to discuss schemes to reduce the family's expenses by dismissing servants and the like but such measures would, they agreed, merely have scratched the surface of the problem. The only viable solution, they concluded, was to sell Hamilton Manor, although, once rumours of their desperate circumstances began to circulate, it was unlikely the offer they would be forced to accept, would reflect anywhere near the house's true value. This, combined with the settlement of their outstanding affairs, would result in a sum estimated to last the family no more than ten years provided they lived frugally.

Once Charlotte had recovered from the shock of the revelation, she had deliberated for days on whether she should make her father aware of her knowledge. But then, out of the blue, had come the proposal from Frederick Farrell. Charlotte had thanked God that she had not spoken to her father regarding his conversation with the solicitor. If she had, then he would have immediately guessed the reason for her acceptance. As it was, she had done a commendable job in convincing him that she was happy to accept the offer. The weight removed from Lord Hamilton's previously hunched shoulders had been visible at once. Of course, Charlotte knew that if her father ever guessed the truth about her feelings towards Frederick Farrell and how unhappy she was at the forthcoming union, he would instantly forbid the marriage, insisting that he would find some other way of solving their predicament. But, as she had heard from his own mouth during the conversation with his man of law, there was no other way and, if the price Charlotte had to pay to see her father happy again and to save her brother and sister from destitution was marriage to Frederick Farrell, then it was a small price indeed.

She was still in this sanguine frame of mind when she arrived back at Hamilton Manor. Having handed the gig over to one of the stable boys, she headed straight for the stairs in order to visit her brother. She was some halfway up, when Dr Leigh came bounding down towards her. Charlotte stopped immediately upon seeing him. He was dressed in a pair of tight beige pantaloons and another crumpled white shirt, which looked as though it had never so much as seen a flat iron. He stopped two stairs above her.

'Good afternoon, Lady Charlotte,' he said, with a gracious bow.

'Doctor Leigh,' she rejoined politely, desperately attempting to calm her racing heart. 'How is my brother, sir? I was just on my way to see him.'

'I am delighted to say that he is in exceptional spirits, ma'am,' replied the doctor, beaming broadly. 'If he follows my orders, I envisage him making a full recovery in no time.'

'Well, thank, um, goodness for that,' stammered Charlotte. Conscious of his gaze upon her and the colour that was subsequently rising in her cheeks, she added hurriedly, 'Well, um, if you will excuse me, Doctor, I shall be on my way. I have a, er, great deal to do today.'

The doctor's lips slanted upwards in a lazy smile, causing Charlotte's stomach to somersault. 'Of course, my lady,' he said. 'But, before you go, I have a message for you from Lady Farrell. She requests that you visit Wetherington at eleven o'clock tomorrow morning.'

The frantic racing of Charlotte's heart stopped abruptly and all colour drained from her face. With the countess apparently so discomposed yesterday, she had hoped to have several days' reprieve from the ghastly family. But, to her great chagrin, it appeared that that was not to be the case.

'I see. Well, then you may inform Lady Farrell that I shall be there. Thank you, Dr Leigh.' She stood for a moment, gripping the banister. Her nerves were already beginning to jangle at the thought of the forthcoming meeting and were not being eased by the doctor standing so close to her, regarding her with his large, dark – and disturbingly perspicacious – eyes.

'If I may say so, my lady,' he remarked, his smile now completely vanished, 'my message seems to have caused you some distress.'

Charlotte gazed at him aghast. Were her feelings so apparent? She attempted to pull herself together. 'Of course not, Doctor. I am extremely pleased to hear that her ladyship is again well enough to continue with the discussions of the wedding. As I am sure you are aware, the subject of weddings is one favoured by all us young ladies.' She attempted a girlish titter, but no sooner had the affected sound vacated her throat, than she regretted it, cringing at its transparency.

The doctor said nothing, his gaze continuing to burn right through her as he narrowed his eyes. 'Then I shall inform her ladyship that you will be there tomorrow,' he said at length.

Charlotte was aware of another deep flush creeping over her neck. 'Thank you, Doctor. That would be most, um, kind of you.' And with that, she gathered up her skirts and, sidling around him, continued her ascent of the staircase, hoping desperately that he did not notice her quaking legs in the process.

Out of sight at the top of the stairs, Charlotte leaned against the cool wall of the corridor. Closing her eyes, she attempted to regain some of her equilibrium. Her previously positive frame of mind had now diminished to be replaced by a deep, gnawing concern. She had no doubt that the newly arrived Dr Daniel Leigh had managed to correctly gauge her true feelings towards the Farrells. If her father's intuition were half as strong, then he would immediately cancel the arrangement and her family would find themselves, once again, on the verge of destitution. Panic began surging through her. She could not allow that to happen. She *would* not allow that to happen. Her marriage to Frederick Farrell was their only hope and, in order not to jeopardize that hope, she realized she would simply have to do better.

Chapter Seven

CONTRARY to the past few days, the weather the following morning was dull and dreary, with a leaden sky and a strong, unforgiving wind. It matched Charlotte's dejected mood perfectly. Yet again sleep had eluded her for the greater part of the night but, during the long hours she had lain awake, her resolution to portray the role of a dutiful and loving bride-to-be had strengthened. No one, no matter how deep their suspicions, would be allowed so much as a hint of her true feelings. And so it was, with this resolution at the forefront of her mind, that Charlotte entered Wetherington Hall at precisely eleven o'clock. Once again, she was directed to the dark, depressing drawing-room.

As the butler pushed open the door, Charlotte saw that this time all three of the room's occupants were lying on *chaises-longues*, placed side-by-side, in front of the roaring fire. Despite the stifling heat, each was covered with a pile of blankets. Charlotte sensed immediately that the mood of this meeting was to differ little from that of the previous one. The only thing for which she was grateful, was that there was no sign of Dr Leigh. The execution of her resolution was going to be difficult enough, without the added pressure of such a perceptive audience.

'Lady Hamilton, my lady,' announced the butler, before turning on his heel and, fanning his face with his hand, marching back down the corridor.

Charlotte, standing in the open doorway, waited for one of her three future relatives to acknowledge her presence, but the only sounds were the crackling of the fire and a rasping snore coming from Perdita. All at once, Frederick's mother, who was nearest the door, gave a rattling cough and swivelled her head around.

'Good God, girl. Come in and close the door this instant, or we shall all catch our death of cold,' she expostulated loudly.

Charlotte did as she was requested and, with a thudding heart, walked over to the countess. She came to a halt at the side of the woman's makeshift bed and dipped a curtsy.

'Good morning, my lady.'

'Well, quite what is good about it, I fail to see,' muttered Frederick, who was in the middle of the row of three.

Charlotte twisted her features into what she hoped was a sympathetic countenance.

'Are you feeling ill … dear?'

From beneath his eiderdown, Frederick twisted around and gaped at her. 'I beg your pardon?'

'I merely asked if you were feeling out of sorts, er, dearest,' repeated Charlotte, wincing at her own insincerity.

Frederick continued staring at her for several uncomfortable seconds before spitting out, 'Of course I am ill, girl. Why else would I be lying here like a slice of boiled ham?'

'Oh,' murmured Charlotte, quelling an urge to slap the man's supercilious face. 'Well, in that case, is there anything I can, um, do for you?'

Frederick regarded her once more in disbelief before informing her, in a tone which implied he considered her well below average intelligence, 'I am suffering with one of my headaches. Doctor Leigh is mixing me a draught and should return forthwith.'

At this announcement, Charlotte's spirits plunged at exactly the same moment as the door opened and Dr Leigh strode into the room. Her resolve to be pleasant to her fiancé, which had already come dangerously close to waning, immediately stiffened.

The doctor inclined his head to her. 'Good morning, my lady.'

'Doctor Leigh,' rejoined Charlotte stiffly, determined that he should not see through her newly fortified façade. Then, wasting no time on inanities, she said, 'I see that you have brought the draught, Doctor. May I request that you pass it to my fiancé at once? He is not feeling at all the thing this morning.'

A look of scepticism crept over the doctor's face, but, before he could say a word, the countess forestalled him.

'I, too, am in need of a draught, Doctor. My head has begun to pound quite dreadfully during these last few minutes.'

At this proclamation, the doctor closed his eyes for several seconds before turning to the older woman. 'As I have already told you this morning, Lady Farrell,' he intoned in the manner of one out of all patience, 'the heat in this room is far too oppressive. If you would only permit me to open the windows and let in some fresh air – and indeed some light – I can assure you, you would all feel infinitely better than supping yet another draught.'

Lady Farrell whipped her head around to him. 'And I have already told you this morning, Dr Leigh, that fresh air does not agree with me in the slightest. I cannot bear to think of where else it has been, blowing about as it does. It is my considered opinion that one is much better off keeping one's air to oneself.' She then thrust out her arm. 'Now, Doctor, I demand you take my pulse again. My heart is beating most erratically.'

The doctor rolled his eyes. 'I can assure you there is nothing whatsoever wrong with your heart, ma'am,' he informed tersely.

She was not convinced. 'If you recall, that was not your opinion two days ago, Doctor. Why, I believe your opinion then, was that I might be suffering from quite a serious condition, was it not?'

The doctor pulled a rueful face. 'I may have been a little hasty in making that statement, ma'am.'

'Many a true word is uttered in haste, Dr Leigh,' pronounced the older woman. 'Now, my pulse if you please, man, and, Charlotte, do stop hovering like a fly over a rotting corpse.'

More deflated than ever, Charlotte sidled over to a chair at the side of the snoring Perdita and sank into it. No sooner had she done so than, to her dismay, Perdita's eyes sprang open and attached themselves to Charlotte's face. Charlotte was aware of goosebumps breaking out all over her body at the disconcerting intensity of the girl's gaze. She was grateful when a timely cough from the doctor diverted Perdita's attention.

'Oh, Dr Leigh,' fluttered Perdita, turning her head to him, 'it is the strangest thing, but I cannot feel my legs at all. I think, perhaps, I may have need of a poultice.' The nauseating smile which followed this announcement made Charlotte feel quite discomposed. From the look which flickered across the doctor's countenance as he took the countess's pulse, it appeared he was experiencing a similar feeling.

He fixed Perdita with an icy glare. 'I know of a much more effective remedy than a poultice, my lady,' he pronounced.

Perdita widened her colourless eyes. 'If it concerns your healing hands, Doctor, then I agree wholeheartedly that such a treatment is much more likely to be beneficial to me.' She followed this outrageous statement with a flirtatious giggle.

The doctor's expression remained impassive. 'I am suggesting a brisk walk around the gardens, ma'am,' he rejoined coolly. 'That, I can assure you, will restore your circulation much better than any poultice.'

Disappointment swept over Perdita's ugly features, but, before she could give voice to her thoughts, the older lady cut in.

'Now, Charlotte, you are aware that at the time of your acceptance of Frederick's very generous offer of marriage' – she flashed a beatific smile at her son, which he returned with equal virtuousness – 'we spoke of a ball to mark the occasion.'

Charlotte wrinkled her forehead. Try as she might, she found she had absolutely no recollection of such a conversation.

'Well,' she ploughed on regardless, 'as we discussed, the ball is to take place here at Wetherington tomorrow evening. I have, as usual, taken complete responsibility for the event myself and no, Doctor, please do not protest that my strength is not up to it. Where one's social obligations are concerned, I am afraid that when one is a Farrell, one's health must always take second place.'

The doctor dropped the woman's scrawny wrist. 'I was not about to protest, Lady Farrell. As far as I am able to ascertain, there is nothing at all wrong with your health. And your heartbeat is perfectly regular.'

The countess slanted him a suspicious look. 'I can assure you there is no need to tiptoe around me, Doctor. If I am suffering from something more serious, then I am perfectly capable of coping with it.'

'So brave, Mama,' muttered Frederick, only his head, gleaming with perspiration, now visible from under the blankets which he had tucked right up under his neck. 'Such an admirable woman.'

Lady Farrell gave a martyr-like sigh. 'It is a simple fact, Frederick, that some of us are born to suffer throughout our lifetime. Ill-health is merely one of the many heavy crosses I have been forced to bear.'

'Well then, I am happy to inform you that whatever you have been bearing all these years, seems to have completely vanished, ma'am,' declared the doctor.

'For the moment perhaps,' huffed the countess. 'But only the Lord knows when it may decide to rear its head again. Now, where was I? Ah, yes. The ball shall begin at seven o'clock tomorrow evening, Charlotte. I have, naturally, invited the very cream of Society although with that dreadful highwayman terrifying everyone half to death, I have no idea how many of my friends will be honouring us with their presence. It is nothing short of appalling the way such a criminal can disrupt one's social engagements.'

'From what I have heard, it is only a matter of time before the man murders someone, Mama,' piped up Perdita, her eyes alight with something Charlotte disturbingly identified as eager anticipation. 'I would wager that he will slit their throat from ear to ear with one clean sweep of a knife. Either that or stab them to death.' She emulated a stabbing action with her bony hand. 'Stab, stab, stab, until they—'

'That is enough, thank you, Perdita,' broke in the countess, shooting her daughter an admonishing glare. 'I think we are all aware of the possibilities. Now, Charlotte, I shall, of course, expect those members of your family who attend the ball, to make the greatest of effort with their appearance. One can never go to too much trouble when one is to be mixing with the *haut ton* and we Farrells have our reputation to maintain. The Hamiltons, by association, will now be required to meet our high standards. Do I make myself clear?'

'Very clear, ma'am,' muttered Charlotte.

'Good. Then that is all,' concluded the countess.

Grasping this as her cue to leave, Charlotte rose from her seat and bobbed a curtsy. 'Until tomorrow then, my lady. Perdita. Goodbye, Frederick, er, darling.'

Frederick did not reply, his insipid blue eyes regarding her warily. But, as Charlotte walked from the room, constraining herself not to run, it was not the watery, suspicious gaze of Frederick Farrell that she could feel boring into her back, but the dark, questioning one of Dr Daniel Leigh.

As the butler dragged open the door of Wetherington Hall, the fresh outside air hit Charlotte in the face with the same startling intensity as a bucket of cold water. With her own head now thumping from the exhausting combination of the over-heated room; the enormous effort it had taken to be courteous to the Farrells, and the growing awkwardness she was feeling in Dr Leigh's presence, she felt, once again, on the increasingly familiar verge of tears.

'If you don't mind me saying so, miss,' commented Albert, as he held open the carriage door for her, 'you ain't looking at all yourself.'

Charlotte gave a weak smile. 'I'm fine, really, Albert.'

Evidently unconvinced, Albert added, 'I hope I'm not speaking out of turn nor nothing, miss, but if you're asking me, you could do with a slice of Mrs Tomms's meat 'n' potato pie. Fatten you up a bit. Should be just about ready by the time we get back. And I know our Kate'd love to see you. Thinks the world of you, so she does.'

At the thought of sitting around the Tomms's kitchen table with Albert, Kate, Mrs Tomms and a slice of delicious meat 'n' potato pie, Charlotte felt instantly better. 'Do you know, Albert,' she replied, with a grateful smile, 'I believe there is nothing I should like more.'

Albert Tomms had been in the employ of the Hamilton family for some thirty years. Not only was he the family's long-standing and trusted carriage driver, but he could turn his hand to many of the odd jobs which constantly needed attention at the manor. Being a little shy when it came to matters of the opposite sex, Albert had married relatively late in life but still believed, some twenty years on, that his wife, the plump and pretty Roberta, had been well worth the wait. During their contented life together, Roberta had provided her husband with two children: William, who was now almost 18 and as fond of food as his father, and 15-year-old, Kate who, with her head of red curls and her milky skin was as pretty as a picture and as shy as a church mouse.

By the time they reached the estate, the first drops of rain were beginning to fall.

'I'll drop you off at the cottage, miss,' Albert shouted down to Charlotte inside the carriage, 'before I take the horses round to the stables.'

'Thank you, Albert,' she called back.

The Tomms's pretty cottage was located just inside the gates of Hamilton Manor. It consisted of three rooms upstairs and a parlour and a kitchen downstairs. The house was not at all large, yet, despite its meagre proportions, it was one of Charlotte's favourite places in the whole world. In all but the most extreme weather conditions, the cottage's gleaming green front door was thrust open, allowing the smell of mouth-watering baking to tickle the tastebuds of any passer-by. Even today, despite the rain, the door was ajar and the surrounding air redolent with delicious meat and potato pie.

'Oh, Miss Charlotte! What a lovely surprise!' exclaimed Roberta Tomms as Charlotte stepped out of the carriage a few minutes later.

'Invited her for a bit of pie, so I have,' informed Albert, as he helped Charlotte down the carriage steps. 'Could do with a bit of fattening up if you ask me.'

Mrs Tomms's appraising green eyes raked Charlotte's slender frame as she came to stand before her. 'Hmm. You are looking a bit on the thin side, miss,' she said. Then, brightening her tone, 'Still, I expect it's all the excitement over your wedding and all.'

'I, er, expect so,' concurred Charlotte. Then, in a hasty attempt to change the subject, she added, 'The pie smells delicious, Mrs Tomms.'

'Our Will's favourite,' declared the older woman, a proud smile spreading across her round, rosy face. 'We'll keep a bit back for him for when he comes home from work tonight. Now, come on in, miss. We don't want you getting wet and catching a chill.'

As Charlotte smiled her thanks and stepped inside, Mrs Tomms shouted up the stairs, 'Kate! Look who's here!'

In a flash, Kate Tomms appeared on the landing, her long red hair, constrained in two fat pigtails. She peered down the stairs.

'Hello, Kate,' grinned Charlotte. 'How are you?'

'Miss Charlotte,' enthused the girl, her face lighting up. 'Gosh, what a treat.' She bounded down the stairs towards her.

'Well, I'm not sure about that,' chuckled Charlotte, as the two of them embraced.

'Oh, but it is, miss,' insisted Mrs Tomms, ushering the two girls into the kitchen and gesturing to Charlotte to remove her coat and bonnet. 'Why, we haven't seen so much as a hair on your head since your betrothal to Lord Farrell was announced. And I know our Kate is dying to hear about all the wedding plans. Got a little romantic on our hands, so we have.' She turned her back to Charlotte and began busying herself with the bubbling pots on the stove.

'Oh, do tell me about your wedding gown, Miss Charlotte,' pleaded Kate, colouring slightly. Charlotte, having removed her coat and bonnet and hung them on the pegs in the hall, slid on to the wooden bench at the opposite side of the large wooden table to Kate. 'Is it a very beautiful gown, miss?'

Charlotte attempted a smile. 'Well, I don't know, Kate. It's not yet ready. One can only hope that it will be beautiful.'

'And I'd wager you are going to have lots of pretty flowers,' ventured the girl.

Charlotte thought of the roses her mother had so adored and felt a pang of sadness. 'Er, quite pretty, I suppose,' she muttered, with as much enthusiasm as she could muster.

'Oh, I bet Father Jameson is beside himself with excitement,' gushed Mrs Tomms, still with her back to the girls. 'Why, it's not every day he'll have the pleasure of marrying off a young lady he had the honour of baptizing. And one so dear to him at that.'

Charlotte cringed. 'Actually, Mrs Tomms,' she explained ruefully, 'Lady Farrell has requested that Father Bartholomew take the ceremony.'

Mrs Tomms spun around and regarded Charlotte for a moment before turning back to her pots. 'Oh well, I don't suppose it really matters who marries you,' she declared briskly. 'The most important thing is that the pair of you'll be wed. Oh, your mother would be so proud of you, Miss Charlotte.'

At the mention of her mother, Charlotte's hand flew to her necklace.

'Do you really think so, Mrs Tomms?' she uttered, suspecting that, for all her good intentions, her mother would not have approved of her callousness.

'Of course,' replied the older woman brightly. 'Why, them Farrells is one of the most important families around here.'

'And one of the richest,' added Kate.

A tide of misery swept over Charlotte. 'Yes, I know,' she agreed. 'But they are not—'

Mrs Tomms whipped her head around to her. 'Not what, miss?'

Charlotte's eyes brimmed with tears. 'They are not—'

'What is it, love?' implored Mrs Tomms, wiping her hands on her apron as she left her position by the stove and walked around to Charlotte.

Silently remonstrating with herself for allowing her shield to slip, Charlotte blinked away the tears, took a deep breath and forced a smile. 'Nothing. Nothing at all, Mrs Tomms.'

The intensity of the moment was broken as one of the pans began boiling over. But, while Mrs Tomms rushed back to the stove to salvage the situation, muttering something about potatoes all the while, Kate's clear green eyes continued to observe Charlotte unblinkingly.

'A betrothal ball?' echoed Harriet, when they were all gathered in Edward's bedchamber later that afternoon. 'Tomorrow evening? Oh, how simply wonderful.'

'Indeed it is not, Harriet,' countered Edward. 'How can it possibly be wonderful when I shall be unable to attend?'

'Oh, you are far too young for balls anyway, Edward,' replied Harriet dismissively. 'But tell me, Charlotte, why have you only found out about it the day before? Surely, you should have had much more notice in order to prepare yourself.'

Charlotte shrugged. 'Lady Farrell was under the impression that she had already informed me of the arrangements.'

'Hmm,' mused Harriet. Then in a lighter tone, 'Still, I am sure it shall be perfectly marvellous. Oh, but please may I ask Mirabelle, Charlotte? She can take Edward's place.'

At the mere mention of Mirabelle, Charlotte's spirits usually plummeted. Today, however, already being on rock bottom, she found herself replying, 'Why not?' After all, the evening was assured to be such an unbearable affair anyway, that it was unlikely even the venomous Mirabelle McGregor could make it any worse.

Chapter Eight

NOT being in the centre of Society, Charlotte's choice of gowns for the ball was limited. She attempted not to dwell on the fact that, had she had a little more notice of the event, then she could have acquired a new dress. To inform her of the occasion merely hours beforehand was obviously another of Lady Farrell's tactics to reiterate her position of power and place Charlotte at a disadvantage.

After much deliberation, she opted for a rose-pink silk creation with a beaded trim. It was a pretty dress, but Charlotte was under no illusion that this would exclude it from the old lady's invective. This depressing thought served only to increase her anxiety at the evening ahead but, rather than spending all day moping about it, she determined to do something constructive. With two more baskets of food, she therefore set off once again in the gig to Murphy's Mansion.

Receiving just as effusive a greeting as on her previous visit, Charlotte was relieved to see that the young family appeared to be faring well in their new accommodation and the fresh country air. She was delighted when Emmy timidly asked her if she would like to take a look inside the cottage and had been unable to suppress her amazement at the transformation. Every bit of the dusty, damp debris, which had littered the property on her last visit, had been cleared away and, with the door thrown open, the smell of damp had all but disappeared. Charlotte was also overjoyed to see her gifts very much in evidence: two of the candles had pride of place in their brass holders on the mantel; on the hearth stood the copper saucepans; and in one of the rear rooms, makeshift beds had been arranged using the blankets. The huge effort which had been employed in making the place a home tugged at Charlotte's heartstrings. In fact, so enjoyable was her time with the young family, that she almost forgot her problems. But, as a ghostly mist began snaking its way over the landscape later that afternoon – providing a fitting analogy to Charlotte's own declining mood – she reluctantly announced that she had better be making her way home.

Charlotte was approximately half-a-mile from Hamilton Manor when the mist thickened into what Albert, with his obsession with food, would appropriately have termed a 'pea-souper'. It reduced Charlotte's visibility dramatically. She tried to remain calm as her driving skills were tested to the limit – the gig almost veering off-track on two hair-raising occasions. Upon reaching the crossroads which led on to a wider thoroughfare, she gave a huge sigh of relief and was just about to swing the conveyance into the main road when a lone figure on horseback came hurtling out of the mist. Charlotte pulled the gig to a halt as the horse thundered past. The appalling conditions allowed her no more than a brief glimpse of its rider but it was long enough to discern that it was a female, dressed in a green riding-habit, with a veiled hat covering her face. In a flash, the woman and her mount had disappeared, swallowed up by the fog.

'Lovely evening, ma'am,' sighed Adams, as he opened the door to her.

Charlotte lifted her brows, wondering how anyone could possibly favour such dire conditions. But she did not have long to dwell on the matter as Harriet came flying down the stairs.

'Goodness, Charlotte, where in heaven's name have you been? We have been beside ourselves with worry.'

'I, er, lost track of time,' mumbled Charlotte, as she continued to observe Adams. He had not yet closed the door and was standing on the top step, looking longingly at the swirling fog as it lapped about his legs. Harriet paid the man not the slightest heed, evidently having much more pressing matters on her mind.

'Well then, allow me to enlighten you as to the time, Sister,' she flustered. 'It is precisely ten minutes before six, which means that you have less than one hour to prepare yourself for your own betrothal ball.'

'That is time enough, Harriet,' replied Charlotte wearily, as Adams – with a great deal of obvious reluctance – slowly creaked the door shut.

Harriet's eyes grew wide. 'Time enough? Why, *I* have spent the best part of the day in preparations. The only thing that remains for me to do is to slip on my gown.' Then, unable to contain her excitement a moment longer, her tone changed completely. 'Oh, it is so thrilling, Charlotte, I can scarcely wait. And I hope you don't mind, but I extended your invitation to Mirabelle *and* her brother. They both paid us a visit earlier.'

Charlotte pulled a disgusted face. If there was one man who repulsed her equally as much as Frederick Farrell, it was Mirabelle's odious brother, Bertie.

Harriet, ignoring her sister's reaction, carried on. 'I own, Charlotte, I feel quite sorry for Bertie McGregor. In my opinion, the poor man is completely devastated you are to be married. It is my sincere belief that he has quite a *tendre* for you.'

'Lucky me,' muttered Charlotte under her breath.

'Your maid has, of course, prepared everything for you,' continued Harriet, 'but we were all so tired of waiting for you that I sent her down to the kitchens for something to eat. I shall send word to her now that you are arrived.'

Charlotte nodded her acquiescence and, turning on her heel, crossed the hall to the staircase. Despite the fact that time was of the essence, she mounted the stairs slowly, her legs feeling heavy as an uneasy sense of foreboding wrapped itself around her.

Reaching her bedchamber, she pushed open the door and came to an abrupt standstill, her heart leaping into her mouth at the unbelievable sight before her. Lying on her bed, was her rose-pink silk beaded gown – cut completely in half.

Between making the shocking discovery and leaving for the ball, there was little time to dwell on what her maid had termed 'the spiteful act'. What time there was, Charlotte employed in attempting to calm the long-standing servant who was hysterical with remorse for having left the room, thereby allowing the culprit the opportunity to carry out their intentions. Not wishing to aggravate matters further, Charlotte swore the girl to secrecy and, despite her protestations, ordered her straight to her room until she calmed down. Charlotte then made her own hasty toilette, selecting another gown – of cream satin – and quickly arranged her hair which had, from the spell in the damp fog, developed such an unattractive frizz that she didn't have the first idea what to do with it. In the absence of any better ideas, she twisted it up crudely and added a diamond clip to hold it in place. Then, aware that she was dreadfully late, she flew downstairs to join her father and Harriet who were waiting in the hall. Charlotte affected a cheerful countenance as she did her best to ignore her sister's silent, critical assessment of her appearance. Allowing the girl no time to voice her findings, she proceeded to usher the pair towards the door and into the waiting carriage where Lord Hamilton, much to Charlotte's relief immediately struck up a jolly conversation.

'Dr Leigh informed me today that Edward is making a marvellous recovery,' he announced, as the carriage rattled down the fog-filled drive.

'That is excellent news, Father,' replied Charlotte, determining not to allow him the slightest hint of either her exhaustion or her distress.

'And, it could not have worked out better,' beamed the old man. 'With the doctor now residing at Wetherington, he is to visit regularly to keep an eye on the young rascal – much better than us having to employ a nurse. Young Edward does not know how lucky he is. Why, do you know, I once knew a man who broke his arm and his leg and the doctor said to him …'

But Charlotte heard nothing else of her father's amusing tale. Her mind turned yet again to the unsettling incident of her ruined gown. Who on earth, she pondered, as an icy shard of fear slithered down her spine, could possibly hate her enough to do such a thing?

Despite the abysmal weather conditions, the Hamilton party arrived at Wetherington safely – courtesy of Albert's diligent driving – but some forty minutes late. As the carriage drew nearer to the building and the outline of the menacing pointed turrets peeped out above the mist, a heavy sense of dread enveloped Charlotte.

From the large number of conveyances outside the hall, it was clear that neither the weather nor the infamous Courteous Criminal highwayman had deterred the majority of invitees from attending. This fact was confirmed the moment the Hamiltons set foot inside. Within seconds, Lord Hamilton was accosted by a group of acquaintances he had not seen for some time. Harriet, meanwhile, visibly agitated at the thought of Mirabelle's reaction to her late arrival, instantly vanished into the throng to seek out her friend. Consequently, Charlotte was left with the task of greeting the Farrells alone. Finding that their hosts had already abandoned their reception party by the door, Charlotte went directly into the ballroom, in search of her future relatives. It did not take long for her to spot her future mother-in-law. She was holding court amongst a crowd in the centre of the vast room. Her bony form was attired in a gown of the deepest blue, with a shimmering silver overlay and matching demi-train. A glittering diamond tiara nestled in her white hair, whilst her wrists, neck and ears were all adorned with the famous family sapphires.

Threading her way through the crowd, Charlotte noticed, with a sinking heart, that not only was Frederick standing alongside his mother, but that the pair had obviously gone to a great deal of effort to co-ordinate their outfits. Frederick was dressed in knee-length velvet breeches – exactly the same shade of blue as his mother's dress – and a silver shirt with a large froth of lace at his throat.

The crowd surrounding the Farrells drifted away before Charlotte reached them. Only one other person remained. Charlotte's breath caught in her throat as she realized that that person was none other than Dr Daniel Leigh. She had to confess that, although she had considered the man handsome in his dishevelled day clothes, it was nothing to her opinion of him now. Attired in the very latest mode in evening wear: a dark-blue tail coat, beige knee breeches, white silk stockings and an intricately folded neck-cloth, with his dark hair gleaming under the light of the candles, he looked, she thought, positively striking.

Taking a deep breath, Charlotte marched up to the three as assertively as her shaking legs would allow. Her arrival, just as she had expected, was not greeted with an ounce of enthusiasm. Frederick and his mother regarded her with obvious disdain, whilst the doctor managed a courteous, but noticeably cool, bow of his head. Charlotte ignored him. She had far more important matters to deal with than concerning herself with the suspicions of a stranger, however handsome he may be – her first priority being to placate the obviously disgruntled Farrells.

'Good evening, my lady,' she began, forcing a smile on to her face. 'And you too, Frederick, um, my sweet.'

Frederick's wary expression was quickly replaced with a contemptible sneer as his mother wasted no time in launching into her tirade.

'Well, I am relieved to see that you have at last decided to honour us with your presence, Charlotte,' she sniffed. 'Clearly, you do not consider the occasion of your own betrothal ball of sufficient import to arrive in a timely fashion. I, on the other hand, have dragged myself from my sickbed to host the event. Although, with the anxiety forced upon us by your late arrival, I fear I may be returning there sooner than I had hoped. You should only be grateful, my girl, that I am under constant medical supervision. My health is so precarious that, save for a short visit to your brother today, Dr Leigh has not dared leave my side for a moment.'

Feeling, at that moment, in desperate need of an ally and recalling the way the doctor had winked at her when he had first examined Lady Farrell, Charlotte sneaked a glance at him, hoping, despite herself, for another such conspiratorial gesture. She found none. The doctor's expression remained as neutral as that with which he had greeted her.

'And,' ploughed on the old lady, running a disapproving eye over Charlotte's person, 'to exacerbate matters further, I see that you have clearly not wasted any of your precious time on your toilette – despite my quite clear instructions.'

Endeavouring to heave herself out of the swamp of mortification into which she was slowly sinking, Charlotte squared her shoulders to the older woman.

'I apologize for my late arrival and my appearance, ma'am. I am afraid both are due to some rather, um, *unforeseen* circumstances.'

'Unforeseen circumstances must always be foreseen, Charlotte,' countered Lady Farrell. 'We Farrells have a reputation to withhold – a reputation which I will not allow to be sullied by tardiness and poorly arranged hair.'

'Of course not, ma'am,' rejoined Charlotte in a rueful tone. 'I can assure you it will not happen again.'

'Indeed it will not,' affirmed the older woman. 'For I can assure you that when you are the wife of my son and residing under my roof, you will not be permitted to leave the house until I am completely satisfied with your appearance. It is obvious that you are going to require a great deal of supervision before you achieve the standards of the Farrells.'

Flooded with humiliation, Charlotte called upon every ounce of her restraint not to tell the countess exactly what she could do with her standards. Instead, she affected an ingenuous smile, aware that the doctor was, once again, observing her intently.

'It shall be my greatest pleasure, ma'am, to achieve the high standards which you and your family attain so effortlessly. In fact, may I say how utterly charming you look this evening, Frederick … dearest?'

Frederick screwed up his face to her. 'I beg your pardon, madam?'

Charlotte gulped, aware that all three were now observing her as though she were newly escaped from Bedlam.

'I, er, said that you are in exceptionally good looks this evening, my lord.'

Frederick and his mother exchanged a questioning look, whilst a flicker of disbelief hovered over the doctor's features.

'We Farrells are always in good looks,' replied Frederick, ruffling the mound of lace at his neck. 'Why, one rarely sees Mama without her jewels or Perdita dressed in anything but the very finest of gowns.'

'Indeed one does not,' concurred Charlotte with forced alacrity. 'And where, may I ask, is dear Perdita?'

Frederick heaved an impatient sigh. 'She will be joining us later when her strength allows. Despite the fact that the girl's condition is so far beyond delicate that she has not left her bed all day, she is a Farrell and we Farrells do not permit our poor health to interfere with our duty.'

Before Charlotte had a chance to comment on this observation, a stout woman, dressed in a sumptuous gown of puce satin and a matching jewelled turban from which two large ostrich feathers protruded, appeared at Lady Farrell's side. Despite the elaborateness of her attire, Charlotte noticed that her most striking features were her dark bushy eyebrows, which met seamlessly in the middle of her forehead.

The countess's previously sour expression melted effortlessly into one of beatific charm. 'Ah, Duchess of Lonsdale. What a great pleasure,' she gushed. 'I own, I was a little concerned if you would be honouring us with your presence this evening, your grace. We have, needless to say, heard all about your recent ordeal at the hands of that wicked highwayman.'

'Alas, it is that very ordeal, Lady Farrell,' began the duchess, 'that has resulted in my tardiness. Not only has it taken me a great deal of courage to leave the house this evening, but I also engaged the services of every one of my footmen in accompanying me. It will, I fear, be quite some time before I am recovered from the incident.'

The countess shook her head. 'The audacity of these criminals is beyond contemplation.'

'Well, I certainly cannot disagree with you there, Lady Farrell,' concurred the duchess. 'Do you know, the man aimed his pistol directly at my head.' To demonstrate her point, she directed two fingers towards the middle of her eyebrow.

Four sets of eyes regarded it curiously before Frederick announced, 'It is my sincere opinion, Lady Lonsdale, that no punishment would be good enough for the cad, terrifying the aristocracy as he is. It is nothing less than scandalous.'

His mother nodded her agreement. 'News of such incidents does not help my shattered nerves at all.'

'Then one can only hope you never meet with such an incident in person, Lady Farrell,' rejoined the duchess. 'Although, I must confess that, given the peculiar circumstances, the man was exceedingly polite.'

'Polite or not, I fully intend to write to the Bow Street Runners and inform them that it is high time they caught the scoundrel,' pronounced the countess. 'Several of my acquaintances have sent word that they will not be attending this evening, due to that man's appalling antics. One can only wonder, when one's social engagements begin to be disrupted, where it will all end.'

'Where indeed,' remarked the duchess. 'If the man is not caught soon, I fear we will all be stuck at home during the long winter evenings twiddling our thumbs. I dare not even contemplate such a dreadful state of affairs. Now, please do excuse me, Lady Farrell. I see Viscount Cunningham over there and I have not yet shared my experience with him. The man is, I am certain, desperate to hear every one of the details.' And, with that, she whisked around and began elbowing her way through the crowd, towards her unsuspecting target.

Chapter Nine

NO sooner had the Duchess of Lonsdale taken her leave of the group, than the countess pressed the palm of her hand to her forehead.

'Doctor Leigh, I feel a distinct fit of the vapours overtaking me. I insist you do not leave my side for a moment. Absolutely anything could happen to me.'

'I think it unlikely, ma'am,' countered the doctor.

'One must always be prepared for the worst,' she snapped.

'It could not get much worse,' muttered the physician. But neither Frederick nor his mother appeared to hear this remark, the countess busily engrossed in disentangling the cord of her ivory fan from her wrist. Having succeeded in her task, she proffered the item to the doctor.

'Talk of that odious criminal has sapped me of the strength to use my own fan, Doctor. I insist you cool me down, if, that is, you do not wish to be picking me up from the floor within the next few minutes.'

'I really do not think, ma'am—' protested the doctor, clearly appalled at the request.

'I am paying you well for your services, am I not, Dr Leigh?' butted in the countess.

'Yes, ma'am.'

'Then I think the very least you can do is oblige me. Don't you?'

The flash of anger which flittered over the doctor's face did not escape Charlotte's notice. Without saying another word, he snatched the fan from Lady Farrell's scrawny hand and began half-heartedly fluttering it in front of the woman's face. No sooner had he begun this activity, than Charlotte felt a tug on her arm. She whisked around to find a beaming Harriet, accompanied by Mirabelle McGregor and her brother, Bertie.

'Look who I have found, Charlotte,' announced Harriet proudly.

Aware of Mirabelle scrutinizing her less than impeccable appearance, Charlotte forced the corners of her lips upwards. 'Mirabelle! Bertie! How lovely to see you both.'

Mirabelle's smile failed to melt the ice in both her eyes and her tone. 'Charlotte. And looking so, er—'

'Lovely,' interjected Harriet loyally. 'Perfectly lovely, as always.'

Bertie nodded, his beady eyes adhering themselves to Charlotte's bosom.

Charlotte quailed inwardly. Whilst Bertie McGregor had a much taller frame than his sister, and a not displeasing build, there remained, unfortunately, very little else that could be said in the man's favour. His hair was exactly the same shade of muddied water as that of his sister and his wide nose – with several dark hairs protruding from the nostrils – spread proprietorially over the centre of his podgy, spot-ridden face. But it was not just Bertie McGregor's appearance that Charlotte found offensive. Indeed, all physical defects could, she believed, be more than redeemed by a person's other qualities. The problem with Bertie McGregor was that he did not appear to have one redeeming quality. Whenever she found herself in the man's presence, Charlotte could not fail to notice the lascivious way he stared at her, a stare that had the unfailing effect of rendering her discomfited – exactly how she was feeling right now.

'So, you are to be married, Lady Charlotte,' remarked Bertie. 'Lord Farrell is a lucky man.' His eyes shifted again to her chest and, at the implication, Charlotte felt bile rising.

Mirabelle, meanwhile, gave a snort of mocking laughter. 'There will be no one luckier than you, Bertie, when you are married. If, of course, you ever are.'

'And why wouldn't I be?' asked Bertie, clearly affronted.

'Well, just look at you,' scoffed Mirabelle, raking her eyes down his frame. 'What lady could ever fall in love with you?'

'Wh-what is wrong with me?' stammered Bertie.

Mirabelle gave another derisive cackle. 'What is wrong with you? I think it much less time-consuming to ask what is right with you? I am sorry to have to inform you yet again, dear Brother, that you are lacking in every one of the qualities we ladies seek in either a husband or a lover.'

Bertie flushed a deep shade of crimson, effectively joining together all the red blotches on his face. 'S-Sarah Cataract does not agree with you, Sister. She stood up with me twice last week.'

Mirabelle gave a chilling snort of laughter. 'Forgive me for shattering your pathetic illusions, Bertie, but the only reason Sarah Cataract so much as spoke to you was because her family have just lost their entire fortune and are desperately seeking a half-decent husband for her. I suppose, given that you may eventually qualify as a man of law, and inherit Papa's legal firm, the Cataracts consider you to fall into that category. Where money is concerned, we ladies can, of course, willingly forego all other considerations. Am I not correct, Charlotte dear?'

As Bertie, Mirabelle and an uncomfortable-looking Harriet all stared at her expectantly, a stain of red began snaking its way over Charlotte's cheeks.

'I confess I have, er, no idea, Mirabelle.'

Mirabelle threw her a sardonic smile. 'Of course you don't. Why, how could I possibly expect an innocent like you to comprehend such motives when you would marry for nothing other than love?'

'Love is a wonderful thing,' professed Bertie, focusing again on Charlotte's cleavage.

Mirabelle gave a roar of laughter so icy that it cut through Charlotte like a knife. 'Love is a wonderful thing?' she echoed. 'And what pray, do you know about it, dear Brother?'

'More than you think,' retorted Bertie, so vehemently that Charlotte's toes curled in her silk slippers.

'Good lord, Bertie, you really are a lost cause,' sniggered Mirabelle. 'But for me, you would have not the first idea about the real world. I can see, however, that there remains a great deal to teach you – particularly in the workings of the female mind. Still, all is not lost, I suppose. If Sarah Cataract does not have the doubtful privilege of becoming Mrs Bertie McGregor, then there will no doubt be others who are equally as desperate.'

Bertie's ugly face was now a deep shade of scarlet as he stared at his sister, his eyes full of something Charlotte could only identify as contempt. And she could not blame the man. As odious as he was, the relief Charlotte had felt when Mirabelle had directed her noxious comments away from her and on to Bertie, was now replaced by something akin to pity for the man. Even the fact that he was some seven years Mirabelle's senior, and her own flesh and blood, obviously did not entitle him to any concessions where the girl's malicious tongue was concerned.

Harriet, evidently experiencing similar thoughts, made a valiant effort to change the subject. 'I, er, see you were speaking to the Duchess of Lonsdale, Charlotte. Did she happen to relate anything of her recent ordeal at the hands of the Courteous Criminal?'

Charlotte nodded her head, grateful to her sister for the diversion. 'Indeed she did, Harriet. She has been greatly distressed by the incident.'

'But did she confirm that the man is all he is rumoured to be?' asked Harriet, unable to curb the excitement in her voice.

'All he is rumoured to be?' echoed Bertie, his cheeks still flaming. 'What rumours have you heard, Lady Harriet?'

Harriet flushed. 'Well,' she began, a little apprehensively, 'I have heard that he is very handsome, extremely charming and quite, quite dashing. A most romantic figure in fact.'

'Really?' mused Bertie.

'Well, handsome or not,' sniffed Mirabelle, 'I am certain I would not surrender my jewels to such a criminal.'

'Not even if he held a pistol to your head?' asked an astounded Harriet.

'Not even if he held two pistols to my head,' confirmed Mirabelle, with a toss of her murky ringlets. 'I would not tolerate such insolence for a moment. No common criminal will order me around as though I were a mere servant.'

While Harriet regarded her friend in wide-eyed admiration, Charlotte and Bertie did not appear so convinced. As all three of them continued to stare at Mirabelle, Charlotte became aware of Dr Leigh's deep voice. She had all but forgotten that he was standing directly behind her and had most likely heard every word of their conversation. She turned her head to look at him.

'Just as I told you, ma'am,' he declared, snapping shut the countess's fan. 'There was no question of you suffering a fit of the vapours.' But, as his words were directed to the countess, his eyes, Charlotte noticed, were coolly observing Mirabelle McGregor.

Apart from a brief exchange of formalities with the Farrells, Charlotte saw little of her father and her sister during the course of the evening. She was only grateful that, whenever the crowd did allow her a fleeting glimpse, they both appeared to be having a fine time. The same could not, unfortunately, be said of herself. The countess had insisted that Charlotte remain constantly by her side whilst she introduced her to any number of people – each one as dull and pompous as the next. From the haughty manner in which she had directed Charlotte's movements throughout the evening, she had little doubt that the woman was already looking upon her as another of the Farrells' many acquisitions. This, she recognized with a sinking feeling, was to be her life from now on: Lady Farrell ruling her, just as she did her offspring – with an invisible iron rod, liberally brandished before anyone who dared to question her authority.

Charlotte realized that she was not alone in this unfortunate predicament. Despite her increasing irritation at the man's perceptiveness, Dr Daniel Leigh was another of the countess's victims, tied to the family for exactly the same reason as Charlotte: the Farrell family fortune. Not, of course, that she could blame the man: the offer to pay him five times his usual fee would have been exceedingly difficult for anyone to turn down. But there was, she acknowledged, one marked difference between the two of them: whereas the doctor's sentence was but temporary, Charlotte's was to last the remainder of her days.

Two interminably long hours had gone by before Perdita Farrell appeared in the ballroom. She was dressed in an elaborate creation of turquoise silk adorned with more spangles than Charlotte had ever set eyes on. Despite its opulence, the dress hung languidly on the girl's skeletal frame, highlighting her complete lack of feminine curves. A spangled bandeau of the same colour held back her hair, permitting an unhindered view of her bland, elongated face.

'Ah, Perdita dear. How very brave of you to join us,' gushed her mother. 'How are you feeling, my love?'

Perdita gave a diffident smile. 'A little better, Mama.'

'Thank the Lord,' sighed Lady Farrell. 'Quite what we Farrells have done to suffer so with our health, is completely beyond me. But we shall, of course, not permit ourselves to dwell on such matters. Now, I must say, my dear, that is quite the most charming of gowns. It brings out the colour of your eyes beautifully.'

Charlotte wrinkled her brow, trying to ascertain exactly what colour the countess was referring to. As far as she could see, Perdita's eyes, despite her glittering, gaudy dress, remained as colourless as ever.

But, evidently delighted at her mother's compliment, Perdita gave a satisfied grin and began swishing her skirts from side to side. 'Do you like my gown, Dr Leigh?' she twittered, lowering her pale lashes and casting a flirtatious look at the man.

A shadow of horror fell over Dr Leigh's countenance. 'I, er, beg your pardon, ma'am?'

Perdita attempted a coy smile, which served only to cause her thin lips to disappear inside the rim of her mouth. 'I asked, Doctor, if you liked my gown. Do you agree with Mama that it brings out the colour of my eyes?'

'It, er suits you very, um, well, ma'am,' floundered the physician.

The girl emitted a contented sigh and began fluttering her fan. 'Oh, I do so love balls. They are the most romantic of occasions. And I do believe I feel strong enough to engage in a little dancing. May I borrow Dr Leigh for a waltz, Mama?'

The countess regarded her daughter concernedly. 'Are you sure you are well enough, my dear?'

'Quite well … for the moment,' confirmed Perdita.

'Well, if you insist,' acquiesced her mother, 'then I am sure Dr Leigh would be only too delighted to take to the floor with such an eminent partner. After all, it cannot be every day that a doctor is presented with the opportunity to hold such an esteemed member of Society in his arms. Am I correct, Doctor?'

Before the astounded physician had a chance to reply, Perdita laid her bony hand upon his arm, causing him to flinch and leaving him with little choice but to escort his eager partner to the dance floor. Charlotte watched with interest as he took Perdita's thin frame in his arms and began whisking her around the floor. From the strained look upon his face, it was obvious to her that he was finding the experience exceedingly unpleasant. Frederick, on the other hand, appeared to have a completely different view.

'Oh, Perdita is such a worthy woman,' he muttered. 'Just like you, Mama.'

The countess heaved another of her sighs. 'You see, Charlotte, one must learn to put on one's best face when one is a Farrell. Society expects nothing but the very highest of standards from us at all times.'

Frederick nodded his agreement. 'But I think we should make the girl aware, Mama, that she will never be considered a true Farrell. She will never, after all, have the Farrell breeding.'

'That, of course, is very true, Frederick,' concurred the older woman. 'Unfortunately, we can only make the best of what we have and even that will require a great deal of effort.'

They both sighed resignedly, regarding Charlotte as though she were an unruly puppy in dire need of house-training. But their insulting comments had swung the spotlight once more to the same tiresome question which still disturbed Charlotte's brief snatches of sleep with alarming regularity; the question to which she was still failing to find, no matter how hard she tried, any answer to at all: with both his and his mother's obvious dislike of her, why exactly was it that Frederick Farrell wished to take her as his wife?

Chapter Ten

ALONG with the Farrells' motives for her marriage, the issue of who was responsible for ruining her ball gown was now vying for supremacy on Charlotte's increasing list of worries. Despite the many long, dark hours she had spent puzzling over who could possibly hate her enough to do such a thing and who, indeed, had had the opportunity, she remained completely baffled by the incident. In a more anxious state than usual that morning, it did not take her long to conclude that she was in no mood to face Harriet's bright chatter and in-depth analysis of the previous evening's ball. To that end, she slipped out of bed, pulled on her riding breeches and made her way around to the stables before all but a handful of servants had begun their daily activities.

The dense fog of the previous evening had now completely dissipated and the sky was streaked with orange as the sun began its ascent. Charlotte urged Victor to a gallop as soon as they were clear of the house. Riding out long and hard over the colourful patchwork of fields, she relished the cool clear air whistling through her head, momentarily flushing it of its chaotic thoughts.

On Charlotte's return, the sun had completed its daily undertaking and was high in the clear blue sky, indicating that she had been out several hours. This fact was confirmed by her stomach as it rumbled loudly, evidently not impressed that she had left the house before breakfast. With her spirits a little restored, she steered Victor through the gates of the manor only to come upon the McGregors' mustard-coloured coach.

At exactly the same moment, she heard Harriet calling her from Edward's bedchamber window. Her thought processes weighted down with other matters, Charlotte was too slow to pretend she had neither seen nor heard her sister. Reluctantly raising her hand in acknowledgement of Harriet's cries, she kicked Victor on towards the house, feeling all at once as miserable as she had when she had left it.

A particularly dismal Adams opened the door to her. 'Lady Harriet left instructions that you are to join her in Master Edward's chamber at once, my lady.' This announcement was followed by a tremulous sigh as the servant then turned on his heel and shuffled silently towards one of the doors leading off from the hall.

Charlotte groaned inwardly as she watched him go. Had she been presented with the choice, she would have preferred to spend the entire day – nay, week – in the haunting presence of Adams, than face Mirabelle McGregor for some thirty minutes. But she did not have the choice. They would all now know that she had returned to the house. Avoiding Mirabelle would serve only to antagonize the girl and increase her already strong suspicions regarding the reasons behind her marriage to Frederick Farrell. Having Dr Daniel Leigh already apparently questioning her every move was bad enough; to add Mirabelle McGregor to the equation was beyond consideration.

Excited chatter drifted along the corridor as Charlotte approached her brother's rooms. On reaching the door, she steeled herself for a moment, wondering if, on a much lesser scale of course, this was how a soldier must feel before going into battle. The analogy, given Mirabelle as an adversary, could not have been more fitting. She pushed open the door and stood for a few seconds on the threshold, absorbing the scene. Edward was lying atop his counterpane; Harriet was seated in the chair on his left and Mirabelle in a matching chair on the right. On the bottom of the bed was perched Bertie McGregor, looking particularly hideous with a fresh outbreak of red and yellow pimples on his chin and, just when Charlotte had thought the little gathering complete, Dr Daniel Leigh stepped out of the bathroom. Charlotte's stomach turned over. Mirabelle and Bertie were more than enough to cope with this morning, but Mirabelle, Bertie *and* Dr Leigh.... She was not at all sure she had the strength. She met the doctor's eyes defiantly, but, rather than the impassive way in which he had regarded her at the previous evening's ball, she now noticed that his lips were twitching. Bertie McGregor also appeared to be regarding her strangely.

'Charlotte! What on earth possessed you to go out riding so ridiculously early? And for so long?' demanded Harriet.

Charlotte opened her mouth to reply, but, before she could do so, Mirabelle forestalled her, an unsettling smirk upon her face.

'And wearing, what appears to be a pair of boy's riding breeches?'

With a pang of dismay, Charlotte dropped her head and took in her attire. Of course everyone at the manor was used to seeing her dressed so, which made it easy to forget that a lady in breeches was not at all the thing. She was aware of two stains of pink appearing on her cheeks as Bertie and the doctor gawped at her long legs, the shapeliness of which was clearly defined for all to see.

'Oh, don't be such a ninny, Mirabelle,' chuckled Edward. 'Charlotte always dresses so to go riding. She finds it impossible to ride astride in a lady's riding-habit.'

Bertie's beady eyes grew wide. 'You ride *astride*, Lady Charlotte?'

Charlotte cast a despairing look around the room. Every one of its inhabitants was staring at her, but it was the look on the doctor's face that was causing her most annoyance. If she was not mistaken, the man was choking back a laugh. She tilted her chin upwards.

'If you will excuse me, as my dress is obviously causing such offence, I shall go and change at once,' she announced.

Harriet gasped. 'Oh no, Charlotte, don't waste time doing that. Mirabelle and Bertie have brought us such exciting news. Why, you will never guess what happened after the ball yesterday evening. There has been' – she paused for effect – 'yet another hold up by the Courteous Criminal. The Countess of Montague no less. And he even took her diamond tiara which has been in her family since the days of King John.'

Now Charlotte felt her own eyes widen. Another hold up by the Courteous Criminal? Was the man ever going to stop, or would he only do so when he was hanging from the gallows?

'Really, Harriet, you do recount a shockingly poor tale,' remonstrated Mirabelle, shaking her head at her friend. 'I can see that *I* shall have to provide your sister with all the details.' She turned to Charlotte, still hovering at the door. 'The Countess of Montague, Charlotte, was travelling home alone from your betrothal ball yesterday evening when, out of the fog, appeared a lone figure dressed entirely in black, save for a blue silk cravat around his face. This, as we all know, is the ensemble favoured by the man known as the Courteous Criminal. Well, the woman's driver brought the coach to a halt, of course. Then the highwayman ordered him and the footmen to step down while he held the gun at the countess's head. He then proceeded to rob the poor woman of every one of her jewels.'

'But she did admit, did she not, Mirabelle,' said Harriet, looking to her friend for confirmation, 'that he was perfectly courteous and very handsome?'

Edward gave a snort of laughter. 'How could she see if he was handsome when the place was covered in fog so thick you could scarce see a hand before your eyes? You ladies do have some strange romantic notions in your heads.'

'But I believe it is true, sir,' cut in Bertie. 'I, too, have heard, from several different sources now, that the man is both courteous and handsome.'

'Well, I hope,' chortled Edward, 'that my good looks and gracious manners are not the only attributes people recall when I am famous. I should much prefer them to remember my scientific discoveries just as I imagine the Courteous Criminal should prefer to be remembered for his long-running and, although we do not wish to admit it, extremely successful campaign of robbing the rich – much more laudable than just being remembered for being handsome and courteous. What say you, Bertie?'

Bertie gazed at Edward for several seconds before replying, 'I confess I should be happy with merely being remembered at all, my lord.'

The stunned silence that followed this remark was broken by one of Mirabelle's chilling snorts of laughter. 'Oh Bertie, you really are a pitiful soul. Who on earth would wish to remember you? There is simply, dear Brother, nothing at all to remember.'

Bertie's face turned puce as he flashed his sister a look overflowing with loathing. But Bertie's was not the only shocking response that Charlotte noticed. From the contemptuous look on Dr Leigh's face, there was little doubt that he, too, was both repulsed and appalled by Mirabelle McGregor's sour observations.

Albert was up a ladder, fixing a piece of loose guttering when Charlotte eventually found him later that afternoon.

'Do you think Kate would like to accompany me to the mantuamaker tomorrow, Albert? I'm due another fitting for my wedding gown.'

Albert stopped what he was doing and stared down at her in amazement. 'Our Kate, miss?'

Charlotte nodded. 'But if you don't think that she would, then I won't—'

'Don't think she would?' repeated Albert, his mouth stretching into a proud smile. 'Why, I'd be hard pushed to think of anything she'd like better.'

'Good,' declared Charlotte, already looking forward to the girl's company. 'Then I shall ask her myself later.'

'It'll fair make her week, so it will,' chuckled the old man. 'Now, if you don't mind just holding the ladder 'til I climb down, Miss Charlotte, I think we'll be having ourselves a slice of that ham 'n' egg pie Mrs Tomms wrapped up for me afternoon snack.'

Having done as she was bid and with Albert safely on the ground, he and Charlotte sat down on the grass together, leaning against the wall of the house. Albert unwrapped the pie from its muslin cloth and offered a slice to Charlotte. Although not the least bit hungry, she accepted it, anxious not to have him launch into another concerned speech about her dwindling weight.

'My,' sighed Albert, wiping his hands on the cloth as he swallowed his last morsel, 'I have to admit that it's not goin' to be the same without you round here, Miss Charlotte.'

'Things never stay the same, Albert,' murmured Charlotte.

Albert nodded his white head. 'That's right enough, miss. More's the pity.'

'More is indeed the pity,' concurred Charlotte, as she blinked back a tear.

*

Knowing his daughter as well as he did, Albert Tomms had been correct in his confident assumption. Kate had leaped at Charlotte's invitation and given her such an effusive hug that Charlotte, unable to breathe, had had to employ all of her strength to wriggle out of it. As Kate joined her in the carriage that morning, dressed in her best beige pelisse and straw bonnet, her pretty face was awash with excitement.

'Oh, I feel like such a grand lady, Miss Charlotte,' she giggled, as she took her seat opposite. 'I can't thank you enough for inviting me. This is one of the best days of my life.'

'Oh, believe me, Kate,' replied Charlotte, with complete sincerity, 'it is I who should be thanking you. Your company will make the trip all the more bearable.'

Kate regarded her incredulously. 'But aren't you excited, miss? I should think there would be nothing more thrilling than having a beautiful gown made for your own grand wedding.'

Charlotte forced a smile upon her face, which stopped short of her eyes. 'Of course I am, Kate,' she rejoined, as sanguinely as she could manage. 'I should be very grateful, I know.'

Kate said nothing, but began nibbling her bottom lip as she studied Charlotte's face. Breaking the ensuing uncomfortable, silence and determining not to allow the poor girl another insight into her true feelings, Charlotte piped up, 'But tell me about you, Kate. I would wager there are lots of young men who are sweet on you. Have you taken a shine to any of them?'

Kate flushed to the brim of her bonnet. 'Well,' she all but whispered, 'I haven't told anyone else, miss, not even me ma, but there's a boy called Thomas on the farm where our William works and he's ever so kind and handsome and …'

As Kate, in the throes of young, uncomplicated love, began recounting the tale of the boy who had caught her eye and she evidently his, and of how he had shyly approached her and they had been out walking a couple of times, Charlotte observed the high colour in the girl's cheeks and the happy glint in her eyes. How wonderful, she thought, to be so free, without the burdening weight about her shoulders which Charlotte knew would now be with her for the rest of her life. At that particular moment, she wanted nothing more than to be Kate Tomms.

*

At the mantuamaker's the dress had taken another large leap towards completion.

Kate was speechless as she took in the classic simplicity of the ivory gown; the tiny pearls shimmering on the bodice and the discreet edging of lace on the puffed sleeves.

'Two more fittings and it should be ready, miss,' beamed the mantuamaker proudly. 'And then you'll be the prettiest bride that ever wore one of my dresses.'

'And the happiest,' added Kate, her voice subtly lilting upwards.

Was it a question or a statement? Either way, Charlotte could not find it within herself to reply.

Chapter Eleven

THERE was a great deal of hilarity at Murphy's Mansion the following day when Charlotte arrived with more provisions for the family. Little Harry had surprised them all that morning by taking his first tentative steps. His siblings, all delighted at this momentous occasion, were taking turns in holding his chubby hands as he waddled up and down the grass verge outside. He really was a beautiful child, thought Charlotte, as she watched Becky and Tommy attempting to coax him to walk between the two of them. Each had their arms outstretched, ready to catch the tot if he teetered in his mission and flopped down on to his well-padded bottom. For all it was unlikely that little Harry would ever achieve great wealth in the material sense of the word, she mused, there could be no one richer when it came to being loved. And indeed the same could be said of all the members of the young family, who were so fiercely proud and protective of one another.

When Emmy came and sat down on the blanket alongside Charlotte, thanking her yet again for her generous gifts, Charlotte found herself so overcome with emotion that she could do nothing but squeeze the girl's hand. If only Emmy knew that it should be Charlotte who was thanking her and her family for bringing into her complicated life some of the simplest of pleasures.

Simple pleasures were, unfortunately, not the order of the day at Hamilton Manor. Awaiting Charlotte upon her return some hours later, was an invitation to one Lady Fisher's birthday celebrations that evening, accompanied by a note from Lady Farrell demanding Charlotte's attendance. Charlotte's heart sank as she read it. She had done her utmost to avoid such tedious social occasions in the past, but she now realized, with an increasingly familiar leaden feeling, that her days of doing so were over. As the wife of Frederick Farrell and the new Countess of Wetherington, her presence would be expected at all such events and, as Lady Farrell insisted upon telling her, as a Farrell she would have to put on her best face.

Charlotte, accompanied by her maid, arrived punctually at Lady Fisher's stately country house, where she had been instructed to meet her future in-laws. She waited in the entrance hall, peering out of the floor-to-ceiling window at the line of carriages depositing their occupants at the foot of the steps. From her dwindling selection, she had chosen a gown of dove silk with two layers of frills about the hem. It was a flattering creation which suited her very well. But, observing the three Farrells as they alighted their carriage, dressed in their usual opulent style – Perdita in scarlet satin covered with a profusion of bugles, the countess in bilious green and Frederick in gold breeches – she felt instantly under-dressed. The last person to appear from the Farrells' carriage was Dr Leigh. Wearing the same classic evening dress he had worn to the betrothal ball, he looked just as dashing. Looking up at the house, his eyes fused with Charlotte's. She realized she had been staring at him. With a pang of embarrassment, she shifted her attention to the Farrells who were mounting the steep set of steps. She walked over to greet them as they entered the building, forcing the corners of her lips into a smile.

'Good evening, my lord,' she said, dipping a curtsy before Frederick. 'I was, um, very much looking forward to seeing you this evening.'

Frederick, obviously not considering his fiancée's comment worthy of reply, merely glared at her contemptuously as he straightened his neckcloth. Instead, it was the countess who addressed Charlotte first, employing her usual derisive tones.

'Well,' she began, casting an appraising eye over the girl's appearance. 'Thank goodness you have not only arrived on time, but are also looking somewhat presentable.'

Before Charlotte could reply, Perdita gave an almighty sigh. 'Hmm,' she huffed. 'I own there is *some* improvement in the girl's appearance, Mama. Although I believe myself to be in much finer looks this evening, eh, Dr Leigh?'

'Wh–what?' stammered the doctor, who had now joined the group and accorded Charlotte a courteous bow.

'I said, Doctor,' repeated Perdita, making another of her futile attempts at a demure smile, 'that Lady Charlotte is in nowhere near as fine looks as myself this evening. Do you not agree, sir?'

The doctor looked from Charlotte to Perdita and back again. 'Well, I, er, confess I really have not given the matter much, um, thought, ma'am.'

'I should not have thought that much thought would be required, Doctor,' tittered Perdita.

Lady Farrell threw her daughter an admonishing glare. 'Really, Perdita, I would have thought that having been blessed with the Farrell good looks, you would not stoop so low as to compare your appearance with those families of lesser quality. Now enough of this idle chatter, Lady Fisher is waiting to greet us.' She swung around and began marching towards the door of the ballroom where their hostess was hovering. Frederick and Perdita followed.

Despair engulfed Charlotte as she watched the three of them go. She had no inclination at all to join them. So absorbed was she in her miserable musings in fact, that she had not realized Dr Leigh was still standing alongside her. His voice brought an end to her reverie.

'If I might be so bold as to say, Lady Charlotte,' he began, his dark eyes glinting with humour, 'in answer to Lady Perdita's question, I find yourself in much better looks this evening and the matter did indeed, as Lady Perdita pointed out, require no thought at all. I should have reached exactly the same conclusion were you standing before me now in your riding breeches.'

Utterly astonished at this confession, Charlotte stood rooted to the spot as the physician took his leave of her. Had he been laughing at her again, or had he just paid her a compliment? The stab of indignation which pulsed through her at the realization that it was most likely the former, was tempered, ever so slightly, by the faint ray of hope that it could possibly have been the latter. She did not debate the matter long though, as she realized that Perdita was staring back at her. The look on the girl's face caused every one of the hairs on the back of Charlotte's neck to stand immediately on end.

Any further rays of hope Charlotte had been harbouring that perhaps Lady Fisher's birthday celebrations would not be quite as dire as she had envisaged, were quickly extinguished as the evening dragged by tediously. Frederick, adopting his usual scathing manner, paid her scant attention all evening, in spite of Charlotte's efforts to portray the image of the perfect fiancée – an image which was becoming increasingly difficult to maintain under Dr Leigh's constant enquiring gaze. So mentally exhausted was she, that Charlotte was almost grateful to Perdita for her simpering attentions towards the doctor. As nauseating as these were, they did, at least, serve to intermittently divert the man's suspicious attentions away from her. After several long, unbearable hours, Charlotte could almost have hugged the countess, when the woman announced that she was quite fatigued and that they were all to take their leave.

Having bid their farewells, they made their way to the hall, where the butler threw open the door. Charlotte shivered as the chilled night air cut right through to her bones. She pulled her cloak tightly about her and gathered up her skirts, ready to descend the steep steps. She was some halfway down the steps when Perdita, who was behind her, suddenly emitted a blood-curdling shriek. Charlotte came to an immediate stop and whisked around to face the girl. At exactly the same moment, she felt something at her feet and, a second later, she lost her footing and tumbled, headlong, down the steps. She crashed in a heap at the bottom, a blinding pain splitting her head and every one of her bones aching. Trying to open her eyes, she found that every effort to do so merely intensified the pain. Instead, she surrendered herself to the soft blanket of darkness that was gradually smothering her.

'What on earth made her fall like that?' she heard Perdita asking.

'Perhaps it had something to do with your screaming, ma'am,' remarked the doctor archly.

'But I only screamed because a bat flew directly by me, Doctor,' twittered the girl.

'I doubt very much that it had anything at all to do with bats or screams,' butted in Frederick, not a hint of concern in his tone. 'Clearly, the girl is incapable of even walking down a set of steps. Now do, pray, do something with her, Dr Leigh. It is enough having these wretched carriage drivers fussing about. Before we know it, we shall have the entire house out here gawping at us and I cannot abide being made a spectacle of.'

Charlotte sensed two strong arms scooping her up with ease. 'If you will permit me, Lady Farrell,' she heard the doctor saying, 'I think it best if I accompany Lady Charlotte home this evening. I fear she has suffered a concussion.'

Charlotte was aware of the countess heaving an impatient sigh. 'Very well, then,' she said, evidently unimpressed at the suggestion. 'But on your head be it, Doctor, if anything happens to *me* this evening.'

'Or to me, Doctor,' huffed Perdita. 'Why, I'm sure the girl has done nothing more than broken a fingernail.'

'Let us hope that that is indeed the case, ma'am,' retorted the doctor tersely. 'Now, if you will excuse me, I think it best we get her home without further delay.'

Charlotte was conscious of the capable arms carrying her. She heard Albert Tomms's anxious voice, followed by that of her maid and then … nothing.

Charlotte awoke in her bed the next morning feeling like she had endured several rounds in a boxing ring. Her entire body ached and there was a large, throbbing lump on her head. She sensed immediately that she was not alone. She looked around, expecting to see her maid, but, to her amazement, she found a sleeping Dr Leigh in the chair next to her. Sweeping aside both the shock at this discovery and the discomfort of her aches and pains, she allowed herself the luxury of studying him. The first thing she noted, was that he was dressed in the same clothes he had worn to the party the previous evening, minus his cravat. One side of his shirt had come un-tucked from his breeches and both his sleeves were rolled up, exposing the muscular arms which she was certain had carried her so effortlessly to her carriage the evening before. His head was tilted slightly to one side and she took in the sweep of long, dark lashes resting on his cheeks; the stubble covering his chin and jaw; and his lips – full, pink, moist lips which were parted slightly. She stared at them – transfixed –

wondering what it would be like to feel them on her own; wondering how many women they had kissed; how many words of love they had uttered; how many hearts they had broken. So lost was she in these musings, that it was not until several seconds later, she realized the doctor had opened his eyes and was staring at her. A deep flush suffused her cheeks as the very lips she had been studying so intently, curled upwards into a languid smile, setting forth a swarm of butterflies in her stomach.

'Good morning,' he all but whispered, his voice husky with sleep. 'How are you feeling?'

Mortified was the first word that sprang to Charlotte's mind as she concluded, from the way he was looking at her, that he had, yet again, read her thoughts. Instead, she cleared her throat and mumbled, 'Um, extremely sore, Doctor. And my, er, head is throbbing dreadfully.'

He nodded sympathetically. 'That is to be expected, I am afraid. You suffered quite a blow. But, fortunately, a bout of concussion seems to have been your most serious injury. I examined you quite thoroughly yesterday evening and found the beginnings of a great many bruises but no broken bones.'

At this pronouncement, Charlotte said nothing, the thought of his hands upon her causing her skin to tingle in the strangest manner.

All at once, the doctor shifted from his chair to perch on the side of the bed. Charlotte's heart began pounding. What on earth was he going to do? Was he going to kiss her? Was it really possible that he knew what she had been thinking? She tilted her head upwards to look at him. His hand moved to her face, his fingers lightly brushing her cheek. Charlotte quivered at his touch. But, in a flash, in through the door burst Harriet, breaking the tension as effectively as stepping on a dry twig.

Charlotte stared aghast at her sister, wondering what she must be making of the scene in front of her. The doctor, conversely, appeared wholly unperturbed.

'Good morning, Lady Harriet,' he announced. 'I was just carrying out one last check on your sister, before moving on to your brother.' He lifted each of Charlotte's eyelids in turn and, apparently satisfied, stood up from the bed.

Charlotte's already pounding head began reeling, not only with the throbbing pain, but also with the mixture of emotions coursing through her. Had she completely misread the man's actions? Had he only meant to examine her all the while? Had the blow to her head resulted in her imagination running riot? The doctor raised his arms above his head, stretching out his spine. Charlotte's eyes moved to the muscles evident in his taut stomach as the side of the shirt, which hung loose, rose several inches above the waistband of his breeches. She swallowed, attempting to repress yet another torrent of outrageous thoughts.

'Goodness, we are keeping you busy, are we not, Dr Leigh?' smiled Harriet, entirely oblivious to the undercurrent swirling about the room. 'How is my sister this morning, sir?'

The doctor began busying himself with his medicine bag, which he retrieved from the floor alongside him. 'I am glad to report that she appears to have suffered no serious side-effects, ma'am. Although she will be covered in a great many bruises for a week or so.'

'Well, we shall be grateful that bruises are the only consequences she will have to bear,' said Harriet, on a sigh of relief. 'I imagine it could have been a great deal worse.'

'Indeed it could, ma'am,' affirmed the doctor. 'She could well have broken her neck. Now, if you will excuse me, I must attend to your brother before returning to Wetherington. Good-day to you both.' He inclined his head before turning on his heel and heading for the door.

Charlotte could not bring herself to speak, awash with disappointment as he took his leave of her. But Harriet's chatter allowed her no opportunity to ponder the situation further.

'Well, Charlotte,' exclaimed the younger girl, flopping down into the chair so recently vacated by the doctor, 'you did give us all a fright yesterday. What on earth caused you to fall down those wretched steps?'

Charlotte's mind cast back to the incident: Perdita Farrell's shriek and the awareness of something at her feet. Had Perdita set out to cause a commotion? Had she intended to distract Charlotte before deliberately wrong-footing her? Did Perdita find people falling down steps and potentially breaking their necks as 'fascinating' as being devoured by wild bears? She shuddered as she recalled the incident with her gown the evening of the betrothal ball. Was a girl who was capable of causing her to tumble headlong down a flight of steps also capable of cutting up a dress? The question required very little deliberation.

*

Charlotte spent all of that day and the following one in bed. Doctor Leigh had left specific orders that she was to have complete rest and these orders were followed rigidly: firstly, because Charlotte had neither the strength nor the inclination to do anything else; secondly, because her father, her sister and her maid would not allow her to raise so much as a spoon to her mouth.

Doctor Leigh did not return to the manor the following day and for that Charlotte was grateful. After much consideration, she had concluded that her ridiculous notions regarding the man kissing her, were due purely to the blow to her head. The accident had, obviously, caused some imbalance in her brain, resulting in outlandish thoughts. Why, in all her one-and-twenty years, the thought of kissing any man had never before crossed her mind. Besides which, she was betrothed to Frederick and, although she had no wish to dwell on the matter of kissing him, she was just weeks away from becoming his wife. Now that she was feeling much improved, she resolved to push aside any further rogue notions regarding kissing and the like and, instead, use every ounce of her determination to carry on with her portrayal of the perfect fiancée – even if such sentiments were not in the least reciprocated. Certainly, Dr Leigh's was not the only notable absence from the manor. Not one of the Farrells had so far deigned to call upon her, although the countess had forwarded a brief missive, which had been no more personal than if it had been sent to a member of the woman's household staff. Despite their obvious disregard for her, Charlotte was grateful for her future relatives' lack of attentiveness. In fact, she was even considering prolonging her symptoms to take full advantage of the respite from the Farrells. But, at the beginning of the third day of lying in bed, she had to confess that she was feeling much stronger, and, as the same familiar worries began haunting the recesses of her mind, it did not take her long to conclude that she was in need of some distraction. No sooner had her maid whisked out of the door with her breakfast tray, than Charlotte slipped on her robe and padded along the corridor.

'What on earth are you doing up, Charlotte?' proclaimed Edward, as she peeped her head around his bedchamber door. 'Father will not be at all pleased.'

'As you can see, I am perfectly fine, Edward,' replied Charlotte, slipping into the room. 'But I am tired of lying in bed now.'

'Huh,' huffed Edward. 'You have only had two days of it. Imagine how I must feel.'

'Your circumstances are of your own doing, dear Brother,' said Charlotte, plumping down on the edge of his bed. 'Mine, on the other hand, are purely accidental.' As the words left her mouth, she wondered at their accuracy, but, not wishing to involve her brother in her suspicions, she moved on swiftly. 'The only thing from which I am now suffering is a severe case of boredom. I am, I fear, in desperate need of some entertainment.'

'Are you indeed, ma'am?' remarked Dr Leigh, who had entered the room at that very moment. 'And who, may I ask, gave you permission to leave your bed?'

Charlotte's heart stopped for a second as she turned to look at him. While she had spent two entire days convincing herself that her attraction to the physician was purely the result of the blow to her head, the butterflies swarming inside her, appeared to be of a different opinion. As devastatingly handsome as the man looked, though, his steely expression told her that he was not at all impressed with her. Colour flew to her cheeks.

'I, um, can assure you, Doctor, that I am feeling perfectly well.'

'*I* shall decide when you are well enough to leave your bed, Lady Charlotte,' he asserted, his tone leaving no doubt of his disapproval. 'I am only sorry that, with their constant stream of ailments, the Farrells did not permit me to leave Wetherington yesterday.'

At the mention of the Farrells, Charlotte recalled, with a jolt, her resolution. 'Oh. And, er, how is my, um, dear fiancé, Doctor?'

The doctor's already grave expression visibly hardened. Narrowing his eyes, he replied at length, 'Lord Farrell suffered another of his headaches yesterday which, so he informs me, is not at all improved today.'

'I, er, see,' stammered Charlotte, unable to meet his eyes. 'How very, um, dreadful for him.'

'Dreadful is indeed one word for him, ma'am,' replied the physician archly.

Before Charlotte could ascertain exactly what was meant by this remark, Edward broke in.

'Well, as much as *I* am following your instructions, Doctor, I fear you will find it a great deal harder to persuade my sister to stay indoors. As you obviously heard, after only two days in bed, she is already in need of some diversion.'

The colour in Charlotte's cheeks deepened. In the doctor's presence, she found she was contemplating a quite different set of diversions to that which she had originally intended. Silently remonstrating with herself for allowing her thoughts to once again stray down such ludicrous avenues, she steeled herself for another chiding from the physician. But, to her surprise, the man set down his medicine bag on Edward's night-stand and began rummaging inside it.

'Well, if it is diversion Lady Charlotte is after,' he declared gravely, 'then I think I may have the perfect remedy.'

Charlotte grimaced, convinced that he was about to administer her a foul-tasting draught as punishment for disobeying his orders, but, to both her and Edward's amazement, he produced a pack of playing cards.

'Cards, Doctor!' exclaimed Edward. 'At this hour of the morning?'

The doctor pulled up the chair to the bed and settled himself into it. He was so close to Charlotte now that she could smell the light fragrance of his soap.

'Ah, but these are special cards,' he professed, his previously steely expression now replaced by one of amusement. He began shuffling the cards with an expert hand then cut the pack into four, placing each pile face down on the counterpane, in the space between Charlotte and Edward.

'Now, Lady Charlotte,' he said, 'would you please select a card from one of the piles. You may show it to your brother, but not to me.'

Intrigued, Charlotte did as she was bid. She chose a card from the second pile – the four of spades. She showed it to Edward, who nodded his head, beaming broadly.

'Now put it back in the pack. Anywhere you like.'

Charlotte pushed it halfway into the third pile.

The doctor gathered all four piles together and cut the pack in half.

He then began spreading the cards out, face up, on the counterpane. He carried on doing this for several seconds before stopping.

'Hmm,' he muttered, rubbing his chin. 'If I am not mistaken, I think one of the cards is trying to tell me something.' To his audience's bewilderment, he picked up the card bearing the image of the queen of hearts and held it to his ear.

'Well, well, well,' he declared. 'This lady is telling me that this is your card.' He pulled out the four of spades.

Charlotte's mouth fell open while Edward, clearly delighted, clapped his hands together.

'Oh, do show us how it is done, Doctor,' he implored.

'Well, I'm not sure I should,' replied the physician earnestly. 'I do, normally, only allow such special privileges to my most well-behaved patients. Not those who go wandering around when they should be resting.'

He raised his brows to Charlotte. The colour returned to her cheeks with renewed heat.

'Then send Charlotte back to her room, Doctor and show me,' begged Edward.

Charlotte gulped, sensing that that was to be her fate while hoping desperately that it was not. Not only would she relish learning such a trick, but it would also allow her more time in the doctor's company – for no other reason, of course, she quickly reassured herself, than to relieve the tedium of yet another long day indoors.

'Hmm,' mused the doctor, regarding her pensively. 'Would you like to learn how to do the trick, Lady Charlotte?'

'I should like it very well, Doctor,' she muttered.

His gaze lingered on her for a few more seconds, before he pronounced, 'Very well then. You may stay. But, before we go any further, the three of us shall have to make a pact. We must swear that we will not divulge the workings of the trick to anyone else for at least six months.' He held out one hand to Charlotte and the other to Edward. Charlotte reached out and took hold of it. Feeling the warmth of his roughened skin against hers, she felt a strange stirring deep in the pit of her stomach. Perhaps the doctor had been correct after all, she pondered: she really should not have left her bed, for she was suddenly feeling extremely light-headed.

*

Some forty minutes later, following a great deal of hilarity, Lord Hamilton entered the room, his hair giving the impression that he had been out walking for several miles in a strong headwind. 'Now, what on earth is going on in here?' he demanded. 'And whatever are you doing out of bed, Charlotte?'

'Oh, we are having the most marvellous time, sir,' replied Edward. 'Please may I try out the trick on my father, Dr Leigh?'

'Of course,' said the doctor, vacating his chair and gesturing to the old man to take his place. With Lord Hamilton seated, they all then watched as Edward diligently followed the steps the doctor had shown him, before revealing his father's card.

'Well, well, well,' chuckled Lord Hamilton. 'Whatever next? And I must say, Doctor, you appear to have done a remarkable job in cheering up young Charlotte here.'

'I find the trick a most reliable tonic, my lord,' informed the doctor. 'However, I must insist that Lady Charlotte now returns to her own chambers. She has had quite enough excitement for one day.'

Charlotte opened her mouth to protest but the look on the doctor's face told her she would be wasting her time.

Tucked up in her bed, Charlotte could not help but wonder at how remarkable she found the doctor. Although of course, she quickly reminded herself, the fact that he was remarkable or not, mattered little to her. In all but a matter of days – should she dare to count them – she would be married to Frederick Farrell and, to that end, she would not permit herself another minute's thought about Dr Daniel Leigh.

Chapter Twelve

IT was the following day that Frederick Farrell deigned to visit Hamilton Manor. Charlotte was only grateful that she was dressed and sitting in the morning-room with her father. The notion of her fiancé in her bedchamber was too much for her to bear.

'How good of you to come over, Farrell,' gushed Lord Hamilton, greeting their visitor in his usual effusive manner. 'Particularly as Dr Leigh informs us you have been feeling quite out of frame yourself, young man.'

'It is true that I have been out of sorts for several days now, sir,' sniffed Frederick, paying Charlotte not the slightest heed.

'Well,' proclaimed Lord Hamilton. 'Then we must be grateful that everyone appears to be on the mend. Charlotte here is doing splendidly. Indeed, the doctor says she should be back to herself in the next day or so.'

Frederick threw Charlotte a perfunctory glance before turning his attention back to Lord Hamilton. 'My mother wished me to enquire, sir, if Charlotte will be well enough to attend Lord and Lady Metcalfe's ball on Friday.'

Charlotte's heart sank to the floor, but, before she could gather her wits, her father forestalled her.

'Why, Friday is four whole days away,' he declared, with a broad smile. 'I am sure you will be back to fighting form by then, Charlotte, and ready for a spot of merriment. Will you not?'

At a loss as to what else to say, Charlotte found herself muttering, 'Yes, Father. I'm sure I shall.'

*

Charlotte was seated by the fire in the morning-room again the following day when Dr Leigh came to call. Harriet was also present, absorbed in her embroidery as she sat in the window-seat. Charlotte did not permit the fact that the doctor appeared more handsome than ever to distract her in the slightest. In addition, she completely resisted the urge to push back the lock of glossy hair which insisted on falling across his face, and the melting sensation she experienced as he held her wrist and took her pulse was paid no heed at all.

'So,' said the physician, upon completing his examination of her and running through an extensive list of questions pertaining to her health, 'I hear you are to attend the Metcalfes' ball on Friday. Are you sure you will be strong enough?'

'I imagine so,' replied Charlotte, with a feeble attempt at a smile. 'After all, as you have no doubt heard the countess state on numerous occasions, Dr Leigh, when one is a Farrell one cannot allow one's health to interfere with one's social obligations.'

To her surprise, the doctor fixed her with an extremely earnest expression. Lowering his voice to little more than a whisper, he said, 'If I may be so bold, Lady Charlotte, I should like to point out that you are not yet a member of the Farrell family – and you never have to be.'

Charlotte regarded him in astonishment. 'I-I have not the first idea what you mean, Dr Leigh.'

'I mean,' he hissed, 'that it is not too late for you to pull out of this marriage.'

Charlotte's jaw dropped. 'B-but why ever should you imagine I would wish to do such a thing?'

The doctor's dark eyes narrowed to two slits. But, before he could say another word, Lord Hamilton entered the room and, to Charlotte's relief, the subject was dropped as effectively as if it had been a hot brick.

Two hours later, Charlotte could scarcely contemplate the fact that, only days before, she had considered allowing Dr Leigh to kiss her. The blow to her head had obviously been far more detrimental than she had first imagined. Now, all she could think about was slapping the man. How dare he suggest that she pull out of the marriage to Frederick? Who did he think he was interfering in her private affairs? She was only sorry that the anger raging through her now at his audacity, had not reared its head as soon as he had made the remark. But, so stunned had she been, that it was only when she was alone and had had time to reconsider the conversation, that she had fully comprehended his meaning. Her act at playing the perfect fiancée had obviously not fooled Dr Leigh at all. Charlotte was only grateful that Harriet appeared not to have overheard him. If she had, her suspicions would have been immediately alerted, setting forth an uncomfortable barrage of questions. Doctor Leigh's impudent remarks could have ruined not only Charlotte's plan, but her family's entire future. To that end, she would, she concluded as another wave of fury washed over her, tell the physician exactly what she thought of his meddling – just as soon as she was presented with an opportunity to do so.

Despite the fact that Lord and Lady Metcalfe resided in one of the biggest houses Charlotte had ever seen, the opulent surroundings did little to distract her. Instead, her thoughts were entirely occupied by the members of her own party. It was the first time she had been in the company of the countess and Perdita since her fall. Despite this fact, Perdita had failed to enquire once about Charlotte's health, choosing only to pass a rude remark about her impressive array of bruises. Charlotte, now fully convinced that Perdita had deliberately caused the accident, could scarcely bring herself to look at the girl. Any evidence of the countess's concern for her future daughter-in-law, meanwhile, seemed only to surface at exactly the same moment any witness to the incident expressed an interest. Then, in front of an avid audience, the woman would launch forth into a concerned speech about what a dreadful occurrence the mishap had been and the detrimental effect the anguish over poor Charlotte had had on her own shattered nerves.

The person paying Charlotte the most genuine attention was Dr Leigh. But, still seething at his meddlesome comments at the manor several days earlier, Charlotte did her utmost to ignore him. She would not speak another word to the man until such time as she was presented with an opportunity to tell him exactly what she thought of his interfering.

The exhausting effect of all of the above, combined with Frederick's usual snubs, made Charlotte wish desperately that she had adhered to her intention to prolong her symptoms and was tucked up in bed with a book. Instead, she found herself sitting alongside her future in-laws and the doctor in one of the many side rooms of the enormous house – the countess having declared that the overpowering smell of perfume in the ballroom was making her nauseous. Charlotte was on the verge of making an excuse and slipping off to the ladies' withdrawing-room for five minutes' much-needed reprieve, when into the room came a group of four distinguished, white-haired gentlemen.

'Oh, my goodness,' exclaimed the countess, as she studied the new arrivals. 'If my failing eyesight does not deceive me, that is Dr Reuss – my previous physician, who recently took his leave of England to carry out some wretched experiments overseas. Quite why you doctors insist on experimenting with one thing or another when you have patients to attend to, is beyond me, Dr Leigh. I was all but abandoned when the man left, was I not, Frederick?'

Frederick shook his head disparagingly. 'It was the very height of impudence, Mama, leaving you in the lurch like that.'

'Still,' she sighed, 'the man is supposedly one of the most eminent physicians of our time and we Farrells shall therefore be expected to pay our courtesies. Come along children.' In a flash, she rose to her feet and sailed towards her unsuspecting target, her green silk skirts swishing vigorously from side-to-side. Frederick, Perdita and Dr Leigh followed, with Charlotte lagging behind at a more reluctant pace.

'Ah, Lady Farrell,' beamed Dr Reuss, upon setting eyes on his former patient. 'And looking in the very best of health I am delighted to see.'

The countess released a quivering breath. 'Alas, I am not, Dr Reuss. I am afraid I am on the very verge of my palpitations – or something more serious. I have employed Dr Leigh here to remain by my side at all times, lest something quite dreadful strikes me down.'

Doctor Reuss turned his head to the young man to whom she was referring. 'Good God!' he exclaimed, his eyes growing wide. 'Not Dr *Daniel* Leigh? The man who has been carrying out such fascinating research into the smallpox vaccine?'

All eyes shifted in bewilderment to Dr Leigh, over whose countenance an amused expression was hovering.

'Guilty as charged, sir,' he confessed, bowing his head to the older gentleman.

An obviously awe-struck Dr Reuss shook his head. 'My, my, my,' he declared. 'You cannot know how honoured I am to make your acquaintance, Doctor. I have heard wonderful things about your work. And, if you would permit me the very great honour, I should be delighted to discuss with you some of the more intricate workings of your new drug. You should consider yourself extremely fortunate, Lady Farrell, to be in the hands of such a young genius and an extremely modest one too, so I have heard.'

Lady Farrell gawped at him. 'Well, of course I, er, do, Dr Reuss,' she floundered. 'As you yourself are aware, nothing but the best is good enough for us Farrells – particularly where our shockingly poor health is concerned.'

'Well, you certainly have the best here,' pronounced a clearly elated Dr Reuss. 'Now, you will permit me, I hope, Lady Farrell, to borrow Dr Leigh for a short while and introduce him to several of my colleagues who are present here this evening. I know they, like myself, would be most delighted to make the acquaintance of one who is, quite radically, changing the face of modern medicine.'

The countess attempted to twist her countenance into an understanding expression, which sat awkwardly alongside her frosty features.

'Of course, Dr Reuss. I am feeling a little stronger this evening and therefore do not envisage a serious occurrence within the next hour or so. I shall go and sit in the supper-room and take a little light refreshment.'

'Marvellous,' beamed Dr Reuss. 'Well then, if everybody's happy, please do excuse us.' He began to lead Dr Leigh away by the arm.

'Oh,' sighed Perdita, pressing a hand to her chest as she watched the two men wind their way across the floor. 'I do so think that success adds to a gentleman's appeal.'

As Charlotte watched the doctor's retreating back, she found that, despite her raging annoyance at the man, she could not disagree.

Sitting in the supper-room with Lady Farrell, Frederick and Perdita – not one of them enjoying any refreshments due to the extensive list of allergies which had been reeled off as they perused the plates of food – a palpable buzz snaked around the room as a tall, sylph-like figure wound its elegant way through the tables. Wearing a low-cut silver gown so sheer it was almost possible to see her creamy skin beneath it, the woman's mane of glossy red hair was arranged in a tumble of curls to one side of her face, showing off her exquisite features to perfection.

'Goodness,' gulped Charlotte. 'Who is that?'

The countess glanced fleetingly at the woman. 'Why, it is Antonia, Lady Devers, of course,' she informed her, in a tone which insinuated that everyone, other than a complete imbecile, was aware of that fact.

The countess's tone notwithstanding, Charlotte could only stare as she observed Lady Devers's graceful progress. And she was not the only spectator. The woman's striking beauty was attracting a great deal of attention from those present – the males in admiration and the females in envy.

Although Charlotte had never before set eyes upon Lady Devers, even she was aware of the woman's colourful reputation. Widowed some two years before, Lady Devers had been left a hefty fortune by her elderly late husband and had made good use of the money in her quest to live life to the full. She had, apparently, a constant stream of lovers, amongst them, according to the rumours, the Prince of Wales himself.

No sooner had she slipped into a seat at one of the tables, than she was surrounded by a throng of male admirers. Charlotte observed with some fascination as, with well-honed skill, Lady Devers dispensed one-by-one with the men, as though they were nothing more than a swarm of annoying flies. She had only just completed this task when Dr Reuss entered the room, accompanied by two of his white-haired colleagues and Dr Leigh. Much to Charlotte's amazement, upon setting eyes on Lady Devers, Dr Reuss made an immediate beeline for her. What on earth could an eminent physician have in common with such a woman? she pondered. But then she remembered: it was not just Lady Devers's physical attributes and her bedchamber antics that caused so much interest amongst the *ton*. Adding to her enigma was the fact that the woman was said to have a brilliant mind, with a particular interest in the sciences. And, unlike many of her contemporaries, she made no effort to hide her intelligence. In fact, from their warm greeting of one another, it appeared that Lady Devers was a very dear friend of Dr Reuss.

Now completely detached from the conversation taking place at her own table which, the last time she had paid it any attention, was concerned with an outbreak of pimples Frederick had discovered on his chest that morning, which Dr Leigh had dared to dismiss as nothing more than a heat rash, Charlotte continued to watch as Dr Reuss introduced his colleagues to Lady Devers. Was she mistaken, or did a look of particular interest flicker over the woman's face at her introduction to Dr Leigh?

'Charlotte!'

Charlotte jumped as the countess's strident voice interrupted her thoughts. 'Have you been listening to a word I said?'

'Er, mostly, ma'am,' blustered Charlotte.

Perdita sucked in a disapproving breath while Lady Farrell shook her head in despair.

'Really, girl, *mostly* is not good enough. One day – which I fear may be sooner than we all should wish – you will be representing the Farrell family and do you think it will be good enough for such a prominent figure to *mostly* listen to those in her company?'

Humiliation swept over Charlotte. 'No, my lady,' she muttered.

'No indeed,' confirmed Frederick, regarding his fiancée as though she were nothing more than a speck of dirt that had dared to spoil the appearance of his white silk stockings.

Some time later, having not dared let her eyes stray from her own table, lest she face more remonstrations, Lady Farrell announced that they were to return to the ballroom. Making their way out of the supper-room, Charlotte risked a glance across the room. Doctor Reuss and his two colleagues were nowhere to be seen, but, still seated at the table were Dr Leigh and Lady Devers, deep in conversation. Charlotte watched as the woman threw back her head of gleaming curls, to laugh heartily at something the doctor had said. Observing the pair sharing their private joke, an unfamiliar feeling washed over her. She had no time to consider what it was, before the countess, once again, rudely intruded upon her thoughts.

'Charlotte! Do come along, girl.'

Charlotte averted her eyes and followed the Farrells back into the ballroom, which was packed with swaying couples. As they took their seats on the periphery, Perdita, claiming the chair next to Charlotte, emitted a sigh so heavy that Charlotte immediately whipped her head around to her. She found the girl staring wistfully at the dancers.

'Oh, it is the very greatest of pities that I do not yet have a husband with whom to dance,' Perdita huffed. 'I am sure I should have made a grand Duchess of Wittingsall or indeed a most suitable Countess of Sly. And I could also have been wed to the Viscount Viceroy, you know? Mama's arrangements were proceeding awfully well until one day we received the strangest note from his family saying that the man had quite lost his mind and was to be sent to an asylum.'

'Really,' murmured Charlotte, feeling not the least bit comfortable in the girl's presence.

'But I am quite confident I shall find a husband soon,' continued Perdita, smoothing down her pale-red hair. 'Quite, quite certain of it in fact.'

Charlotte stared at Perdita's bland features. She could not help but wonder if such a series of 'unfortunate events' was actually nothing more than an impressive array of excuses, all desperately constructed in order to prevent the poor gentlemen concerned tying themselves to Perdita for the rest of their days. And, from her own short acquaintance with the girl, Charlotte could not blame them. There was no doubt in her mind that Perdita Farrell was quite mad and that the girl had not only caused her fall, but had also ruined her gown the evening of the betrothal ball. The only answer which was still eluding her, was how Perdita could have gained access to Hamilton Manor to carry out the venomous act. She was silently debating the matter once again, when she caught sight of a stunning couple – Dr Leigh and Lady Devers. All thoughts of Perdita ceased as Charlotte observed the pair. What was immediately apparent to her was that, contrary to the awkward way in which the doctor had danced with Perdita at the betrothal ball, his manner with Lady Devers was markedly different. In fact, the doctor now appeared a very accomplished dancer. Charlotte watched as he whispered something into Lady Devers's shell-like ear. The woman's mouth broke out into a broad smile and, as she laughed, a combination of anger and indignation flooded Charlotte's veins.

'I think, Frederick, that I should like to dance,' she announced to her fiancé, who was seated to the other side of her.

'Dance?' balked Frederick. 'What on earth for?'

'Why, because that is what people do at balls, er, darling.'

'Well, I am not feeling at all up to it,' replied Frederick, shaking his head. 'I have been quite out of frame this evening with these pains in my lower leg.'

'Alas,' broke in his mother, sitting next to her son. 'Pains in the lower leg are yet another affliction borne by generations of Farrells. But, that aside, Frederick, I think perhaps you should dance with the girl. After all, it is what is expected of one at these occasions.'

Frederick sighed mournfully. 'But I really do not have the strength, Mama.'

'Nevertheless,' countered Lady Farrell, 'you are well aware that we Farrells are often obliged to set aside our numerous complaints in order to do what is expected of us.'

'Oh, very well then, Mama,' huffed Frederick peevishly. 'If you think it best.' He rose, half-heartedly, to his feet, bowed before Charlotte and held out his arm to her. Charlotte responded with a shaky smile of gratitude, before standing up and laying her hand upon the proffered limb. As she did so, bile flooded her throat. This, to her horror, increased with some ferocity the moment Frederick took her in his arms on the dance floor. With the combination of his bony form and the cloying odour of his cologne, she found herself having to employ every one of her resources not to vomit all over the man. So wrapped up was she in these exertions, that she almost did not notice Dr Leigh, as he whirled past with Lady Devers. Unwittingly catching his eye, she noted, with a stab of panic, that, from the look upon his face, the doctor had yet again managed to interpret her thoughts perfectly. Her anger towards the physician instantly flared. Did she not, after all, have enough to worry about without adding Dr Leigh's opinions to her ever-increasing list? That man was becoming a veritable thorn in her side.

Chapter Thirteen

CHARLOTTE had managed so little sleep that, each time she attempted to open her eyes the next morning, she found the lids insisted upon closing again. Once more, the over-industrious cogs of her mind had been whirring throughout the darkened hours. Try as she might – and she had tried exceedingly hard – she had been unable to erase from her memory the repulsive feelings Frederick Farrell's close proximity had evoked in her. How on earth, she wondered with mounting despondency, was she to cope when they were married? The very thought made her sick to the core.

But her revulsion at Frederick had formed only part of her night-time torment. Shortly after their dance together, Charlotte had observed Dr Leigh and Lady Devers leave the ballroom together. Neither of them had been seen since, even when the countess, with much consternation, had decided that they should all take their leave and had ordered an extensive search for the man. Their strong attraction to one another was obvious, and Charlotte had little doubt that Dr Leigh was the latest addition to Lady Devers's list of conquests. Much to her confusion, she found that this thought sapped her of both the inclination and the strength to face the new day. She therefore burrowed herself under the covers where sleep eventually overtook her.

Charlotte awoke with a start two hours later. Casting a look around the room, she was suddenly filled with a crushing urge to be outside. With newfound energy, she leaped from her bed and pulled on her riding breeches. She decided to have breakfast before she went to the stables, and bounded down the stairs and into the breakfast-room. No sooner had she entered the room, though, than she stopped dead in her tracks for there, sitting at the table, was Dr Leigh. A range of emotions – from relief to anger – swept through her, but it was shock that clung most tenaciously as she remained in the doorway gawping at him.

The doctor, much to her annoyance, appeared not the least bit agitated by her presence as he calmly reached for the silver coffee pot. 'Good morning, Lady Charlotte,' he pronounced, tipping up the pot to replenish his cup.

Charlotte gathered her wits. This man could, she recalled with some discomfiture, all but read her mind. She forced a deep reassuring breath.

'Doctor Leigh,' she replied coolly. 'I did not expect to find you here this morning.'

Despite being acutely aware that she was dressed in her riding breeches – a fact which had previously caused the physician so much amusement, he fixed her with what could only be described as an impassive gaze.

'I came early to attend your brother, my lady. Your father invited me to breakfast but was called upon to attend an urgent matter regarding one of the horses.'

Charlotte pursed her lips as she considered her options. This could, of course, present her with the very opportunity she had been waiting for. She could now tell the man exactly what she thought of his impertinent insinuations regarding her forthcoming marriage. In fact, she had been mentally formulating her speech for several days now. But, given the events of the previous evening, she found her anger regarding his comments on that subject entirely usurped by another matter: that of him and Lady Devers. And on that delicate matter she could, of course, say nothing: how the doctor spent his time was no concern of hers.

Her second option, much more appealing and straightforward than the first, was that she could simply excuse herself. Swiftly concluding that this was by far the more attractive alternative, she was in the process of assembling the words to do so, when the smell of bacon caught her nostrils causing her stomach to rumble loudly.

'Well,' remarked the doctor with a satirical smile, 'it would appear that your dancing yesterday evening has given you something of an appetite, Lady Charlotte.'

From the mountain of ham and eggs piled high upon the doctor's plate, it took very little of Charlotte's imagination to consider what had inspired his own, obviously voracious, hunger. Suppressing the images, a spurt of fury bolstered her confidence. Tilting her head upwards, she marched over to the sideboard upon which sat a number of silver domes. Picking up a plate, she lifted one of the domes and helped herself to two rashers of bacon and some eggs. She then strode over to the table and took a seat directly opposite the doctor, aware that he was regarding her all the while.

'So,' he began, 'did you enjoy the ball yesterday evening, ma'am?'

Deciding that nonchalance was most likely the best policy, Charlotte did not raise her eyes to him as she concentrated on cutting up her bacon. 'Of course, Doctor,' she replied, in what she hoped was an airy tone. 'It was quite splendid.'

The doctor said nothing. Disconcerted by his lack of response, Charlotte sneaked a glance at him. But, no sooner had she done so, than she regretted the action. He was gazing at her so intensely that her heart skipped a beat. She diverted her eyes swiftly back to her plate.

'You did not, if I may say so, give the impression of a young lady who was enjoying herself,' he observed matter-of-factly.

Charlotte jerked her head upwards him. 'I have no idea what you are referring to, Dr Leigh.'

The doctor's countenance remained neutral. 'I am merely saying, ma'am, that I think it would be extremely difficult for anyone to enjoy themselves in the company of the man to whom you are to pledge yourself.'

'I beg your pardon!' exclaimed Charlotte, her tone resonating with disbelief.

The doctor raised a questioning eyebrow and folded his arms over his chest. 'Surely it has not escaped your notice, Lady Charlotte, that Frederick Farrell is nothing more than a pompous, arrogant hypochondriac.'

All her attempts at indifference now flew out of the window. 'How dare you!' protested Charlotte. 'Lord Farrell is a highly-respected member of Society. His family is one of the most—'

'Do you love him?'

His bluntness stunned her. It was several seconds before she could bring herself to answer, although she had no idea what her answer was to be.

'I—' she stammered, averting her gaze from his.

'Do you love him, Charlotte?' he persisted.

Completely flustered, Charlotte picked up her napkin and began dabbing at her mouth. 'Really, Dr Leigh, I find your behaviour quite out of order. You have absolutely no right to question me so.'

'Exactly as I thought then.' He uncrossed his arms and, placing them on the table, leaned towards her. 'I have not known you long, Charlotte Hamilton, but I would wager I have a good idea of the type of man who would make you happy and Frederick Farrell is not that man.'

Charlotte lifted her chin to him. 'I beg to differ, sir. You know nothing at all about me.'

'I disagree,' he countered, so calmly that Charlotte battled with an urge to raise her hand to him and slap his impudent face. 'I can assure you that I am very perceptive concerning matters of the fairer sex.'

'Huh!' snapped Charlotte, her eyes flashing with anger. 'Of that I have no doubt, Doctor. Why, I am sure you very much enjoyed practising your … *perception* skills yesterday evening.'

'Yesterday evening?' he echoed, furrowing his brow. 'I am not sure to what you are referring, madam.'

'I am referring, Doctor,' she replied, every nerve in her body now on edge, 'to Lady Devers, with whom you appeared on quite *intimate* terms.'

The doctor leaned back in his chair, crossing his arms again. 'Aaahh,' he replied, nodding his head. 'I see. The lovely Antonia, eh?'

Mirroring his actions, Charlotte crossed her own arms. Throwing him a look of contempt, she noted how his lips were twitching with suppressed laughter. This served only to increase her annoyance.

'Hmph,' she snorted. Then she turned her head away and stared at the clock on the mantel, pouting furiously.

'And what, may I ask,' continued the doctor, 'do you think happened between myself and Lady Devers yesterday evening?'

No sooner were the words out of his mouth, than an outrageous image of naked, entwined limbs flashed across Charlotte's mind – one of the many she had conjured up during the long night.

'I confess, I have given the matter very little thought, Doctor,' she replied, directing her comment to the mantel. 'However, one can only assume that when two people display such shocking behaviour in public, that the end result is quite predictable.'

'I see,' he mused.

Charlotte flushed an even deeper shade of red, silently cursing herself for having said so much.

'So,' he continued, at length, 'you think I spent the entire night in Lady Devers's company?'

Again, she flinched at his directness. She turned her head to him. 'I can assure you, Doctor, that who you spent the night with, does not interest me in the slightest.'

To her great surprise, the doctor then pushed back his chair and rose from the table. 'Then, if you will excuse me, my lady, it is time I returned to Wetherington.'

Charlotte's mouth dropped open. They were in the middle of an argument. How dare he leave now? Her bewilderment robbing her of the ability to speak, she could only watch as he strode towards the door. No sooner had it closed behind him, than boiling rage began bubbling in her veins. She could not remember ever feeling so angry in her entire life. But what was it, she wondered, that was making her so angry. Was it the fact that the doctor had insulted Frederick Farrell? Was it the fact that he had dared to speak to her so directly? Or was it the fact that, while she had suffered an unbearable few minutes in the arms of her repulsive fiancé, Daniel Leigh had spent the entire night in the arms of the *lovely* Antonia Devers?

Marching furiously around to the stables, it occurred to Charlotte that she had no idea how she would cope, were it not for her outings on Victor. In fact, she had a strong inkling that she would not have coped at all. But even her ride that morning was not without problems, Victor doing an impressive job of jamming a stone in one of his shoes. Using the sharp little knife she kept tucked in the waistband of her breeches for just such emergencies, it had taken Charlotte almost fifteen minutes to dislodge the offending item.

Several hours later, with Victor well and truly exhausted, she was reluctantly heading home, when she heard playful shouts and giggling coming from one of the fields. As she drew nearer, she made out the slim figure of Kate Tomms, running around the meadow, her mass of red curls streaming out behind her. She appeared to be with a small group of friends. Unsure of Charlotte's reaction to their antics, the group stopped their game as she approached them.

'Hello, Kate,' said Charlotte, as the younger girl ran towards her. 'It looks like you are all having fun.' As the words left her lips she was conscious that they were coloured with envy.

'Oh, we are, miss,' giggled Kate, her cheeks flushed pink. 'In fact I don't think I've ever laughed so much in all my life.'

Charlotte attempted to recall the last time she had laughed so uninhibitedly. She found it was so long ago that she had no recollection of it. In fact, for all it had been only a matter of weeks, she could barely remember her previously contented life before that fateful day when she had overheard her father's conversation with his solicitor.

All at once, she became aware that Kate was speaking to her. Returning to her senses, she noted that the girl was regarding her anxiously, deep lines of concern etched into her brow.

'Why don't you join us, miss?'

'Wh-what?' stammered Charlotte.

'Come and join us. I promise you'll enjoy yourself.'

Charlotte cast a look around the group of young, happy faces – Kate's friends – who were standing a little way from her, chatting amongst themselves.

'All right, Kate. If your friends won't mind.'

'They won't mind a bit,' confirmed Kate, with a broad grin.

Charlotte slipped down from the saddle.

'I'll tether your horse up for you, if you like, miss,' offered a young man with hair as red as Kate's. He came to stand directly before the two girls, inclining his head to Charlotte.

'This is Thomas, miss,' announced Kate, blushing furiously.

'Very pleased to meet you, Thomas,' said Charlotte. 'Kate has told me a great deal about you.'

A look of pride swept over the boy's handsome features. 'Really, miss?'

He turned his head to Kate and the two of them exchanged an intimate look.

Charlotte then handed him the reins of the horse and the boy led Victor away.

'He seems a very nice young man, Kate,' remarked Charlotte, as the pair of them watched Thomas tethering the reins to a branch. 'You are very lucky.'

Kate sighed contentedly. 'I know, miss. And so are you.'

Charlotte stared at her for several seconds, wondering what the girl was referring to. 'Oh, yes, of course I am,' she said, realizing that she meant her forthcoming union with Frederick Farrell. 'We are both very lucky. Now, am I going to have the pleasure of meeting the rest of your friends?' she smiled.

The shadow of concern hanging over Kate's features did not disappear as she continued to regard Charlotte.

'Your friends, Kate?' chivvied Charlotte, raising her brows.

'Oh. Of course, miss,' said Kate, shaken from her thoughts. 'Come on now and I'll introduce you.'

As the two girls walked towards the group, Kate chattering all the while, something caught the corner of Charlotte's eye. Squinting against the sunlight, she noticed a lone figure on horseback galloping across the fields. The figure was female, dressed in a green riding-habit and a veiled hat. Although she could not be certain from such a distance, it looked suspiciously like the woman who had thundered past her in the fog the evening of her betrothal ball.

After luncheon, Lord Hamilton requested his eldest daughter accompany him on a trip to London. Welcoming anything that provided a distraction to her depressing musings, Charlotte accepted. The two of them went to Lock's, with the intention of purchasing a new hat for the old man. Despite the fact that the hat-changing activity had played havoc with Lord Hamilton's hair, resulting in a state of chaotic disarray, it filled Charlotte with pleasure to see her father back to his old self again. They passed a most pleasant afternoon together. Until, that was, they were making their way home.

'Oh, I have just had the most marvellous idea, Charlotte,' pronounced

Lord Hamilton, banging the top of his cane against the roof of the carriage. 'Albert, take us to Wetherington Hall.'

Charlotte's stomach lurched. 'Wetherington Hall, Father? But why on earth do you wish to go there?'

'We are all but passing,' explained Lord Hamilton, leaning back against the squabs. 'So why not pay a call? It will provide the perfect opportunity for me to thank Lady Farrell for hosting such a marvellous betrothal ball, thereby saving me the trouble of penning yet another wretched letter, which, I confess, I ought to have done long before now.' He followed this confession with a complacent chuckle.

Complacency, however, was nowhere to be found amongst Charlotte's emotions. She had no desire at all to see the Farrells and even less desire to see Dr Leigh following their row that morning.

'B–but,' she spluttered, 'I really do not think it a good idea, Father. The countess is known only to accept callers in the morning.'

'*Ordinary* callers, Charlotte. Not her future relatives as we now are. I have always maintained that family should be permitted to call upon one another whenever the urge takes them,' intoned Lord Hamilton.

If only that were true, pondered Charlotte. For, if she had the choice of calling on the Farrells whenever the urge took her, she would never see their ugly faces ever again.

Just as Charlotte had predicted, their spontaneous visit did not receive the rapturous reception her father had been anticipating. In the gloomy drawing-room, they found the three Farrells languishing on their *chaises-longues*, with Dr Leigh, much to Charlotte's chagrin, seated in a chair alongside them. As she entered the room, she observed the muscles in his face tighten. Determining to show him that she was not the least bit affected by his presence, she ignored him, focusing instead on the Farrells and their lukewarm greeting.

'Lord Hamilton,' proclaimed the countess, regarding him – and his dishevelled hair – with obvious disdain. 'What a, er, surprise. Whatever are you doing here?'

'Please do forgive the intrusion, my lady,' chuckled Lord Hamilton, 'but we were passing by the house and, as I am always remiss with my correspondence, I thought it an ideal opportunity to call in and express my gratitude for the marvellous betrothal ball you held for my daughter and young Frederick. Harriet has spoken of little else since.'

'Really,' sniffed Lady Farrell, evidently not at all interested at this revelation. 'Well, as you are here, I suppose you had better sit down and take some refreshment.'

'Oh, but we couldn't possibly,' protested Lord Hamilton. 'Not when you are all so obviously indisposed – and on this most beautiful of days.'

'Alas, many a beautiful day passes us Farrells by, Lord Hamilton, our poor health being as it is,' she remarked.

Lord Hamilton affected a sympathetic countenance and was obviously searching his mind for some other platitude when there was a sharp rap at the door. It was pulled open by Higgins, the butler, who was bearing a silver salver.

'An urgent missive has just been delivered for you, ma'am,' he informed the countess.

'Good lord. What now?' huffed the woman. 'Am I not permitted a moment's peace in this house? Bring it here at once, man.'

The servant did as he was bid. She snatched up the note from the tray and ripped open the seal. Folding out the sheet of white paper, she then proceeded to read.

'Oh, it is more than my nerves can bear,' she exclaimed, clutching a hand to her chest.

'Whatever is it, Mama?' asked Frederick.

She shuddered. 'It appears that, on the way home from the Metcalfes' ball yesterday evening, the Duke of Langley's coach was attacked – and by that blackguard they are calling the Courteous Criminal no less. The man took every bit of jewellery from both the poor duke and Lady Devers.'

Charlotte's ears pricked up. 'Lady Devers?' she echoed. '*Antonia* Devers? But how—? I mean – whatever was Lady Devers doing in the Duke of Langley's coach?'

'The Duke of Langley and Lady Devers are good … *friends*,' informed Frederick. 'A fact of which *everyone* is aware.'

A shade of deep red began staining Charlotte's cheeks as the doctor loudly cleared his throat. 'I, er, *I* was not aware of that fact, my lord.'

'Really, Charlotte,' berated the countess. 'You simply must keep up-to-date with such matters. As the future Countess of Wetherington, you will be expected to know all the latest *on dits*.'

'Of course, ma'am,' muttered Charlotte. Her tone hinted at regret, but inside her stomach was performing a series of somersaults. Lady Devers had been with the Duke of Langley and not Dr Leigh. She turned slightly, observing the doctor out of the corner of her eye. His dark mood appeared to have completely subsided. His head was tilted to one side, one brow arched quizzically. Amusement was pushing at the corners of his mouth, as he correctly read her mind for what seemed like the umpteenth time. With a pang of embarrassment, Charlotte whipped her head back to face Lady Farrell. Why, oh why had she lost her temper and all but accused the man of spending the night with Lady Devers? The answer slapped her in the face. It was perfectly obvious why: she had been racked with jealousy. Jealousy for a man she scarcely knew; a man who was occupying her thoughts with far more regularity than was healthy; and a man who now thought her a complete and utter lackwit.

Chapter Fourteen

'WHAT is it, Edward?' enquired Charlotte anxiously, later that afternoon. Her brother's brow was coated in a film of sweat and he was deathly pale.

'I'm not sure,' murmured Edward, grimacing. 'But I've been feeling quite out of sorts all afternoon.'

Charlotte placed her hand on his brow. It was burning hot. 'I shall fetch Father,' she declared, attempting to keep the concern from her voice.

As Charlotte had predicted, Lord Hamilton's feelings were the same as her own. 'I shall send immediately to Wetherington for the doctor,' he announced, panic washing over his features.

Charlotte nodded her head in agreement. For all she was devoid of any desire to see the doctor again following her ridiculous and embarrassing accusations of him, she knew that, if there was one man she could trust implicitly to help her brother, it was Dr Leigh.

It was less than an hour later and already early evening, when Charlotte spotted Dr Leigh's curricle clattering up the drive. She had not left her brother for a second since the man had been sent for, despite Edward having long since drifted into a fevered sleep. Completely sapped of all strength to face yet another encounter with the physician, she made her way down to the library before he had even reached the house.

Outside, the sun was providing an impressive finale to the day, flooding the library with a brilliant pink and orange hue. In an effort to distract herself from her anxiety about Edward, Charlotte decided to hunt out a book to read to him. Employing all her concentration on perusing the floor-to-ceiling shelves that lined two walls of the room, she almost jumped out of her skin when the door was thrust open and in marched her father, followed by the doctor.

'Ah, there you are, Charlotte,' boomed Lord Hamilton. 'Been hiding away have you?'

Charlotte cringed at her father's unwittingly accurate choice of words but not before her heart had missed a beat at the thought of why the pair were looking for her.

'How is Edward, Father? Is it bad news?' she asked, bracing herself for the worst.

'Thanks to Dr Leigh here, it is not,' informed the old man, breaking into a smile. 'He has a slight infection in the cut in his leg, but Leigh has given him a draught which should cure it within a few days.'

Relief seeped through Charlotte. 'Thank God,' she muttered, flicking a grateful look at the doctor who remained standing in the doorway.

'Now then,' continued Lord Hamilton, rubbing his chin. 'I've promised the doctor here a book but I'm damned if I can remember where I put it.'

'I too am looking for a book, Father,' piped up Charlotte, aware of the doctor's eyes upon her. 'One which I shall read to Edward tomorrow. In fact,' – she spun around to face the shelves and reached for the first tome in front of her – 'I think this one will serve very well.' Tilting her chin upwards and avoiding looking at the doctor, she took the book and glided as elegantly as she could, given the sudden weakness in her knees, over to the fireplace. Sinking into one of the four leather wing-chairs there, she opened the text and, despite the fact that her whirling head merged all the words into one great jumble, feigned instant absorption in it.

'Now then, Leigh,' mumbled Lord Hamilton, continuing to rub his chin as he scanned the shelves. 'I'm sure it's here somewhere. Best have a seat, man, while I hunt the devil out.'

No sooner had the words left the old man's mouth, than Charlotte's stomach began to churn. She held her breath as the doctor slipped into the chair opposite hers but still she refused to look at him, keeping her eyes firmly fixed on the book.

'Blast! That's not it,' mumbled Lord Hamilton, pulling out a volume and, upon viewing the title, promptly replacing it. 'Confounded thing must be here somewhere.'

Charlotte, aware that her every move was being observed by the physician, buried her nose even deeper into her book, her left hand nervously twirling a lock of stray hair. The only sounds in the room were Lord Hamilton's incessant mutterings accompanied by the crackling of the fire.

All at once, Charlotte's heart skipped a beat as the doctor addressed her directly in a low, intimate voice.

'May I congratulate you on selecting such an interesting text, my lady. I am sure your brother will be most ... delighted with your choice.'

Charlotte did not reply. Instead, she tossed him a contemptuous glare which, to her annoyance, he seemingly failed to notice.

'In fact,' continued the doctor, a hint of humour now evident in his tone, 'I do believe that is a most considered choice for a convalescing young man.'

Charlotte flinched. What on earth was he talking about? She urged herself to focus on the words, but her head was too fuddled. 'Indeed it is, sir,' she sniffed, refusing to look at him.

'I must confess that I never thought of offering my convalescing patients such an interesting ... topic,' he remarked with a snort of laughter, which he attempted, unsuccessfully, to disguise as a cough.

Charlotte slammed the book shut and turned it over so she could read its title: *The Feeding Habits of Flat Fish in Southern Europe*. A deep flush suffused her entire body, starting from her toes and spreading upwards to her cheeks. Damn! Why, in her haste, had she pulled out the first book to hand? Now the doctor would think her even more of a paperskull than he had before – if that were possible. Her mind raced in an attempt to salvage the situation.

'Er, yes, Doctor,' she declared, her eyes glued to the book. 'Were you not aware, sir, that Edward and I maintain a keen interest in flat fish and particularly their, er, feeding habits?'

'Surprisingly, I was not, my lady,' he replied, his shoulders shaking with suppressed laughter.

'It began when we were children,' continued Charlotte. 'In fact our mother was quite an expert on the subject.'

The doctor raised a doubtful eyebrow. 'Was she really?'

Still Charlotte refused to look at him. 'And several of her friends,' she went on, the words now tumbling from her mouth.

He gave another snort of laughter. 'You don't say.'

'In fact, this very book was one of our mother's favourites, Doctor, and one which I would highly recommend.'

'Really? Well in that case, perhaps you would like to enlighten me a little on the subject before I decide whether or not the topic is one I wish to pursue,' he said.

'Wh–what?' stammered Charlotte, her head jerking upwards.

'The subject, my lady. Would you care to share with me some of the feeding habits of these, er, flat fish?'

Charlotte felt as though she had been wedged into a very uncomfortable corner. 'Well,' she hastily flicked through several pages. 'Were you aware for instance, Doctor, that flat fish like to eat, er—' Her eyes fell on a chapter entitled 'Plankton'. 'Plankton,' she pronounced with some relief.

'Really,' said the doctor archly. 'How very … fascinating.'

'That it is, sir,' concurred Charlotte, lifting a hand and smoothing down her hair. 'Most fascinating.'

'And may I ask, my lady, if your fiancé shares your interest in this, er, fascinating subject?'

'He, er, we, um, have not yet had the opportunity to discuss the topic,' she blustered, fidgeting uncomfortably with the fabric of her skirt.

'I see. And I suppose with the news of the Courteous Criminal's latest attack, that there was little opportunity to discuss the topic at Wetherington this afternoon?'

Charlotte had to confess that his skill in steering the conversation to the subject she was desperately trying to avoid, was admirable.

'It was interesting, was it not,' he continued blithely, 'the news regarding the Duke of Langley and Lady Devers?' He affected a look of wide-eyed innocence but, as Charlotte glanced at him, she noticed that he was making very little effort to control his twitching lips.

She averted her eyes back to her skirt. 'It was very interesting, Doctor,' she replied sheepishly, searching for a witty retort. But, all retorts, witty or otherwise, appeared to have disappeared. 'I, er, believe I owe you something of an apology for my behaviour this morning, sir,' she found herself muttering.

'I beg your pardon, my lady?' He turned his ear to her.

Charlotte pursed her lips and raised her chin. 'I said, Doctor, that I wish to apologize to you for my rather unnecessary outburst this morning.'

'Oh,' he said, now holding a finger to his mouth as if trying to recall the information. 'Forgive me, but I have forgotten exactly what it was we were discussing this morning.'

Charlotte stiffened. 'I am doing my best to apologize, Doctor. I therefore think that, as a gentleman, the very least you could do would be to accept my apology.'

'I shall give it some thought, ma'am,' he replied. Then his tone suddenly turned serious. 'If you will give some thought to the other matter we discussed. The one regarding your forthcoming marriage.'

Charlotte regarded him icily. 'I'm afraid I cannot do that, Dr Leigh. I shall be marrying Lord Farrell in a few weeks, exactly as I had planned. And I can therefore assure you that your concern for me is both unwarranted and unwelcome.'

His expression hardened. 'As you wish then,' he said coolly.

Taken aback by his abrupt change of tone, Charlotte held his gaze for several seconds, feeling completely nonplussed. At a loss as to what else to do, and afraid that she might, at any moment, burst into an impromptu flood of tears, she sprang to her feet and, with the book in her hand, whisked out of the room, just as she heard her father declaring triumphantly, 'Ah, there it is, Leigh. Knew the damned thing was here somewhere.'

Chapter Fifteen

'OH, thank goodness you are returned, Charlotte,' flustered Harriet, the moment Charlotte returned from her ride the next morning. 'An urgent message has been delivered from Wetherington. Lady Farrell requests your presence forthwith.'

Charlotte's stomach lurched. 'Forthwith? But why? Is anyone ill?' No sooner were the words out of her mouth, than she realized the futility of the question.

'Well, most likely,' replied Harriet, 'although that may not, of course, be the reason for your summons.'

'Oh well,' murmured Charlotte, heading for the stairs, 'I'm sure I shall find out soon enough.' She resisted the urge to add, 'And I am sure that, whatever it is, it is not good news.'

Charlotte had a strong presentiment of just how bad the news was to be, when, on her arrival at Wetherington, she was shown not to the usual drawing-room, but up several flights of stairs – to the countess's bedchamber.

Not even daring to contemplate what she was about to encounter, her heart was in her mouth as the butler pushed open the creaking door. The stifling heat of the room and the strong smell of laudanum hit her immediately. Peering into the dimness inside, she saw Lady Farrell propped up against a pile of pillows in a large four-poster bed. Seated in a chair on either side, were Frederick and Perdita, each with a blanket over their laps. All three, she noted with rising panic, were regarding her with strong disapproval. Her heart began racing as she stepped inside the room, allowing the door to swing shut behind her.

'You, er, sent for me, my lady,' she stammered, bobbing a curtsy.

The woman's icy stare sent ripples of terror surging through Charlotte.

'You are aware, are you not, girl, that we Farrells have the very highest of reputations to uphold in Society?'

Having no idea at all where the conversation was leading, Charlotte muttered, 'Er, yes, ma'am.'

'And you are aware, are you not, that I will not tolerate the slightest deviation from the impeccable standards on which our reputation has been built?'

'Yes, ma'am.'

'Then why—' But, no sooner had Lady Farrell uttered the two words, than she began wheezing. Whipping out a hand from under the pile of bedcovers, she held it to her throat, gasping for breath.

Charlotte, filled with panic, stared in bewilderment.

'For goodness sake, girl, can you not see that your shocking behaviour is to be the death of her?' exclaimed Frederick wrathfully.

Having not the first clue as to what shocking behaviour she had allegedly engaged in, Charlotte shifted awkwardly from one foot to the other.

'Where is that blasted doctor when you need him?' grumbled Frederick. 'Dr Leigh!' he roared. 'Dr Leigh!'

Two seconds later, Dr Leigh crashed through the door, almost knocking over Charlotte in the process. Charlotte's racing heart skipped a beat as she set eyes upon him but he paid her no attention.

'What is it now?' he demanded, in a tone which made no effort to conceal his exasperation.

'My mother, man!' retorted Frederick. 'Can you not see that she is fighting for her life?'

The doctor rolled his eyes. 'It is nothing that a sip of lemonade will not cure.' Striding over to the nightstand, he filled a glass from the jug there. Propping up the countess's head, he held the glass to her lips. As the woman slurped at it noisily, all wheezing and gasping subsided.

'Oh,' remarked Perdita, who had been observing the drama with an air of morbid fascination. 'So she is not to die then, Doctor?' Charlotte could not be sure but did she detect an edge of disappointment to the girl's tone?

The doctor set down the glass. 'One rarely dies of a dry throat,' he informed archly.

Lady Farrell, who had now sunk back on to her pile of pillows, gave a shuddering sigh. 'But I think you and I know that it was much more than that, was it not, Doctor?'

The doctor regarded her with acute impatience. 'I am pleased to inform you, Lady Farrell, that it was not. A dry throat is, I fear, a common consequence of spending too much time in over-heated rooms.'

Through narrowed eyes, she shot him an admonishing glare. 'Sometimes I believe that were it not for your outstanding reputation in the field of medicine, Dr Leigh, I might be forced to reconsider your appointment here.'

'Oh, please do not allow my reputation to deter you, ma'am,' replied the doctor sardonically.

She ignored the retort. 'As it is, we Farrells have our reputation to uphold of dealing only with those at the very height of their profession. You will, therefore, remain under this roof until such time as I say otherwise. Now, you will stay in this room, Doctor, lest I take another turn for the worst, which may well occur given all I have to deal with today.'

Her watery-blue eyes swivelled to Charlotte, now standing at the foot of the bed. As the doctor turned around and headed for the chair in the corner of the room, Charlotte noticed the anger colouring his face. He was muttering something under his breath. Although she was not at all sure she had heard correctly, her brows shot to her hairline nonetheless. But her mind was soon turned from the doctor's imprecations and back to the reason for her summons to Wetherington, as Lady Farrell resumed her speech.

'Now, where was I?' she demanded irritably.

'You were asking, Mama, if the girl was aware of the high standards which are expected of the Farrells,' piped up Perdita, rather too helpfully for Charlotte's liking.

'Ah yes. You should be aware that the reputation of the Farrells has remained untarnished for centuries, Charlotte.'

'I'm, er, sure it has, ma'am,' muttered Charlotte.

'Well then, you can no doubt imagine my reaction when I received the letter this morning.'

Charlotte wrinkled her brow. 'I'm, er, not sure to which letter you are referring, my lady.'

The countess cast her eyes to the ceiling. 'I am referring to the letter informing me of your outrageous behaviour. Behaviour so shocking that it caused me to take to my bed immediately.'

Charlotte racked her brains. The only behaviour that she had engaged in recently which could possibly have caused such a flurry was her row with the doctor regarding Lady Devers. But how could the Farrells possibly know about that? 'I really have no idea to what behaviour you are referring, ma'am,' she confessed.

'Hah! She is denying it, Mama,' chipped in Perdita triumphantly. 'Did I not tell you that she would?'

'I am not denying anything,' clarified Charlotte. 'If only you could tell me what it is I am supposed to have—'

'Breeches!' proclaimed the countess. 'The letter informed me that not only do you parade around on horseback in a pair of gentleman's riding breeches, but that you also ride astride. Can you deny these accusations?'

As three sets of disdainful eyes bore through her, Charlotte had some notion of how it must feel to stand on trial. She was also acutely aware of the doctor's eyes burning into her back, although, unable to see his face, she had no opportunity to gauge his thoughts.

'Well?' demanded the countess.

Charlotte gulped. 'I'm afraid I cannot deny the accusations, ma'am. They are perfectly true.'

Perdita tutted reproachfully whilst Frederick quivered with horror.

'Although of course,' added Charlotte, 'I am aware that, as Countess of Wetherington, such behaviour will be unacceptable.'

'Well, for that at least, we should be grateful,' sighed the countess. 'But the very fact that you are now associated with the Farrells means that such behaviour will not be tolerated. Do you understand me?'

'Yes, ma'am,' mumbled Charlotte, suddenly feeling sick with despair.

'I can only thank the Lord that someone considered it prudent to bring this shocking matter to my attention,' huffed the older woman.

This remark jolted Charlotte from her depressing thoughts. 'May I ask who it was who sent you the note, ma'am?' she asked, wrinkling her brow.

'You may ask all you like,' replied Lady Farrell matter-of-factly, 'but I shall not be able to answer you. I have no idea who sent the note. It simply came into my possession after breakfast this morning, causing me to take to my bed forthwith.'

'Outrageous news,' piped up Frederick. 'So outrageous, it could well have tipped you over the edge, Mama.'

'I can assure you, Frederick, that it has pushed me a great deal closer to it. I am now teetering on the very brink. In fact, one more ghastly matter like this to contend with and that could, I fear, be the end of me. Now, you may go, Charlotte.'

As Charlotte escaped the overbearing atmosphere of the room, her head was once again reeling. Who could possibly have sent that note and what did they have to gain from it? She could only assume that, whoever it was, they were not happy with the prospect of her forthcoming nuptials to Frederick and doing their best to sully her reputation with the Farrells. Could this be the same person who was responsible for cutting up her gown before the betrothal ball and pushing her down Lady Fisher's steps? Her suspicion turned, once again, to Perdita Farrell. Would she not have had the perfect opportunity to write a note and slip it into her mother's possession? The only problem was, so far as Charlotte was aware, Perdita had never seen her in riding breeches.

'I can scarce believe he's going to have his first birthday in a few days, miss,' declared Emmy, as she and Charlotte sat outside Murphy's Mansion the next day, observing the toddler's shaky progress. 'It doesn't seem two minutes since he was born.' Just at that moment, Harry plopped down on to his bottom and began giggling. Becky rushed to his aid.

'He's nothing but a pleasure,' said Emmy, gazing adoringly at the babe.

'He certainly is, Emmy,' agreed Charlotte, who, with the exception of the first time she had discovered the family, had not once heard Harry cry.

Emmy gave a sudden sniff and swiped her hand across her nose. 'It's a shame our ma and pa never got to see him like this,' she said. 'He's fair thriving thanks to all that good stuff you keep bringing us to eat, Miss Charlotte.'

Charlotte smiled. 'I'm sure your parents would be as proud of Harry as they were of you, Emmy – all of you in fact,' she said.

'Do you really think so, miss?' asked the younger girl, her blue eyes brimming with tears.

'Absolutely,' affirmed Charlotte, determining that little Harry's first birthday would be a very special day indeed.

Sitting in the drawing-room, Charlotte cringed as she spotted Adams approaching her, bearing a silver tray. Her spirits sank still further when she noticed what was lying upon it.

'Another note from the Farrells, Adams?'

'I'm afraid so, ma'am. Another invitation, so I believe.' The servant's dour tone intimated there could be no worse news. The way Charlotte was feeling at that precise moment, she could not help but agree with him.

The invitation, accompanied by a list of curt instructions, was to the wedding of the countess's goddaughter, Lady Amelia Augustus. The occasion was to take place at the estate of Lady Amelia's parents, Augustus Hall, which was situated some eight miles from Hamilton Manor. Following her orders, Charlotte awaited the Farrells outside the small Norman church, which was set in the extensive grounds of the ancestral seat. As she did so, she failed to quash the anxiety rising within her. In a matter of days, guests would be attending her wedding – her wedding to Frederick Farrell, the man to whom she was to pledge herself for the rest of her life. Her stomach began to churn – an activity which increased in pace as the Farrells' coach rolled up and out stepped her future mother-in-law, Frederick, Perdita and Dr Leigh.

'As you can see, Charlotte,' announced Lady Farrell, shaking out her maroon skirts as she alighted the carriage, 'I have made the greatest of efforts to attend this wedding, despite, I might add, not yet having recovered from the incident regarding your breeches. I believe my nerves to have been irreparably damaged by that preposterous news. Do you not agree, Doctor?'

Charlotte slanted a look at the physician as he muttered his response. She was shocked to see how jaded and miserable he looked – the very feelings she was experiencing herself. Obviously, it was not just her life the Farrells were making a misery. Had the doctor's behaviour towards her not been so discourteous, then Charlotte might well have felt some sympathy for him; might even have found an ally in him. But she did not. All her previous embarrassment – his amusement at her breeches; her incorrect accusation regarding Lady Devers; the ridiculous book on flat fish – had, in the time since their discussion in the library, completely evaporated. In its place was a deep resentment at his persistent, and potentially damaging interference in her life. As breathtakingly handsome as the man was, she would, she resolved, do her absolute utmost to have as little to do with him as possible.

Unfortunately for Lady Amelia, the little church, with its exquisite stained-glass windows and colourful altar was by far the prettiest thing at the wedding. Although not a direct relative of the Farrells, with her long bland face and pale-red hair, Lady Amelia did bear an unfortunate resemblance to her godmother's family. Even the Farrell theme of ostentation appeared to be favoured by the girl, her gown – an enormous, jewelled creation of white satin adorned with large bows and flounces of lace – completely swamping her fragile frame.

The wedding breakfast was to take place at the family home – a timber-framed, Tudor mansion house. In keeping with the house's heritage, long trestle tables and wooden benches had been laid out for the feast. Charlotte took her place on one of the benches, alongside Perdita and Frederick with the countess and Dr Leigh opposite. Charlotte employed all her resolve not to look at the man.

'Ah, Amelia does make such a lovely bride,' sighed the countess, observing her goddaughter and her new husband at their table, which had been raised slightly above the others on a wooden plinth. 'And such a beautiful gown. One can only hope, Charlotte, that you have made such a wise choice.'

Before Charlotte could reply, Perdita butted in. 'I shall make a lovely bride too, do you not agree, Dr Leigh?' she asked, twiddling one of her limp ringlets.

The doctor's face grew noticeably paler as he stared, somewhat aghast, at Perdita. 'Well, I'm, er, sure you, er, will, ma'am,' he stammered.

A satisfied smile played upon Perdita's thin lips. 'Lovelier than Lady Charlotte, don't you agree, sir?'

The doctor winced as he flashed a cool look at Charlotte. 'I'm afraid that I really can't, um, comm—'

'And I already have my wedding gown. It is quite the most beautiful dress ever created, is it not, Mama?'

Frederick tutted loudly. 'Yes, well, it's all very good having the gown, Perdita, but what use is that without a man?'

Perdita gave a shrewd grin. 'Do not concern yourself, Brother,' she declared, casting a knowing look at the doctor. 'I shall be married before the spring – of that I am quite certain.'

Charlotte had no time to ponder the unabashed confidence ringing in Perdita's words, before the countess turned her attention to her.

'Now, as to *your* wedding gown, Charlotte, needless to say, I am hoping it bears no resemblance to a pair of gentleman's riding breeches.'

'I can assure you it does not, ma'am,' confirmed Charlotte, holding back a sigh.

'And it is, I hope, not too dowdy,' continued the older woman, running a critical eye down Charlotte's elegant soft-apricot dress. 'The wedding will, after all, be attended by the entire *haut ton* and … the Duke of Sussex himself.'

'The Duke of Sussex?' gasped Charlotte. 'Are you of his acquaintance, ma'am?'

'But of course,' she sniffed. 'It appears you are not yet fully aware of the importance of the family into which you are to marry, Charlotte. The Farrells have had royal connections for centuries. In fact, my own grandfather was a personal friend of Queen Anne, until the poor man died of a rather ghastly condition pertaining to his particularly weak blood – a condition which I believe I have inherited. The signs are there, are they not, Dr Leigh?'

'If they are, they are very well concealed, ma'am,' mumbled the doctor distractedly.

The countess glared at him before turning her attention back to Charlotte. 'My grandfather married his cousin, Felicia and the pair produced nine children, only two of whom survived to adulthood. Another example, I am afraid, of the Farrells' delicate constitution.'

As Frederick and Perdita expressed their agreement with resigned sighs and nods, a familiar voice intruded upon the group.

'Why, Charlotte Hamilton, I did not expect to see you here today.'

Charlotte turned around to find Mirabelle McGregor, in an unflattering gown of tobine stripes, accompanied by her brother, Bertie.

'Goodness,' she gulped, at once aware that she was surrounded by her least favourite people in the world. 'What a, er, surprise to see you two here.'

Mirabelle smiled beatifically. 'I take it then, that you are not aware that the Lady Amelia and I are exceedingly well acquainted. In fact, after dear Harriet, I would say the girl is my greatest friend.'

Looking at the poor, hapless Amelia, shrouded in her enormous wedding dress, Charlotte could well imagine that she was yet another of Mirabelle's victims whom the girl could effortlessly bully into submission. She was still gazing at the bride, when she heard Mirabelle saying, 'You don't mind if we join you, do you?'

The horrified expression on Lady Farrell's face left little doubt that the intrusion was most unwelcome. Charlotte, however, at a loss as to what else to do, concluded that she had little choice but to make the best of the situation.

'You will all, er, recall my sister's friend, Miss Mirabelle McGregor and her brother, Mr Bertie McGregor, from the betrothal ball at Wetherington?' she announced.

All three frosty expressions gave little clue as to whether the Farrells recalled the pair or not. But Mirabelle, slipping on to the bench alongside Charlotte, remained completely oblivious to the hostile reception.

'May I say how much my brother and I enjoyed the betrothal ball, Lady Farrell,' she gushed, with a wide smile. 'And here we all are on another such romantic occasion. Why, to think, in just a few short weeks, you will be holding your very own wedding at Wetherington. How dreadfully exciting.'

'Hmph,' huffed the countess.

'Of course, you are exceedingly lucky, Lady Farrell,' continued Mirabelle airily. 'I have heard tell that there were no end of young ladies wishing to set their caps at your son. Our poor Mama, on the other hand, must be pitied at having to find only one to take Bertie here. As you can see, he is such an ugly oaf.'

Bertie, seated alongside the doctor, on the opposite bench, flushed a bright shade of red. 'I am not,' he protested.

Mirabelle gave a snort of contemptuous laughter. 'Just look at the colour of him! Can you imagine any young lady paying him even an ounce of attention?'

'Just because I am not the most handsome of men, does not mean I am uninteresting,' stammered a now glowing Bertie. 'Indeed, I can be most interesting when I wish.'

Mirabelle guffawed. 'What on earth is interesting about you, Brother? I own I have had more scintillating conversations with the topiary.'

Whilst no one but Mirabelle appeared to find her comments the least bit diverting, Bertie speared his sister with such a heated glare that Charlotte would not have been at all surprised if he had then reached over the table and throttled her – a sentiment which, if she was correctly interpreting the look upon Dr Leigh's face, he was also attempting to suppress.

Cook had done an excellent job. Not only was Charlotte of the opinion that little Harry's birthday cake was one of the most delicious creations she had ever seen, but that same sentiment was shared by every member of the infant's family. The cake consisted of two halves, separated by a thick layer of jam and cream. A generous coating of white icing covered the top. As Charlotte did her best to cut it, cream oozed everywhere, much to the delight of her young audience.

Eventually succeeding in her task, Harry, being the guest of honour, was presented with his piece first. With the vigour of an excited one-year-old, he plunged both chubby hands into the mound of cream and plastered it all over his hair. Satisfied, he then sat back and beamed broadly at his laughing siblings.

Determined to make the toddler's first birthday a memorable and enjoyable affair for the family, Charlotte had brought a pile of presents for Harry, more blankets and, ever practical, a new axe. The one they had been using had obviously been lying in the abandoned house for many years and was both rusted and blunt.

'I thought we'd better start giving some thought to the winter, Emmy,' she said, as she handed over the item. 'Prepare a pile of firewood now, whilst the weather is still relatively dry. Do you think you will be able to manage here once the snows come?'

Emmy accepted the axe with a grateful smile. 'We'll be fine, miss,' she replied stoutly. 'There's a lot worse off than us; a lot who haven't even got a roof over their heads.'

Although it grieved her to think of it, Charlotte knew that Emmy was, unfortunately, all too correct in her depressing observations.

Because of the infection in Edward's leg, Dr Leigh had, for the past few days, been visiting Hamilton Manor with far more frequency than Charlotte would have liked. So far, she had done an excellent job in avoiding him. But her luck was soon to run out.

She was mid-way through reading a poem to Edward, seated in the chair to the right of his bed, when the door opened and in came the doctor. A rush of pink flooded Charlotte's cheeks. Following their discussion in the library, the two of them had barely exchanged a word at Lady Amelia's wedding and Charlotte had harboured no inclination to change the situation. Today, though, if she did not wish to arouse the suspicions of her brother, she was left with little choice but to be civil.

'Lady Charlotte,' he said unsmilingly, as he inclined his head to her.

Charlotte could not bring herself to meet his eyes. 'Dr Leigh,' she muttered stiffly.

Obviously aware of the awkwardness between them, but not permitting it to linger, the doctor swiftly moved his attention to his patient. 'Good afternoon, Master Edward,' he declared with a warm smile. 'How are you feeling today?'

'Much better, thank you, Doctor,' informed Edward. 'The draught you gave me appears to have worked splendidly.'

'Thank goodness for that,' replied the doctor.

'And Charlotte here has spent every spare moment of her time reading to me,' Edward went on.

'Very magnanimous,' remarked the doctor, casting an unimpressed look in Charlotte's direction.

'She is the very best of readers, sir. Why, she makes even the most boring texts sound interesting.'

'How very clever of her,' intoned the doctor, sardonically. 'Although I do hope, young man, you are not implying that the feeding habits of flat fish are boring?'

Edward wrinkled his brow. 'Feeding habits of flat fish, sir? I have no idea what you are refer—'

'If you will excuse me, Edward,' broke in Charlotte, 'I think it best if I take my leave of you now in order that Dr Leigh may examine you in peace.'

The doctor fixed her with a frosty gaze. 'I can assure you there is no need to leave on my account, Lady Charlotte.'

Charlotte stiffened. 'I am sure you can imagine that with my forthcoming wedding, I have an inordinate amount of things to do, Doctor. Please do excuse me.' She rose to her feet in what she hoped was a dignified manner and marched resolutely to the door, tripping over her skirts as she did so.

Chapter Sixteen

IF Charlotte had thought – as indeed she had on many occasions – that three Farrells were difficult enough to deal with, she soon discovered that five were more insufferable than even she could have imagined.

As the wedding day drew nearer, the first of the guests began to arrive, in the shape of the countess's Aunt Felicia and her granddaughter, Felicia-Sophia. Charlotte, much to her despair, received a command to attend Wetherington, to make the acquaintance of these soon-to-be relatives.

Initially filled with terror at the thought of such a collection of Farrells under one roof, she had, by the time it reached the appointed hour, almost succeeded in convincing herself that these as yet unknown family members could not possibly be as bad as the three with whom she was already familiar.

She continued to console herself with that thought when, upon her arrival at Wetherington, she was not shown to the bedchamber, but to the dark, airless drawing-room. A fact which, much to her own bemusement, caused her some relief – relief which was, unfortunately, short-lived.

As the butler pushed open the door, Charlotte's eyes fell upon the occupants, seated in five high-backed chairs arranged around the roaring fire. As well as the countess, Frederick and Perdita, there was a young girl, who looked to be of a similar age to Charlotte, and a much older woman with a heavily creased face. Every one of them appeared to be sound asleep.

The butler, normally so assertive in his announcements, appeared to have completely given up. He shook his head despairingly as he opened the door to allow Charlotte entry. Then he turned around and marched back down the corridor mumbling to himself all the while.

Baffled as to what she should do, Charlotte gave a little cough but, to her growing consternation, not one of the party appeared to hear her.

'You will have to do better than that,' announced Dr Leigh, storming into the room behind her. 'Allow me.'

Taken aback by both his sudden presence and his abruptness, Charlotte watched as he marched directly over to the countess and shook her bony shoulder. The woman awoke with a start.

'Good lord! What is it, Doctor? You could well have caused me to have a seizure handling me so roughly. Why, were it not for your rep—'

'Lady Charlotte is here, ma'am,' interjected the physician, his tone belying none of his impatience.

'Oh,' she huffed, turning her head to the door where Charlotte was still standing.

The doctor strode over to a seat at the back of the room and picked up a newspaper from the table beside it. Lady Farrell, meanwhile, reached across and prodded the older woman.

'This is the girl, Felicia.'

'What's that you say?' roared the visitor, clearly disorientated at being woken so rudely.

'I said, that this is the girl.'

'What?' bellowed the old woman.

Lady Farrell shook her head. Then she leaned across and produced an ear trumpet from the side of the old lady's chair. She handed it over and the woman promptly put it to her right ear.

'What's that you say?'

'I said, Felicia,' she repeated, 'that this is the girl.'

The old woman gawped blankly. 'Girl? Girl? What girl?'

The countess rolled her eyes. 'The girl Frederick has offered for.'

'Oh. Her.' The old woman turned her insipid blue eyes – exactly like those of the other Farrells – to examine Charlotte.

'Well,' she sighed, 'she'll do for our purposes I suppose.'

A prick of uneasy curiosity stabbed at Charlotte and, before she had time to consider the consequences, she found herself asking, 'May I enquire as to what purposes you are referring, ma'am?'

Lady Farrell bristled and waved a hand dismissively. 'Nothing to concern yourself with. Now, the fact that you are here, Charlotte, has saved me the trouble of writing yet another note. We are to hold a very important dinner here tomorrow evening. Our guest of honour will be the Duke of Sussex. Needless to say, his grace is a very, *very* important man and one whom we Farrells always strive to impress. Tomorrow evening I shall be handing him, personally, an invitation to your wedding.'

Charlotte stared at the woman with a sinking heart. She had a strong inkling of what was to follow; she was not wrong.

'You will attend this dinner, Charlotte. And you will not, under any circumstances, be late for the occasion.'

'Late?' boomed the visiting Lady Felicia. 'Don't tell me the chit is sometimes late?'

Lady Farrell nodded her head wearily. 'I'm afraid so.'

The visitor cast Charlotte such a disparaging glare that it could not have been worse if she had been standing before them in her riding breeches. She wished fervently for the ground to open and swallow her up. Alas, it did not.

'You will also take the greatest of care with your toilette,' she continued, 'and that includes – although I find it quite incomprehensible that I even have to say this – the state of your hair.'

'Her hair?' repeated Lady Felicia. 'Does the chit not bother with her hair?'

'I'm afraid not, Felicia,' she sighed.

'Good God,' remarked Lady Felicia, gawping at Charlotte in astonishment.

'And that is not all, Felicia,' she continued. 'I received word recently, via an anonymous source, that she has been seen gallivanting around the countryside wearing – of all things – a pair of gentleman's riding breeches. The very thought of it is enough to make me take to my bed again.'

Lady Felicia continued to stare at Charlotte for several long seconds, before emitting a gurgling sound from the back of her throat.

'So,' carried on the countess, ignoring the strange noises coming from her relative, 'do you understand all your instructions?'

A dejected Charlotte nodded her head.

'Good,' she proclaimed. 'This shall be your first true test as a Farrell, Charlotte. Everything must be quite perfect. We Farrells have the very highest of reputations to uphold.'

'The very highest,' chipped in the young Felicia-Sophia, who had now woken up and was staring at Charlotte in the same disconcerting way as Perdita was prone to do. In fact, Charlotte noticed, everything about the girl, from the pale-red hair, to the scrawny form, was astonishingly like Perdita.

'That is all,' piped up Lady Farrell, in such a dismissive tone that Charlotte was left in little doubt that this was her cue to go. She dipped a curtsy and made to leave the room, accompanied by an uneasy feeling that something was most definitely amiss. As she turned around, her eye caught that of the doctor and she realized, with yet another pang of humiliation, that, despite feigning interest in his newspaper, the man had obviously been listening to the entire conversation.

'Blimey, you look worn out, miss,' exclaimed Albert, as Charlotte walked miserably down the steps of Wetherington Hall.

'Worn out or not, Albert,' she replied, 'I have a very, *very* important dinner engagement here tomorrow. Whatever happens, I must not be late for it.'

'Well, then,' said Albert, removing his hat and scratching his head. 'We'll have to do all we can to make sure you're not, miss.'

Charlotte flashed him a smile as, replacing his hat, he offered her his arm and she climbed into the carriage.

Although conditions were not at all ideal for riding the following day, Charlotte spent as long as she possibly could out in the fresh air with Victor. It was only when a drizzly rain began to fall mid-afternoon, that she decided it sensible to return to the manor. Wheeling the horse around, a mysterious female figure in a green riding-habit and veiled hat, caught her eye. For all she caught just a glimpse of her, this time Charlotte was certain that it was exactly the same woman who had passed her in the fog the evening of the betrothal ball. But who was she and what was she doing galloping about the countryside alone?

Having neither the inclination nor the energy to face the wrath of the Farrells yet again, Charlotte adhered strictly to her orders and spent the remainder of the day in preparation for the dinner party that evening. Her maid, who was continually disappointed at her mistress's usual lack of interest in social occasions, was, for once, able to employ all the beauty tricks she had learned in her bible, *The Mirror of the Graces*. Charlotte's skin had been scrubbed and creamed until it glowed; her hair had been washed, oiled and brushed until it shone and she had sat – as patiently as she could – for some two hours, while the girl, with the help of her heating irons, had arranged her hair into an impressive creation of kinks and curls. When Charlotte eventually stepped into her gown, her maid stood back and regarded her in satisfaction. As did Harriet, when she came bowling into the room.

'Goodness, Charlotte you are in fine looks this evening,' enthused the younger girl. 'I can scarce believe that you are to take dinner with the Duke of Sussex. I was so excited that I simply had to pass by Mirabelle's house on my way back from town this afternoon and tell her the exciting news. Bertie says that, once you are married to Frederick Farrell, it is most likely that such royal guests will be the norm.'

'I suppose they will,' muttered Charlotte, with a distinct lack of enthusiasm. She glanced in the mirror and could hardly believe that the reflection staring back at her was the same girl. On the outside appeared a beautiful, refined young woman, worthy of taking her seat alongside any member of the royal family; but, on the inside, it was a very different matter. Her stomach was tied up in so many knots that – royalty or not – she was convinced she would not be able to eat a thing at the wretched dinner. And the weather was not helping matters in the least.

Yet again, a thick fog had wound its eerie way over the surrounding countryside, adding to Charlotte's deepening concern about arriving late for the event. With her nerves on edge, she sent word to Albert that she should like to leave even earlier than the ridiculously early hour they had previously agreed. Ready for her departure, she left her chamber and was walking past Edward's rooms at exactly the same moment the door burst open and she found herself colliding with the large, solid figure of Dr Leigh.

'Oh,' she stammered. 'I, er—'

She tilted her head up to him and, as their eyes met, all thoughts of the dreadful evening ahead, completely evaporated. The only thing she was aware of was the proximity of his body to hers and the fact that his strong hands were holding on to her upper arms.

'Forgive me, Lady Charlotte,' he said, releasing his hold of her and taking a step back. 'I should have looked where I was going.'

His brisk tone jolted Charlotte back to reality. 'Yes, you should Dr Leigh,' she retorted, attempting to quell the disappointment seeping through her. Aware of his gaze sliding over her, she focused on the toes of his boots which were, she noticed, more than a little scuffed.

'I assume you are still to attend the dinner party at Wetherington this evening?' he said at length.

She raised her eyes to his. 'Yes, I am, Doctor,' she replied, in what she hoped was as neutral a tone as his own.

He said nothing for several seconds, his eyes burning into hers. Charlotte swallowed uncomfortably, conscious that the same strange feelings she had had on more than one occasion in the man's presence, were once again overtaking her.

'I am on my way back to Wetherington now,' the doctor suddenly announced. 'However, I hardly think my gig fitting for your journey when you have obviously gone to so much trouble with your toilette.'

Charlotte stiffened. 'I have not gone to the slightest trouble with my toilette, Doctor. And I have my own carriage, thank you.'

Again there was an awkward hiatus before he said, 'Very well then. We will most likely see each other later.'

'Most likely,' muttered Charlotte. Then, having no wish to spend another minute in his presence, she whirled around and marched back along the corridor to her room. She sank down on to the bed and stayed there for ten minutes, until she could be sure the doctor had left.

Word had been sent to Albert at the Tomms's cottage, of the earlier departure time but, as Charlotte waited impatiently in the hall for the carriage to roll up outside the door, she had the same sense of foreboding she had experienced the evening her gown had been ruined. As the minutes ticked by, her concern grew to such an extent that she slipped out of the door and, in the dense fog, began making her way to the coach-house, which adjoined the stables. Scarcely able to see a hand in front of her, her heart flew to her mouth as she walked directly into a bony figure.

'Aahhh!' she screamed as it turned to face her. Upon seeing who it was, her horror soon turned to relief.

'Adams!' she exclaimed. 'What on earth are you doing out here?'

'Enjoying the weather, ma'am,' declared the butler, with more animation in his voice than Charlotte had ever heard in all the years he had worked at the manor. She did not waste time dwelling upon this fact.

'I am on my way to the coach-house, Adams. Would you be good enough to accompany me? I cannot see my own feet in this dreadful fog.'

'It would be my pleasure, ma'am,' said the servant. 'And don't you be worrying about this fog – I've seen much worse than this.'

Charlotte had not the courage to ask where.

As Adams deftly led her around to the coach-house, Charlotte could discern Albert's voice amongst a great deal of commotion.

'Whatever has occurred, Albert?' she asked, upon reaching her destination which was lit up with a number of lanterns.

'It's the coach, miss,' explained Albert, concern etched upon his face. 'Someone's only gone and sawn through the back axle.'

'The back axle?' repeated Charlotte, with more than a hint of panic. 'But surely it can be repaired.'

'Oh, it can be repaired all right. But not tonight. There's no way we'll be able to get it up and running in time to get you to that fancy dinner, miss. Much as I know how much you're wanting to go.'

Charlotte's heart sank to her feet. 'Well, what about the gig?' she asked in desperation. 'Couldn't you drive me over in that. Or I could drive myself.'

'Far too dangerous for any of us to be running around in a gig in these conditions,' countered Albert. 'And there's certainly no way I'm letting you out of these grounds on your own in this weather and with that highwayman gadding about. Lord only knows what could happen to you and I know your father will be of the same mind. You'll just have to stay here and that's all there is to it.'

Prickly tendrils of worry began wrapping themselves around Charlotte as she realized that Albert was absolutely right.

Chapter Seventeen

THE aftermath of Charlotte's non-attendance at the dinner with the Duke of Sussex was not pleasant. In fact, it was so unpleasant, and in front of an audience which had included Dr Leigh and all the Farrells – visiting and resident – that it was all Charlotte could do not to burst into tears and tell the countess and Frederick exactly what they could do with their wretched marriage proposal. But, reminding herself yet again of the reasons why she had accepted it, she succeeded in biting her tongue and saved her crying for the privacy of her own room.

The wrath of the Farrells, though, was not the only thing on Charlotte's mind. Once she had recovered from her initial dismay at having to miss the dinner; and the humiliation of her public scolding, she lay on her bed for several hours dissecting every piece of the same worrying puzzle. There was no doubt that someone had, very deliberately and very painstakingly, sawn through the axle of the coach. Just as someone had very deliberately and very painstakingly taken the trouble of writing a note regarding her riding breeches. And then there was the incident with her gown for the betrothal ball – that too had most definitely not been an accident. Perdita Farrell appeared to be going to a great deal of effort to make her look foolish. But why and, more baffling still, how?

'Will you still come and visit us when you're wed, miss?' asked Becky the following day.

'Of course, Becky,' replied Charlotte. 'Why wouldn't I?'

Becky shrugged her little shoulders and directed her gaze to the spotlessly clean floor. 'I dunno, miss. Maybe your new husband's too grand to have his wife bothering with the likes of us.'

'Becky,' said Charlotte, taking hold of the girl's hand, 'whether my husband is grand or not, he will not stop me coming to visit you.' No sooner had the words left her lips, though, than a sinking sensation engulfed her. She had not, for one moment, considered that her marriage to Frederick would prevent her from visiting Becky and her family. She was aware that Frederick did not give a flying fig what she got up to. But the same, unfortunately, could not be said for Lady Farrell.

Feeling like it was the very last thing on earth she wanted to do – with the obvious exception of marrying Frederick Farrell – Charlotte set off for London for the penultimate fitting of her wedding gown. With Harriet out visiting, and desperate for some light-hearted company, she had once again invited Kate Tomms to join her. This time the girl appeared even more excited than on the previous trip due mainly to the fact that Charlotte had been ordered by the Farrells to procure several new ball gowns.

As the two girls sifted through dozens of fabric samples, Kate's eye fell on a swatch of deep rose-pink satin.

'Oh, is that not the prettiest thing you have ever seen, Miss Charlotte?' she enthused, smoothing the fabric between her slim fingers.

'It certainly goes well with your colouring, Kate,' agreed Charlotte. 'In fact it goes so well that I think we should have a gown made up for you in that very material.'

Kate's eyes grew wide. 'Oh, but I couldn't possibly, miss. I don't have any—'

'It shall be my treat,' asserted Charlotte.

All at once, tears swam in Kate's green eyes. 'After me ma and da and our Will, I think you're the best person in the whole world, Miss Charlotte,' she declared.

'There's no need for that, Kate,' giggled Charlotte. 'Now, come along. Let us choose a flattering style for you. One that will confirm to Thomas that you are the prettiest girl on earth.'

Kate's face flushed exactly the same shade of pink as the piece of fabric she was holding.

*

Charlotte's presence was once again requested at Wetherington. So nervous was she following her most recent chastisement, that she constructed an exhaustive list of excuses for declining the summons. But, she would, she knew, simply be postponing the inevitable and so, swamped by dread, off she set.

Higgins, the butler, had only just opened the door to her, when Charlotte, much to her alarm, found herself face-to-face with Dr Leigh. Her hackles immediately rose, but the doctor greeted her with a disarming smile.

'Ah, Lady Charlotte,' he gushed. 'How very fortuitous. I was hoping to speak to you today on a matter regarding your brother.'

Before Charlotte could say a word, he seized her arm and began marching her across the stone floor of the hall. 'Don't worry, Higgins,' he called back to the servant, who appeared equally as flummoxed as Charlotte by the sudden turn of events. 'Once I have spoken with Lady Charlotte, I shall direct her to Lady Farrell myself.'

'Er, very well, sir,' rejoined the butler, his voice ringing with a little more suspicion than Charlotte was comfortable with.

Not wishing to cause a scene in front of the servant, she allowed the doctor to steer her along a corridor. Upon reaching a door there, he pulled her roughly into a small saloon. As the door swung shut, Charlotte shook her arm from his grip.

'What on earth do you think you are doing, Dr Leigh?' she demanded.

The doctor stood before her. 'I could well ask you the same thing, madam,' he said, his tone dripping with ice.

Charlotte flinched. 'I have no idea what you are talking about.'

'Don't you? Then permit me to clarify. I am referring to your wedding to Frederick Farrell which is due to take place in a little over two weeks.'

'I am quite aware of the timing of my own wedding, thank you, Doctor,' huffed Charlotte.

'Well, I am pleased to hear that at least,' conceded the physician. 'But are you also aware that you are to spend the rest of your life feeling ten times more miserable than you do now?'

Charlotte balked. 'You have no idea what you are talking about, sir; I am perfectly satisfied with my choice of husband.'

'Don't be ridiculous,' he snapped, so sharply that Charlotte gulped. 'Who, in their right mind, could be happy marrying him? And as for his mother, it is nothing short of preposterous the way you allow her to speak to you.'

Charlotte lifted her chin. 'I will remind you, Dr Leigh, that my future mother-in-law is also your employer, who is, I believe, paying you exceedingly well for your services.'

'The arrangement between myself and the countess is of no import and you know it,' he snarled. 'But what does concern me – and a great deal I might add – is why you are insisting on throwing your life away on a pompous dullard like Frederick Farrell.'

Charlotte's eyes narrowed. 'As I have told you now, on several occasions, Dr Leigh, whom I choose to marry has nothing at all to do with you. Now, will you please direct me to Lady Farrell.'

The doctor stared at her, a look of incredulity combined with frustration darkening his face. Charlotte, meanwhile, was aware of hot tears scorching her eyes.

'Time is running out, Charlotte,' he said, gazing at her imploringly. 'I beseech you, once again, to reconsider your decision.'

'I am afraid I will not do that, Doctor,' announced Charlotte, swinging around to face the door. 'Now, if you don't mind, I should like to bring an end to this conversation.'

There was a long silence before the doctor said frostily, 'If that is your wish.'

'It is,' affirmed Charlotte, every nerve in her body screaming otherwise.

Charlotte had almost to run in order to keep up with the doctor as he strode through the corridors of Wetherington Hall. His manner made no attempt to conceal his fury at her, but Charlotte was equally as angry. Why he was persisting in his efforts to persuade her to change her mind regarding the marriage, was beyond her. And the fact that her eyes were constantly being drawn to his legs in the tight black breeches he was wearing was not helping matters in the least. With a great deal of effort she refocused her gaze to the stone floor. Shapely legs the man might have, but she would not allow them to detract from the fact that his meddling could well jeopardize her family's future.

Upon their arrival at the gloomy drawing-room, the doctor burst through the door and headed straight over to a chair at the back of the room. Charlotte tripped in after him and remained standing just inside the threshold. The countess and a dozing Perdita were the only two people present.

'Good God, man,' proclaimed Lady Farrell. 'Must you be so boisterous? You, of all people, should know how dreadfully delicate I am feeling today, Doctor.'

'Lady Charlotte is here, ma'am,' informed the physician tersely.

'Ugh,' she huffed. 'That is all I need, when I was at last managing to gain some comfort. Do help me up, man.'

Making no effort to hide his irritation, the doctor thrust to his feet and strode over to the woman, yanking her to a standing position.

'Really, Dr Leigh!' she exclaimed, as she smoothed down her bottle-green skirts, 'One can only hope you are not so violent with all your patients.'

'That very much depends on who they are,' replied the doctor, before spinning around and reclaiming his chair.

Evidently unimpressed, she turned her attention to Charlotte. 'Your timing, as usual, could not be worse, girl,' she sniffed.

Charlotte wrinkled her brow. 'But you did send for me, ma'am.'

The countess waved a dismissive hand as she began staggering towards the mahogany sideboard on the rear wall. 'That was before I was overcome with this dreadful ache in my back.' Upon reaching the sideboard, she retrieved a small, brass key from a chain around her wrist, inserted it into the lock of the middle drawer and pulled it open. Inside was a scroll of parchment. The countess removed it from the drawer and, with great drama, hobbled over to the armchair alongside that in which Dr Leigh was seated. She lowered herself into it with a painful grimace. The doctor rolled his eyes.

'Now this document,' began the woman, proffering the scroll to Charlotte, 'has been in the Farrell family for over one hundred years. It is our family tree which has been meticulously added to over the generations. Before the wedding, you are to memorize it and learn where every

Farrell who will be attending, fits into the lineage. I shall, of course, be carrying out a rigorous test of your knowledge beforehand.'

'I, er, see,' muttered Charlotte, accepting the scroll.

'Needless to say,' she continued imperiously, 'this is a most valuable and treasured document and you are to treat it as such.'

'Of, course, ma'am,' mumbled Charlotte.

'Now run along,' she instructed. 'Not only do I have shooting pains in my back, but I have just experienced a similar one in my chest. I can only think that my poor heart is beginning to wane, along with everything else. That is, I know, a classic symptom, Dr Leigh, and it is absolutely no good attempting to convince me otherwise.'

'It is indeed a classic symptom, ma'am,' concurred the physician. 'But one of indigestion – resulting, I believe, from too much beef yesterday evening.'

The countess cast him a disparaging glare. 'Your flippant diagnoses do cause me a great deal of concern, Doctor. Indeed, sometimes I have cause to wonder if you would recognize a serious condition if it flared up in front of your very eyes.'

'Oh, believe me, my lady,' replied the doctor, his eyes piercing Charlotte, 'I can assure you that I am acutely aware of when a serious condition is flaring up.'

Having left Wetherington feeling more than a little disconcerted following her encounter with the doctor, Charlotte arrived back at Hamilton Manor with the precious family tree safely tucked away in her reticule. She trooped straight up the stairs, eager for the refreshing, uncomplicated company of her brother. Refreshing and uncomplicated were, unfortunately, not words that could be applied to the two visitors present. Her heart sank to the floor when she pushed open the door to Edward's bedchamber to find not only Harriet inside, but also Mirabelle and Bertie McGregor.

'Oh,' she faltered, 'I was, er, not aware that you were here, Mirabelle. I did not see your carriage outside.'

'Our lump of a driver has taken it around to the stables,' informed Mirabelle. 'Some problem with one of the wheels, or some such, the oaf was twittering about.'

'Do come and join us, Charlotte,' urged Harriet. 'We were just discussing the Courteous Criminal. Are you aware that the man has now carried out some twelve attacks and the Runners are still nowhere near to catching him?'

'Er, no,' replied Charlotte, conscious of Bertie's leering gaze upon her. 'I was, um, not aware of that fact. But I'm afraid I shall not be able to join you, Harriet. Lady Farrell has set me a very important task.'

'What very important task?' enquired Edward.

Charlotte pulled a rueful face. 'I am to learn the lineage of every member of the Farrell family who is to attend the wedding.'

Harriet grimaced. 'Ugh. How dreadfully boring. But how on earth does the woman expect you to do that?'

Charlotte retrieved the scroll from her reticule and held it up for all to see. 'She has loaned me this family tree which has been in the family for over a hundred years.'

'My,' remarked Mirabelle interestedly. 'Such a document must be exceedingly valuable if it has been around that long. And belonging to one of the country's finest families.'

'She informs me that it is extremely valuable,' said Charlotte. 'I dare not even think of the consequences were anything to happen to it.'

Mirabelle's eyebrows shot to her hairline. 'Really?' she mused. 'How perfectly fascinating.'

Charlotte soon discovered that 'perfectly fascinating' was the very antithesis of the Farrell family tree. She spent hours lying on her bed poring over the document. So long did she spend studying it, in fact, that her head was straining with the overload of information. It would not have been half as bad, she pondered, staring at the yellowing piece of paper covered in neat lines of black ink, had the family not been in-breeding for centuries. Not only that, but they insisted upon calling almost every member Felicia, Frederick or Perdita. But Charlotte knew that merely spouting forth one of those names to the countess during the 'rigorous test of her knowledge', would not suffice at all. She would be expected to know if it was Frederick VI, Frederick XVI or Frederick XXVI and the same with the never-ending stream of Felicias and Perditas. With this thought in mind, she shook her head vigorously, hoping that all the information floating around in it would settle in the correct place. She then refocused her attention on the Farrell-Dunworthy branch of the family, the head of which was Lord Frederick Farrell XI or was it XII?

'You're looking a little pasty, girl,' remarked her father over dinner that evening. 'Nothing amiss is there?'

Panic pricked at Charlotte. Was her father beginning to suspect something? She contorted her mouth into a smile. 'Of course not, Father,' she replied, in a tone which she hoped inferred he was quite mad for even suggesting such a thing. 'I am perfectly well. Never better in fact.'

'You sure?' he persisted, narrowing his eyes.

Charlotte gulped. 'Of course. Why, what on earth could possibly be amiss?'

The old man threw her a look which implied he was not wholly convinced but, before he could continue with his line of enquiry, Harriet broke in.

'Oh, you will never guess who I saw when I was taking a stroll in the gardens earlier, Charlotte.'

'I have no idea, Harriet,' replied Charlotte, as lightly as she could manage.

'Kate Tomms,' beamed Harriet. 'And she was accompanied by a very handsome young man by the name of Thomas. The two of them looked head-over-heels in love with one another.'

'Hmm,' sniffed Lord Hamilton. 'Bit too young to be falling in love if you ask me.'

'Oh, don't be so stuffy, Father,' chided Harriet playfully. 'One is never too young – or indeed too old – to fall in love. Is that not correct, Charlotte?'

Charlotte could not answer as a bolt of realization pierced her. Young or old, it was doubtful she would ever have first-hand experience of the condition. She was to spend her entire life without having the first idea about falling in love.

The draining combination of her row with the doctor, hours studying the Farrell family tree and all of dinner feigning a happy persona, resulted in a pounding headache by the time Charlotte came to retire. Totally exhausted, she was looking forward to nothing more than curling up in her bed.

In no mood for the fussing of her maid, she dismissed the girl after she had helped her dress for dinner. Upon returning to her bedchamber, she was just about to step out of her gown when her eyes fell upon a piece of paper smouldering on the marble hearth of the fireplace. Her heart began to pound. Her throat suddenly felt dry. With quaking legs, she walked over to the fireplace and bent down to examine the piece of paper. It couldn't possibly be what she thought it was, could it? But, to her complete and utter horror, she discovered that it was.

'*What?*' demanded the countess, the little colour there was in her cheeks, rapidly dwindling to a startling shade of white.

'Somebody put it on the fire, ma'am,' explained Charlotte, as she stood in the depressing drawing-room, addressing the three Farrells. Fortunately the visiting Lady Felicia and Felicia-Sophia were nowhere to be seen.

'*Somebody*?' repeated the countess, her face contorting with incredulity. 'What do you mean *somebody*?'

'I put the document safely in the drawer of my writing bureau, ma'am. Somebody obviously went into my bedchamber, removed it from the drawer and put it on the fire.'

Lady Farrell shook her head in disbelief. 'Dr Leigh,' she called to the doctor, who, much to Charlotte's regret, was seated in his usual chair at the back of the room, 'do not leave me for a minute. I have the distinct feeling that this might well be my final day upon this earth.'

The doctor rolled his eyes. 'I think it unlikely, ma'am.'

'And do you, Doctor, think it unlikely that *somebody* penetrated Hamilton Manor and put our treasured and extremely valuable family tree on the fire in Lady Charlotte's bedchamber?'

'That is not for me to say, ma'am.'

'Indeed it is not, Doctor,' she concurred. 'It is for me to say, and I say that it is complete and utter nonsense.'

Charlotte gasped. 'But it is true. Why ever would I wish to lie about such a thing?'

'Because,' spat the countess, 'you do not have the nerve to confess to your own completely irresponsible behaviour. You destroyed that document yourself.'

'But I didn't,' protested Charlotte, blinking back tears.

'It does not now signify whether you did or you did not,' retorted the countess. 'The fact remains that the document was ruined whilst it was in your possession. It is you who must therefore accept responsibility and answer to all our relatives who will be equally as distraught as we are. You are a complete and utter disaster, girl, and, were it not for the fact that—' She broke off. 'No matter. I do not wish to discuss the subject for a moment longer.'

Charlotte considered voicing her concerns. She had not slept a wink the night before, pondering the incident. She had, once again, arrived at the same conclusion. Somebody had definitely been in her room with the sole intention of destroying the family tree, just as somebody had purposefully ruined her gown the evening of the betrothal ball, and sabotaged her carriage the evening of the dinner with the Duke of Sussex. But she knew that any attempt to explain all of that would be futile. The countess would not believe a word of it – particularly when the main suspect was the woman's own daughter. Instead, she bit her tongue, waiting for the moment when she would be dismissed. Perdita, however, adding fuel to Charlotte's suspicions, appeared to be taking perverse satisfaction from this latest mishap.

'Oh, it is such a pity that the family tree has been ruined, Mama,' she declared on a breath of disappointment. 'I was so looking forward to adding my own children's names to it in the not-too-distant future. Such a charming tradition, do you not agree, Dr Leigh?'

'I confess I am not a great follower of tradition merely for its own sake, ma'am,' replied the physician coolly.

'Oh, of course, I agree wholeheartedly that some traditions are rather silly,' concurred Perdita with a mirthless giggle. 'But the Farrell family tree was not at all silly. It is, therefore, my sincere opinion that the girl should be punished for her carelessness, Mama.'

Charlotte wondered if Perdita's punishment involved pushing her down another set of steps. Fortunately, Lady Farrell seemed less enthusiastic.

'I have not yet decided what to do about the matter, Perdita,' she informed her daughter wearily. 'But, suffice to say, that if these are my last minutes on this earth, Charlotte – and I suspect very strongly that they are – then I should like you to know that it will be you who is responsible for my demise. Now, Doctor, please arrange for the footmen to carry me upstairs. I do not wish to spend my last precious minutes in this room. It will be a much more dignified death if I am found on my bed. Charlotte, you are dismissed until I send for you again. If, of course, I am here to do so.'

'It is quite beyond me why we are even bothering with the girl, Mama,' piped up Frederick, who had said nothing throughout the tirade, but had shot countless contemptuous looks at his fiancée. 'She is hardly worth all the trouble.'

Lady Farrell raised her eyebrows to her son. 'Oh, but unfortunately she is, Frederick.'

As Charlotte took her leave of Wetherington, the countess's parting words continued to ring in her ears. Whatever had the woman meant when she had suggested that Charlotte was 'worth the trouble'? She racked her brains until she could rack them no more. But it was yet another answer that evaded her.

'Oh, thank goodness it's you, miss,' gushed Becky, as she rushed out of the cottage to greet Charlotte. 'We thought it might have been her again.'

Charlotte furrowed her brow. 'Her? Who are you talking about, Becky?'

Becky inhaled deeply before launching into her explanation, her bright blue eyes shining with excitement. 'There's been a lady riding past here off and on for the last few weeks, but seems to be nearly every day now. We've been hiding, of course, but yesterday she heard our Harry crying – just like you did that time. He'd fallen down and banged his head on the floor, poor little mite.'

The furrows in Charlotte's forehead deepened as it occurred to her just how vulnerable the family were in their new home. 'What did the woman do, Becky?' she asked, making a huge effort to conceal her concern from the child.

Becky wrinkled her tiny nose. 'Well, not much, miss. I was peeping out of the window at her. She just slowed her horse down, listened for a bit and then rode on. Harry didn't cry no more after that, see?'

Charlotte nodded her head, thanking God for that fact. 'Did you get a good look at her?'

'Not her face, miss,' replied Becky. 'She was wearing one of them hats with them veil things on it.'

'And a green riding-habit?'

'Yes, miss. Do you know who she is?'

Charlotte shook her head. 'I'm afraid not, Becky. Although I have no doubt,' she added, injecting her voice with a lightness she did not feel, 'that whoever she is, she will soon tire of riding this route and find another with which to amuse herself. But you must promise me, Becky, if ever any of you are in trouble, you will seek me out at once.'

'Of course, miss,' said Becky, grinning broadly. 'Now come on in and see how tidy we've made the place today.'

Chapter Eighteen

'GOODNESS me,' gasped the mantuamaker, as she stood before Charlotte, clasping her hands together. 'Even if I do say so myself, miss, I think that's the prettiest gown I've ever made.'

Charlotte tried desperately to summon up some enthusiasm for the woman's work. There was no doubting that she had done a first-class job: the dress was truly magnificent. But, the very fact that it was her final fitting and the next time she would see it, the gown would be hanging in her bedchamber ready for her wedding, filled her with clawing panic. Although, none of this, she realized, was the poor mantuamaker's fault.

'Thank you so much for all your hard work, Mrs Chalmers,' she intoned, with what she hoped was an appreciative smile. 'You have done an excellent job.'

'Well, let's hope your new husband thinks so,' replied the woman, with a wink. 'He should be the proudest man alive to have you hanging on his arm.'

Charlotte gave a doubtful smile. Somehow, she knew that, whatever emotions Frederick Farrell was going to be experiencing on his wedding day, it was unlikely that pride would feature amongst them.

As Albert had correctly predicted, the heavy clouds overhead meant that there was little light remaining by the time the carriage made its way out of the city. Charlotte, overcome with fatigue, closed her eyes and fell into a much-needed sleep. Her repose, though, was rudely interrupted as the carriage came to a sudden standstill, the bone-jarring jolt causing her to slam her head against the side and bring her abruptly back to consciousness.

Rubbing her head, it took a moment for her to realize what had happened. She could hear low voices outside. Realizing that she had no idea where they were or how long they had been on the road, she slid aside the green velvet curtain and opened the window.

'What's going on, Albert?' she shouted, squinting into the darkness.

'Stay inside, miss,' commanded Albert. His earnest tone unsettled Charlotte – something was wrong, she could sense it. She leaned forward tentatively and reached for the door handle. But, no sooner had she done so, than it was wrenched open and Charlotte found herself face-to-face with a masked figure attired completely in black. A tricorn hat shaded the upper half of his face, while a blue silk kerchief covered the lower. He was also, she realized with a bolt of panic, pointing a pistol to her chest. Terrified, she pressed herself into the corner of the carriage.

'Wh–what do you want?' she stammered, her heart pounding madly. For a moment, the man didn't answer but, although she couldn't see them, she was aware of his eyes running over her body.

'What have you done with Albert and Jenkins?' she demanded, fury beginning to stoke her courage. 'If you have hurt them, I'll—'

'Forgive me, my lady,' the man interjected, inclining his head to her. 'Please do not be afraid. I have no wish to harm anyone.' His voice sounded strange, muffled almost.

'Then l-leave us alone,' snapped Charlotte. 'Let us be on our way.'

'Indeed I will, madam,' he said. 'Once you have handed over your jewels.' He stretched out his hand encased in a black leather glove.

Charlotte pulled off her own gloves and, fumbling with fear, tugged her two silver rings from her fingers. She then removed her pearl earrings and, placing them with the rings, stretched her hand out to his.

'Thank you,' he said, as she dropped the items into the palm of his glove.

'And now your necklace, if I may.'

Charlotte's hand flew to the string of pearls. 'Indeed you may not, sir. This necklace was my mother's. I am afraid I cannot let you have it.'

'I'm sorry, but I must insist, madam.' He raised the revolver so that it was level with her face.

'No,' countered Charlotte, her hand clenched around the necklace. 'I will not hand it over.'

'Then I am sorry, but you leave me with no choice.' In a flash he swung from his horse into the carriage. Charlotte gasped as he slid into the seat next to her, every one of her nerves on edge.

Placing the revolver to the side of him, the man removed his gloves before turning to face her. Charlotte pressed herself tighter into the corner.

Undeterred, the highwayman placed both his hands around her neck, evidently searching for the clasp of the necklace. Charlotte winced at his touch.

'You–you … *villain*. You have no idea what that necklace means to me. You are a … a *beast*.'

'And you madam,' he replied tartly, 'are far too beautiful for your own good.'

Flooded with anger and indignation Charlotte opened her mouth to protest but, no sooner had she done so, than the man pulled down his kerchief and pulled her to him, kissing her with a strength and a passion which, quite literally, took her breath away. She was aware that she should repulse him, push him away. He was a stranger, a criminal, a blackguard but, although there was no logical explanation for it, something was telling her that he would never harm her; that he had never intended to harm her. Nevertheless, she should not be kissing anyone, let alone rogue highwaymen. But, as the kiss deepened, her thoughts ceased their whirling and her mind became blank, conscious of nothing other than the fire smouldering inside her. All at once, however, the man pulled away from her and replaced his kerchief.

'I beg your pardon, my lady,' he announced, his tone suddenly brisk. 'I will not inconvenience you any further.' He retrieved his gloves and pistol.

'B-but—' stammered Charlotte, her senses spinning from the diverse range of emotions she had experienced in only a few short minutes.

Silencing her, the man placed a fingertip against her lips. 'Thank you, madam,' he whispered. 'I have what I want – for the time being at least.'

His gentle touch and the hidden promise reverberating in his words sent a shiver of excitement shooting down Charlotte's spine. Having lost all sense of reality, she watched in stunned silence as he climbed out of the carriage and on to his waiting stallion, leaving her wide-eyed and panting.

As the sound of the highwayman's galloping horse faded into the background, it took a moment for Charlotte to realize that somebody was calling her name. She immediately came to her senses.

'Miss Charlotte?' shouted Albert. 'Are you all right, miss?'

Leaning across to the open door, Charlotte poked out her head into the blackness.

'I'm fine, Albert. He hasn't harmed either of you, has he?'

'No, miss. But we can't move.'

'Where are you?'

'Over here. Tied to the tree.'

Squinting, Charlotte could just about make out the whiteness of Albert's head, a few feet away.

She jumped out of the carriage and raced over. Albert was tied to one side of the tree and the footman to the other.

'Oh my word. Are you sure he hasn't hurt you?' Her fingers shook as she untied the loose knots.

'No miss,' replied Albert, shaking himself free of the rope. 'He just asked us, dead polite like, to walk over to the tree and tied us up real gentle. He didn't hurt you, miss, did he?'

'No Albert,' professed Charlotte, her lips still burning from the heat of the man's kiss. 'He didn't hurt me at all.'

Upon their return to Hamilton Manor, an almighty commotion erupted as news of their adventure spread like wildfire through the house. Edward insisted on being carried down to the drawing-room, so as not to miss a thing. Seated in a chair at the side of the roaring fire, Albert Tomms was sipping his brandy and animatedly describing the events of the evening to his avid audience of Edward, Mrs Tomms, Kate and Lord Hamilton. Harriet, who would no doubt have found the entire incident thrilling, was out to dinner at a friend's house. Charlotte was relieved to see that the ordeal did not appear to have affected Albert adversely. In fact, if she was not mistaken, he was relishing the attention. She could not help but smile at his numerous embellishments, which were resulting in much ooh-ing and ah-ing from his listeners.

Lord Hamilton, on the other hand, was definitely not smiling. In fact, with his hair standing on end in what would have been, in any other situation, a most comical fashion, the man was positively apoplectic with rage. As Albert recounted the tale, adding his own touch of drama, Lord Hamilton's face grew slowly redder as he furiously paced up and down the thick, patterned carpet.

'Why, the audacity of the man,' he bellowed as Albert explained how he had held the pistol to his temple and ordered him to the tree. 'I will hunt him down personally and have him strung from the gallows.'

Sitting on the sofa opposite the fireplace, Charlotte felt panic rising at the picture her father's threat painted. She rested her elbows on her knees and rubbed two fingers against each of her temples. 'I am sure there is no need for that, Father,' she protested wearily. 'The man did not so much as harm a hair on our heads.'

'That is hardly the point, Charlotte. He was holding a pistol to you.'

'I have no doubt that he never intended to use it,' she countered.

'Oh, I don't know, miss,' piped up Albert. 'You never can tell when those criminal sorts will turn nasty.'

'My sentiments exactly, Albert,' roared Lord Hamilton. 'He could have had your heads off in an instant.'

'I hardly think, Father, that a man who apologizes for the inconvenience of holding up the coach is then likely to shoot off our heads two minutes later.'

'And what, pray, do you know of men who hold up coaches, Charlotte? You are far too trusting for your own good, girl.'

'Trusting I may be, sir, but I am certainly no fool. And I know a gentleman when I meet one.'

'And what *gentleman*, goes about waving a pistol at old men and young ladies exactly?' challenged Lord Hamilton. 'No offence meant to either you or poor Jenkins, of course, Albert,' he added, lowering his voice and inclining his head to the older man.

'None taken, sir,' confirmed Albert, cradling the brandy glass in the palm of his hand.

'I confess, I do not know, Father,' replied Charlotte. 'But I know the man was most certainly not of the lower classes. His manners were impeccable.'

'Impeccable my foot!' barked Lord Hamilton. 'This manners business is nothing more than a ploy to catch you off-guard.'

'I think the mere fact that he held up the carriage is enough to catch anyone off-guard,' mumbled Charlotte.

'What was that you said?'

'Nothing, Father,' she replied, suddenly overcome with fatigue. 'Now, if you will excuse me, I have a splitting headache. If nobody objects, then I think I shall retire.'

Drained of all energy, Charlotte changed into her nightdress and sank into bed, relieved to be away from the drama downstairs. She needed some peace, some time alone to try and make sense of the events of the evening. But how could she make sense of such a ludicrous situation? What explanation could there possibly be for letting a complete stranger – and a criminal at that – take you in his arms and kiss you whilst holding up your carriage and stealing your jewels? Staring at the ceiling, she attempted to analyse the situation and could not help but compare it with the way she had felt when she had been in Frederick Farrell's arms during their dance at the ball the previous week. The thought of it still made her want to vomit. But tonight, in the highwayman's arms, a whole new range of emotions had opened up to her, emotions she would never have dreamed she was capable of. She touched her lips, remembering the heat he had evoked in them; the heat he had evoked in her entire body. Even the thought of him caused something in her belly to sizzle and melt.

Charlotte was so submerged in her thoughts that at first she was not aware of the discreet knock on the door. As it grew more persistent and a little louder, she quickly pulled herself together and managed to call 'Enter', which came out as a painful squeak.

The door was pushed open and Charlotte blinked twice to ensure she wasn't dreaming. 'Dr Leigh,' she exclaimed, feeling thoroughly vulnerable to be caught deep in such irreverent thoughts – and in her nightdress.

Save for her humiliating telling off about the Farrell family tree, she had not seen the doctor since the day at Wetherington when he had all but pleaded with her to call off the wedding. Following that encounter, she had had no wish to see him again and, as he stood in the doorway looking at her now, she wished vehemently that he would go away. Not least of all, she realized with some alarm, because she was afraid he would, once again, sense what she had been thinking.

'Wh–what are you doing here?' she stammered, yanking up the bedcovers to her chin.

'Your father sent for me, my lady,' he informed her. 'He was anxious for me to attend both you and Albert after your distressing incident this evening.'

'I can, um, assure you there is no need, Doctor,' mumbled Charlotte. 'I am perfectly well.'

'I am acting on your father's orders, ma'am,' asserted the physician, perching on the bed and taking hold of her wrist.

At his touch, Charlotte felt her breath catch in her throat. Gazing into his dark eyes, her heart began to race and her head to whirl. She was grateful when, at that moment, Harriet appeared, bristling with a combination of relief and excitement.

'Oh my goodness, Charlotte,' gushed the younger girl. 'I have only just arrived home and Father has told me what happened. How dreadfully exciting. Although I declare I would most likely have had a fit of the vapours on the spot.'

'Oh, it wasn't that bad, Harriet,' replied Charlotte, desperately attempting to regain a little of her composure whilst still acutely aware of the doctor's hand upon her.

'But you must feel dreadful, my dear. How is she, Doctor?'

'Her pulse is a little high,' confirmed the physician, suddenly releasing his hold of Charlotte's wrist and vacating his position on the bed. 'But I think she will live.'

'Well, I want to know absolutely everything the man said and did,' demanded Harriet, kicking off her slippers and tucking her legs under her as she settled into the armchair.

The doctor began rummaging in his medicine bag, which he had placed on the nightstand.

'Er, well,' began Charlotte. 'He-he was, er very … very … *polite*.'

'*Polite*?' echoed Harriet. 'But what did he actually *say* to you?'

'Well,' stammered Charlotte, conscious of the doctor's eyes on her. 'He … er— He said, er— Oh, I really don't remember, Harriet.'

'But do you think it was the Courteous Criminal?' pressed Harriet, unable to hide her exasperation at her sister's lack of detail.

'I don't know,' professed Charlotte, her eyes drawn to the doctor's. 'Perhaps it was.'

'But what did he look like? Was he really as dashing and handsome as they say he is?'

The doctor's gaze was now burning into hers. 'Yes, Harriet,' she found herself saying. 'I do believe he was.'

'Goodness!' exclaimed Harriet. 'How simply thrilling. I can scarcely wait to tell Mirabelle.'

Chapter Nineteen

CHARLOTTE was still abed the following morning when Harriet bowled in once more.

'You will never guess who is here, Charlotte.'

Charlotte, still focused on much more irreverent matters involving a polite highwayman, had not the slightest idea. She stared blankly at her sister.

'Why, the Farrells of course. Is that not the most romantic thing, Sister? Frederick Farrell rushing over to see his betrothed after such an upsetting event?'

Charlotte's heart sank as Harriet whisked out of the room on a wave of excitement. Sharing none of her sister's enthusiasm, she managed, with a great deal of reluctant effort, to drag herself out of bed, pull on a day gown of worked muslin, grace her hair with a fleeting brush and make her way, rather shakily, down the stairs.

In the drawing-room she found her father, the countess, Frederick, Perdita and Dr Leigh, who had taken a seat away from the others, in a corner of the room.

'Now then,' boomed Lord Hamilton amiably. 'Here she is. Safe and sound thank goodness.'

Frederick flashed Charlotte a look which left little doubt that he could not have cared less whether she was safe and sound or not. That of his mother appeared equally as indifferent.

'We came to see for ourselves that you are unharmed,' she intoned, matter-of-factly.

'I am quite well, thank you, my lady,' confirmed Charlotte.

'But what of the highwayman?' piped up Perdita, her colourless eyes shining with glee. 'Did he have a knife? Did he try to cut—'

'Fortunately, I saw no sign of a knife,' interrupted Charlotte, in no mood at all for another of the girl's gory speeches.

A shadow of disappointment fell over Perdita's face.

'Well,' pronounced Lady Farrell, 'now that we have ascertained the facts for ourselves, we must be on our way. We are all feeling quite out of frame this morning although, as you are aware, Lord Hamilton, we Farrells rarely allow our poor health to interfere with our sense of duty.'

'A very admirable trait, if I may say so, ma'am,' remarked Lord Hamilton.

'Quite,' concurred the countess. 'However, I wonder,' – she placed a gloved fingertip against her thin lips – 'as we are here, would you be good enough to permit us a tour of the house?'

Lord Hamilton beamed broadly. 'I should be delighted.'

'How very kind,' she replied, making a weak attempt at gratitude. 'Fortunately it is small enough that my poor back will be able to bear it. Now come along, children.'

As the Farrells all rose to their feet and followed Lord Hamilton from the room, Charlotte found, to her dismay, that Dr Leigh made no attempt to join them. The two of them were, once again, alone. But, before she had a chance to gather her thoughts and leave the room herself, she found the doctor in the seat next to hers.

'Charlotte,' he began, in an imploring voice.

Having a strong suspicion that he was about to launch into another litany on the subject of her marriage, Charlotte raised her eyes to him but, before either of them could say a word, the countess appeared in the doorway.

'Dr Leigh, how many times do I have to tell you that it is essential you remain by my side at all times? Despite this house's distinct lack of proportions, the fact remains that my back may give way at any moment and where would that leave me, hmm?'

'Most likely lying in a heap on the floor, ma'am,' puffed the doctor. He rose to his feet with obvious reluctance and followed her as she swept from the room with as much drama as she had entered it. Charlotte breathed a sigh of relief as she watched him go. There was no denying that she had felt another overpowering pull of attraction to the man whilst he had examined her the previous evening, although that was, of course, simply as a result of her heightened emotions. The man who had occupied her thoughts throughout the greater part of the darkened hours was a complete and utter stranger; a man who held up coaches, terrified their occupants and stole their jewels; a man who was rapidly becoming one of the most notorious highwaymen in history; a man known to her only as the Courteous Criminal.

Over the following days, Charlotte found that her usual nightmares had been replaced by a new set of images – equally as shocking and unsettling – but for quite different reasons. Even the dread of her wedding, now merely days away, no longer consumed her completely, but had been diluted with thoughts of the dashing highwayman. But, as pleasant as these thoughts were, she was ever mindful that they were nothing more than fantasy. The depressing reality of her situation was that she would soon be Frederick Farrell's wife. And the realization that the day was drawing ever nearer, was highlighted by the fact that the wedding guests now appeared to be arriving in droves.

When Charlotte, at Lady Farrell's command, had entered the drawing-room at Wetherington to make the acquaintance of yet more Farrells, her mouth had dropped. To her amazement she discovered that, without exception, every member of the family bore the same long, pallid face, watery-blue eyes and thin, light-red hair. To encounter so many similar looking people in one room was, she found, extremely disconcerting. But, with the collection of Farrells huddled together in the gloomy, overheated room, moaning and groaning, and coughing and spluttering, it soon became apparent that physical characteristics were not the only attributes they shared.

As Dr Leigh, his face clouded with anger and impatience, flitted about the room attending to the various demands, Charlotte sat observing the scene with mounting despair. But the tone of the proceedings was soon to alter dramatically.

'Lord Frederick-Horatio Farrell is here, my lady,' announced the butler from the doorway. 'With his, er, family.'

A loud groan filled the room.

'Well,' shuddered the countess, 'we were expecting them. I suppose you had better show them in, Higgins.'

The butler raised his eyebrows, implying that Lady Farrell might wish to reconsider her decision. With no change of mind forthcoming, he begrudgingly muttered, 'If you insist, ma'am.'

The cloud of silent apprehension that fell over the room as they all awaited these latest visitors, gave Charlotte the distinct impression that Frederick-Horatio Farrell was somehow to differ quite radically from his throng of sickly relatives. She was soon proved correct in her assumption as a loud, brash female voice floated into the room, heavy with an American accent.

'Well, now ain't this a priddy little house, sugar?' it declared.

'It ain't, Ma,' came a child's reply. 'It's old and smelly and horrible. And it don't have no toys.'

Before anyone in the room could comment on this observation, in through the door strode a man of some fifty plus years, dressed in a garish yellow jacket, brown breeches and a lime-green waistcoat. Alongside him, appeared a woman markedly younger. She was wearing a low-cut, red silk dress, which shamelessly displayed her ample cleavage. Protruding from her mass of bright auburn curls was a large ostrich feather, whilst hanging about her skirts was a pale, podgy little boy dressed in an outfit exactly like that of his father.

'Ain't this all mighty fine,' beamed the man, as he cast a look around his relatives. 'All the Farrells together. And for your wedding, Frederick. Whoever would have thought it?'

A startled Frederick shrank back into his chair as the man approached him, holding out an outstretched hand.

'Well, ain't you gonna introduce us all, sugar plum?' asked the woman, with a smile so wide it encompassed everyone in the room.

'Of course, pumpkin,' replied the man, taking a step back from Frederick. 'Everyone. This here is my wife, Fanny-Petunia Farrell and my son, Frederick-Herbert Farrell.'

This announcement was followed by more silence as all twenty

Farrells continued to gawp at the newcomers. This small, and apparently insignificant, fact did not deter Frederick-Horatio from introducing his English relatives to his wife and son.

'This here is my sister-in-law, Felicia. And looking mighty fine if I may so.' He leaned towards the countess, planting a kiss on her wrinkled cheek. The woman recoiled visibly.

'And this here is Aunt Perdita, Aunt Felicia, Felicia-Sophia, Uncle Frederick XVI ...'

'How d'yer all do?' pronounced the woman, bobbing such an enthusiastic curtsy that her voluptuous bosoms wobbled in a fashion Charlotte had never before seen. 'Say how d'yer do, Frederick-Herbert.'

'Don't wanna, Ma,' piped up the boy. 'They're all old and wrinkly and I'm not gonna go anywhere near 'em cos I reckon they'll smell as well.'

'Good God,' exclaimed the countess, looking completely aghast. 'My pills, Dr Leigh. And quickly.'

Charlotte could not deny that the highlight of her introduction to the Farrells *en-masse* had been the moment Frederick-Herbert had removed the currants from the slice of cake he had demanded, shoved them up his nose and proceeded to blow them out all over the countess's skirts. It had to be said, however, that, with the possible exception of Dr Leigh, she was completely alone in her appreciation. In fact, following Frederick-Horatio and his family's arrival, Dr Leigh's services were even more in demand. None more so than when Fanny-Petunia's efforts to exchange a handshake with old Uncle Frederick Farrell XVI, caused one of her bosoms to break free from its tenuous constraints, rudely flopping into the man's prune-like face. This incident, combined with that of the currants, had resulted in three of the most elderly Felicia Farrells partaking of the vapours, the countess and Lady Felicia complaining of chest pains and old Uncle Frederick XVI slipping off his chair and banging his head on the marble table.

But such amusing diversions were, Charlotte realized, only a temporary reprieve from the oppressive life that loomed ahead of her. Her thoughts drifted once again to the Courteous Criminal and her recurring dream of the man rescuing her from her plight, although such fantasies, she knew, remained firmly in the depths of one's imagination.

Instinctively she reached for her mother's necklace. But it was not there.

Charlotte drew Victor to a halt outside Murphy's Mansion. Before she even had a chance to dismount, Becky came hurtling out of the door. 'You've just missed her, miss,' she announced excitedly.

It took but a second for Charlotte to realize to whom the girl was referring. 'The lady in the green riding-habit?'

Becky nodded her blonde head. 'Passed by just a minute or two ago. Went that way so she did.' She pointed down the lane in the opposite direction to which Charlotte had just travelled.

'Wait inside,' ordered Charlotte, as she turned Victor around and galloped off in the direction Becky had indicated. She rode for ten minutes before she gave up. The woman was nowhere to be seen.

'You don't mean to say that you gave that ghastly man your mother's necklace!' exclaimed Mirabelle McGregor. The girl, along with her brother, was obviously visiting Hamilton Manor with the sole purpose of extracting every detail from Charlotte regarding her ordeal at the hands of the highwayman. The pair had arrived shortly after Dr Leigh, who had come to attend Edward. Persisting in her efforts to avoid him, Charlotte had found herself reluctantly dragged along to Edward's room by her sister, in order that she give a first-hand account of matters to their visitors. She had so far done her best to avoid eye contact with the physician.

'I had little choice but to give him the necklace, Mirabelle. The man was, after all, holding a pistol to my head.'

'Hmph,' huffed Mirabelle. 'Well, I know very well what I should have said to him. Quite who the blackguard thinks he is demeaning the Quality in such a fashion, is positively beyond me.'

'But what was *your* opinion of the man, Lady Charlotte?' enquired Bertie.

No sooner had the words left Bertie's mouth than Dr Leigh cleared his throat, causing Charlotte to turn her head towards him. She caught his eye and a suffusion of pink filled her cheeks when she saw how intently he was regarding her.

'I, er, really don't, er, know, Bertie,' she stammered.

'Oh, but you do, Charlotte,' countered Harriet. 'You said that he was all that was charming and handsome.'

'I did not,' denied Charlotte.

'Oh, I believe you did, ma'am,' pointed out Dr Leigh, fiddling with the bottles on Edward's nightstand. 'In fact, if I am not mistaken, "charming" and "handsome" were the very words you used.'

Charlotte shot him a wrathful glare.

Meanwhile, a broad smile spread across Bertie's ugly face. 'Did you indeed, Lady Charlotte?'

'Well, I'm sure I don't know why you are looking so pleased, Bertie,' remarked Mirabelle scornfully. 'Those are hardly words that could be used to describe a lump such as yourself.'

'Indeed they could, Sister,' protested Bertie. 'I can be perfectly charming. My manners are nothing short of impeccable.'

'But I'm afraid "impeccable" cannot be applied to your person, dear Brother.'

'Mama considers me most handsome,' countered Bertie, in an obviously desperate attempt to save face.

'Oh, and Mama is, of course, a most impartial judge,' retorted Mirabelle with a snigger. 'Why, if I had a child who was half as ugly as you, dear Bertie, I should not hesitate in having it farmed out to some peasant family in order that I could deny its very existence.'

At this remark, the doctor slammed down a bottle, causing them all to start.

He turned to Mirabelle. 'If I may say so, Miss McGregor,' he began, in tones so chilling that Charlotte felt a shiver flash down her spine, 'I would suggest you show a little more respect towards your brother. Not only is he a member of your own family, but he is also several years older than yourself.'

Taken aback, Mirabelle glared at the doctor, defiance shining in her eyes. 'As Bertie is my brother, I shall say whatever I like to him, Doctor. And besides,' she continued, attempting to switch her tone to one more jovial, 'I was but jesting.'

The doctor gazed at her for several seconds before saying, 'Then please do excuse me, ma'am, but my sense of humour obviously differs significantly from your own. As, I believe, does that of your brother.'

All eyes now shifted to Bertie, who was cringing with embarrassment. 'Oh, I can assure you, Doctor,' he rejoined, looking disparagingly at his sister, 'that my sense of humour is as far removed from Mirabelle's as is humanly possible.'

Doctor Leigh's outburst at Mirabelle sent a number of varied reactions rippling through the room. Mirabelle, suitably miffed, announced her sudden recollection of another quite pressing engagement she and Bertie had that morning. The pair of them had subsequently taken their leave mere minutes after the girl's chastisement. Bertie dutifully followed his sister from the room, but not before flashing the doctor a look of gratitude for his intervention. Harriet, meanwhile, in an agitated state, retired to her chamber for a lie-down before luncheon. But even she admitted that Mirabelle had, on this occasion, taken matters too far. Edward, in his usual carefree manner, appeared to have found the incident quite amusing.

'About time someone put that woman in her place,' he declared, when he and Charlotte were alone. 'Quite what Harriet sees in the poisonous little toad, I cannot imagine.'

'Me neither,' concurred Charlotte, who had felt nothing but admiration for the doctor and the skilful manner in which he had rebuked Mirabelle.

'I own Dr Leigh is rather clever,' mused Edward aloud.

'Hmm,' sighed Charlotte, reflecting on the man's seemingly never-ending talents. 'I suppose he is.'

'And Harriet thinks him awfully handsome,' he added.

Charlotte felt a flush warm her cheeks. 'Is he?' she replied with a strained lightness. 'I really hadn't noticed.'

Some thirty minutes later, Charlotte was in the library having been ordered there by Edward who had requested she find him something amusing to read. Despite her best efforts to peruse the bookshelves, she found herself staring unseeingly out of the window. Her thoughts were far away from Hamilton Manor as she wondered where her elusive highwayman was at that particular moment. Had he spent as much time thinking about her as she had about him? It occurred to her that perhaps he had not given her a second thought. Perhaps he engaged in such shocking behaviour with all his female victims. After all, kissing a criminal was not a subject most ladies would confess to – particularly if they, like her, had willingly participated in the event. A sharp knock at the door startled her. She spun around as it clicked opened.

'Doctor Leigh,' she exclaimed, once again discomfited that he had caught her indulging in her fantasy. 'I–I thought you had returned to Wetherington.'

'I wanted to have a word with your father before I left, my lady,' he explained, walking slowly towards her. 'And with you.'

Charlotte's heart sank. 'Me?' she repeated, in as light a tone as she could force. 'Why ever do you wish to speak to me?'

He came to stand before her. 'I hope you did not think me out of order this morning, ma'am, when I remonstrated with Miss McGregor.'

'Not at all, Doctor. It was no more than the girl deserved,' said Charlotte, with a diffident smile.

The doctor nodded his head in agreement. 'And you should know, Charlotte, that you deserve much more than to be wedded into the Farrell family.'

At this comment all respect she had previously felt for the man flew out of the window. She rolled her eyes in despair. 'Not this again, Doctor. I have told you that I am marrying Frederick Farrell and that is the end of the matter.'

'It will be the end of your life if you do.'

'Don't be ridiculous,' countered Charlotte, smoothing her hair as she tried to remain calm. 'The Farrells are quite–quite—'

'Hideous,' broke in the doctor. 'For God's sake, can you really imagine yourself sitting around the fire with them all in ten years' time?'

Charlotte squared her shoulders to him. 'I own, I have not thought that far ahead, sir.'

'Obviously not,' he snorted. 'The wedding is less than two weeks away. Please, Charlotte. I beg you – reconsider your decision.'

'I cannot and will not, Doctor,' she retorted. 'And you have absolutely no right to meddle in my affairs.'

'Very well then,' he huffed. 'I may have no right to meddle, but I know someone who does. You leave me with no choice but to speak to your father on the matter.'

Charlotte's blood ran cold. Her hands flew to her face. 'Indeed you will not, sir. You will not say a word to my father. If you do our entire family will be ruined. Ruined, do you hear?'

She watched the doctor's countenance metamorphose from one of anger to one of puzzlement as he digested her words. She quivered as a well of emotions bubbled up inside her. 'Please, I beg you, Doctor,' she pleaded softly.

Time seemed to stand still as the two of them stood staring at one another. Then, without saying another word, the doctor turned on his heel and strode from the room. Charlotte, unable to hold back the tears a moment longer, reached for her mother's pearl necklace. Once again, she found it was not there.

Chapter Twenty

IF Charlotte had thought her sleep pattern erratic before the week leading up to the wedding, as the days slipped by, sleep became but a distant memory. This fact was plain for all to see, the smudges of black underlining her eyes providing a marked contrast to the grey pallor of her skin. Looking like this she would, she realized with ironic despair, fit into her new family perfectly.

With the destruction of the ancient family tree, Charlotte had no idea how many Farrells were to attend the wedding but, each time she visited Wetherington, a whole new batch seemed to have arrived – or so she thought. As each member of the family looked so alike and had the same name, it was rapidly becoming impossible to tell one from the other.

Unfortunately, she had not managed to lose the countess, Frederick or Perdita's face amongst the ever-increasing throng. The three were very much in evidence when she was shown to Lady Farrell's bedchamber that morning. The countess was again tucked up in her four-poster bed, with Frederick and Perdita in a chair either side of her.

'This whole affair is more than my nerves can bear,' she informed her, the moment Charlotte entered the room. 'So much so, that Dr Leigh has ordered me to take to my bed, have you not, Doctor?'

The doctor was sitting in a chair in the corner of the room. 'Indeed I have not, ma'am,' he countered. 'You did, I believe, inform me that you were taking to your bed.'

Charlotte slanted a look at him. Since their heated discussion two days ago during which she had confessed that she had her own ulterior motive for marrying Frederick, she felt even more awkward than usual in the man's presence.

The countess glared at him. 'Well, it is of no import whether the doctor instructed me or not. It signifies only that I felt the need to take to my bed. Of course, this latest decline in my health is attributable to that dreadful American child. The mere sight of him sets my poor heart racing and I'm afraid its racing days are drawing to an all too early close. The child ought to be sent away and not allowed to return until he begins to demonstrate some of the Farrell dignity.'

'Hardly likely, Mama, given the child's mother,' sniffed Frederick.

'Quite,' concurred Lady Farrell. 'However, we should not be discussing such matters now, Frederick.' She threw her son a meaningful look.

'My children will be awfully well behaved, Mama,' piped up Perdita. 'If they are not, then I shall beat them and lock them in the coal-hole until they are improved. Do you not think that the best way to deal with children, Dr Leigh?'

Charlotte's eyes grew wide at this horrific admission. Doctor Leigh appeared equally as appalled.

'Indeed I do not, ma'am. In my opinion, there are much more effective ways of dealing with children which do not involve violence.'

'Oh yes, well, of course I am aware of that, Doctor,' tittered Perdita. 'And I should naturally submit to those methods favoured by my future husband – in all things. In fact, I believe I shall make a perfect, obedient wife, sir. Do you not agree?'

The doctor looked as though the notion of Perdita Farrell becoming anybody's wife filled him with repulsion. 'What is one gentleman's idea of a perfect wife, is not that of another, ma'am,' he replied tactfully.

'Oh, of course not, Doctor,' giggled Perdita. 'But surely there would be few gentlemen who would refuse a wife who was—'

'That is enough idle chatter, Perdita,' broke in her mother. 'My head is fit to burst and I am in dire need of some rest. Given my responsibilities, however, there are, as always, several pressing matters that have need of my attention before I may be permitted that luxury. Now, as you have proved yourself to be quite irresponsible on a number of occasions,

Charlotte, I feel it incumbent upon myself to confirm that the two tasks which were allocated to you, have not met with disaster. The wedding cake, I take it, is ready?'

'Almost, ma'am,' informed Charlotte. 'Cook is taking a great deal of care in icing it but it should be ready within the next two days.'

Lady Farrell nodded her approval. 'And what of your wedding gown?'

'It is to be delivered Wednesday, ma'am.'

The countess pursed her lips. 'Hmm. Well, as all appears to be in order, you may go but do not forget that I shall expect you to look your very best on the day. We will, after all, have the Duke of Sussex in attendance.'

At that moment, Charlotte could not have cared less if King George himself was to attend. As a vine of dread wrapped itself around her, squeezing her ribcage, it was all she could do to force her legs to carry her down the stairs to her carriage.

The only thing which made the days following Charlotte's latest row with Dr Leigh even remotely bearable, was that, to her immense relief, the man did not appear to have carried out his threat to voice his concerns to Lord Hamilton. Not wishing to change this state of affairs, and in an effort to minimize the opportunity for any further such discussions, Charlotte had taken to spending as much time as possible out of the house on her horse.

During one of these excursions, she was just skirting the edge of a forest, when, out of the trees a short way ahead of her, thundered a stallion. With a start, Charlotte noticed that its rider was female, dressed in a green riding-habit and veiled hat; the very figure Charlotte had seen galloping around the countryside on several occasions. And the same figure, she was certain, that Becky had observed riding by Murphy's Mansion. Instinctively she pulled her mount to a halt, watching the rider gallop away from her. But then curiosity overcame her. Consumed with a desire to know who the woman was and what she was about, she spurred Victor on, after her.

Keeping a discreet distance, Charlotte followed the woman over numerous fields, hedges and streams until a small, green cottage came into view. A spiral of ominous thick black smoke was snaking its way from the chimney, but this did not appear to be deterring the woman who was heading directly towards the dwelling. Not wishing to reveal her presence, Charlotte took advantage of a group of nearby trees, from which she could observe the proceedings at a safe distance. She brought Victor to a halt there.

Remaining in her saddle, Charlotte watched as the woman dismounted outside the cottage, tethered her horse to a rail and slipped inside. Charlotte's eyes remained glued to the door as she attempted to calm her ragged nerves and thundering heart. She had accomplished neither of these aims before the woman reappeared, hoisted herself into her saddle and kicked her horse on. With mounting apprehension, Charlotte waited until there was a safe distance between them, before following once again.

This time, to her dismay, the mysterious figure appeared to be heading towards Murphy's Mansion. Charlotte slowed Victor's pace, anxious to avoid the family inadvertently revealing her presence.

Having allowed the elusive female some three minutes to pass the house ahead of her, Charlotte was amazed to see, upon her own approach, the woman's horse standing outside the cottage, minus its rider. Panic for the young family's safety pulsed through her but, as she drew nearer, she noticed a slumped green figure on the ground. Over it were crouched Becky and Emmy.

Becky whipped her head around as she heard Charlotte approaching. 'Oh, miss,' she gabbled. 'She just slipped off the saddle. Right here in front of us.'

Charlotte drew Victor to a halt alongside them and sprang down from the saddle. Kneeling to the woman, she observed at once that she was wholly unconscious. Tentatively, she drew back the veil of the woman's hat. As her identity was revealed, Charlotte's heart increased its already pounding pace for the face before her was none other than that of her future sister-in-law, Perdita Farrell.

It took several seconds for Charlotte to digest this information. Then, sweeping aside her shock, she attempted to take stock of the situation, which was, she feared, extremely critical. Rather than Perdita's usual glinting, colourless eyes, her paper-like lids were closed and her breathing was fast and shallow.

'Bring some blankets, Emmy, and keep her warm,' commanded Charlotte. 'I will go and find the doctor.'

Emmy nodded her acquiescence and darted into the house to carry out her instructions. The other members of the family, all now gathered outside, stared at Charlotte in bemusement as she leaped back into her saddle and clattered down the lane. But what the family could not see was the guilt piercing Charlotte's innards. Perhaps, while she had constantly dismissed Perdita's complaints as nothing more than hypochondria and cries for attention, the girl was really ill after all. She leaned low over Victor's head, spurring him on and hoping desperately that this time Dr Leigh *would* be at Hamilton Manor. If he wasn't, she had no idea what she would do, for she had a strong suspicion that Perdita Farrell's life was in danger.

At the sight of Daniel Leigh's battered gig outside the house, Charlotte was overwhelmed with relief. In a flash, she was off her horse and sprinting up the steps to the front door.

'Is the doctor with Master Edward, Adams?' she enquired of the servant, as she flew past him. Without waiting for his reply, she bounded up the stairs, leaving the butler, nonplussed, staring after her.

'Doctor Leigh,' asserted Charlotte, as she crashed into Edward's bedchamber, causing both her brother and the physician, who was wrapping a clean bandage around Edward's leg, to jump several inches. 'You must come at once.'

The doctor regarded her with an air of incredulity, several creases appearing in his forehead. 'What on earth is amiss, Lady Charlotte?'

'Perdita Farrell,' explained Charlotte, gasping for breath. 'She was out riding and has fallen from her saddle. She is unconscious. Outside Murphy's Mansion.'

'Perdita Farrell?' echoed the physician. 'But the woman rarely leaves the house. And certainly never on horseback.'

'Oh, but I think you will find that she does, Doctor,' contradicted Charlotte. 'As you will shortly see.'

'Good God,' muttered the doctor, swiftly packing up his bag. 'This is going to be interesting.'

'That is indeed one word for it, sir,' muttered Charlotte, as she followed him out of the room, both of them completely ignoring her brother's pleas for more information.

The doctor, assuming control of the situation, informed Charlotte that he would take Victor, who was waiting patiently outside the house, while she should follow in his gig. Making innovative use of the various straps and buckles of the horse's bridle, he attached his medical case to the steed, wheeled him around and thundered down the drive.

When Charlotte arrived at the cottage, some minutes later, it was to discover that he had carried Perdita inside and laid her down on one of the makeshift beds. Emmy, Becky and the three older boys, all huddled together opposite, watched on as, with a clean, dampened handkerchief, the man deftly wiped the sweat from Perdita's wan face. Little Harry, meanwhile, was sleeping peacefully in a makeshift crib in the corner, completely oblivious to the drama going on around him.

'Oh, thank the Lord she is still alive,' declared Charlotte, with another rush of relief.

'But only just,' replied the doctor. 'I have no idea what is wrong with her, but her heart rate appears to have slowed to a dangerously low level. I think it best if we inform the family forthwith.'

Charlotte gulped, but realizing this was no time for cowardice, said, 'You stay with her, Doctor. I shall go and break the news at Wetherington.'

The Farrells' reaction to Charlotte's unexpected arrival was, just as she had anticipated, one of complete bewilderment. And that was before she had even been granted an opportunity to inform them of her news. No sooner had she arrived, than a mask of horror fell over the countess's face.

'What on earth—?' she began, as Charlotte bowled into the dreary drawing-room behind the butler.

A collective disapproving gasp followed from the various relatives present.

'How dare you come here in that … that … *shameful* attire,' she remonstrated, waving an exasperated hand at Charlotte's riding breeches. 'Are you trying to finish me off, girl?'

'No, ma'am,' replied Charlotte, eager to explain herself. 'Please do excuse my apparel. I am come to—'

'And we sincerely wish that you had not come,' broke in the old woman. 'Are you determined to make a laughing stock of us in front of our esteemed relatives?'

'I can assure you I am not, ma'am. I am come regarding Lady Perdita.'

The countess narrowed her eyes. 'And what business, pray, do you have with Perdita?'

'She has met with an accident, ma'am. Whilst she was out riding.'

The countess wrinkled her nose. 'Perdita? Out riding? Really, Charlotte, is it not enough that you insist on turning up here dressed like an … an *actress*, without spouting forth such ridiculous nonsense? Perdita, as you are well aware, is far too indisposed to be out gallivanting – and particularly on horseback. She has not left her bed all day as, indeed, is the case most days.'

'Then I must insist that someone go upstairs and confirm that fact, ma'am,' demanded Charlotte.

The countess regarded her for several seconds before exclaiming tetchily, 'Very well. If that is what it takes to be rid of you and those dreadful breeches.' She turned her head to the footman in attendance. 'Hilton, go upstairs and inform Lady Perdita that her presence is required in the drawing-room forthwith.'

As the servant bowed his head and took his leave of the room, Frederick flicked a disparaging look at Charlotte.

'I don't believe a word of it, Mama,' he sniffed. 'The girl is obviously only here to cause a scandal in those outrageous breeches. Why, the very idea of my sister out on horseback is nothing more than laughable.'

Nobody, however, was laughing. In the footman's absence, a disconcerting silence fell over the room. Charlotte remained standing, aware, all the while, of the collection of watery-blue Farrell eyes regarding her with a mixture of disapproval and suspicion.

At last the footman returned. 'Lady Perdita is not in her room, ma'am.'

'Poppycock!' countered Lady Farrell, shaking her head. 'I saw her lying abed myself not two hours ago.'

'There were several pillows in her bed, ma'am,' explained the footman, 'which may well have given one the impression that her ladyship was sleeping.'

The countess gawped at the footman as she absorbed this information. Then, having obviously digested it, she raised a hand to her throat and boomed, 'Pills, Hilton. And quickly.'

Accompanying Charlotte on her return to Murphy's Mansion was the Farrells' navy-blue carriage and a list of instructions for Perdita's immediate transportation back to Wetherington. The very notion of the diseases which could befall her daughter lying in what the countess had termed 'a hovel' had resulted in another near-attack of the woman's palpitations and brought on one of Frederick's headaches.

Instructions adhered to, Perdita's limp form was carefully transferred to her own bed at Wetherington. The whole scandalous affair being too much for both Lady Farrell and Frederick, they had both taken themselves and their respective complaints to their own chambers, leaving orders that they were only to be disturbed in the event of a change in Perdita's condition.

Doctor Leigh, although handling the situation in the most proficient and professional of manners, made no disguise of the fact that he was completely baffled by Perdita's symptoms.

'I own, I have not the first idea what is wrong with her,' he confessed, with obvious frustration, as he sat on the edge of the bed studying Perdita's ashen face. 'For all her incessant complaining in the past, I have discovered nothing at all wrong with the girl other than a severe case of idleness.'

Charlotte, although reluctant to admit that she had been following Perdita, conceded that it could prove advantageous if she divulged something of the girl's movements that afternoon. They may, after all, provide the doctor with some clue as to what had suddenly overtaken his patient.

'I, um, did spot Perdita whilst I was out riding, Doctor,' she began tentatively.

He whipped his head around sharply. 'How long before she collapsed?'

'About, er, ten minutes,' muttered Charlotte.

'And how did she appear?'

'She appeared quite fine, sir. Until she—'

'She what?'

'She, um—'

'For God's sake, Charlotte, spit it out. Any clue as to what happened to her could well save her life.'

Charlotte gulped. 'She appeared perfectly fine until she paid a short visit to a small cottage up at Beaver's Mount.'

The doctor's brows drew together. 'A small green cottage?'

Charlotte nodded apprehensively.

The doctor clapped his hands together. 'Ah, now we are getting somewhere. Where is the riding-habit she was wearing?'

'Her maid hung it in the armoire, sir,' informed Charlotte, who had helped the servant undress Perdita and put her into her nightgown.

The doctor thrust to his feet. 'Show me.'

Charlotte did as she was bid. With the riding-habit successfully located, several seconds later Dr Leigh began rifling through its pockets.

'Ah ha,' he declared, pulling out a small corked bottle containing a lime-green liquid. 'I think, Lady Charlotte, we have found our answer.'

It was some two hours later when Perdita Farrell gained consciousness. Contrary to her previous 'illnesses', there was no denying that this time the girl looked definitely out of sorts. So weak was she in fact, that she could not even hold a glass of water to her lips. Her mother and Frederick, having been informed of the development, succeeded in dragging themselves along to Perdita's chambers. They were now sitting in a chair, one either side of the girl's bed. Charlotte, meanwhile, had commandeered the window-seat, whilst Dr Leigh was busying mixing a draught from the collection of bottles on the nightstand.

'Well, I can scarce believe what I have heard, Perdita. What on earth were you thinking of going out like that?' demanded her mother, her tone dripping with exasperated disapproval.

'I was in need of some, um, air, Mama,' replied Perdita, with uncharacteristic sheepishness.

'Air!' barked the countess. 'We have plenty of air here. Whatever possessed you to go in search of more of it? I can scarce believe my own daughter – a Farrell – has been gallivanting about unchaperoned and on … on *horseback*? What, in the Lord's name, were you about?'

Tears began rolling freely down Perdita's pale cheeks. 'I really don't know, Mama,' she whispered.

'Oh, but I think you do, ma'am,' cut in the doctor. 'Correct me if I am wrong, but I believe this to be the reason you went out riding. Am I correct, Lady Perdita?'

Perdita jerked her head around. Observing the bottle of green liquid he was holding, a sweep of mortification spread over her face.

'What on earth is that?' demanded Frederick, straining his neck in order to better his view.

'I think your sister is the best person to answer your question, sir,' replied the doctor. 'Would you care to enlighten us, ma'am?'

Perdita sniffed and mumbled something inaudible into her eiderdown.

'I'm afraid we did not quite hear you, ma'am,' said the doctor, throwing the girl a reproving glare.

Perdita lifted her chin to him. 'Very well. If you wish to embarrass me so, Doctor. It is a-a … love potion.'

'A *love potion*?' spat Frederick, his ugly face twisted with incredulity. 'But wherever did you get it?'

'I believe it was obtained from a man who calls himself Cupid, sir,' explained the doctor. 'A quack, who has made a substantial living exploiting the vulnerable hearts and purses of rich ladies. Although the man charges an extortionate amount for his services, his potions usually consist of no more than a few herbs and some scented water. But, in the case of your sister, it appears he has been significantly more ambitious with his ingredients. I suspect some poisonous mushrooms or some such to have been the cause of her reaction.'

'Good lord,' exclaimed Frederick, glaring in astonishment at his sister. 'You have been poisoned. And for a love potion. What in God's name possessed you to visit such an undesirable character, Perdita?'

Perdita wiped her dribbling nose on the eiderdown. 'Because, Brother, it is quite the most humiliating thing that everyone but me is to be wed. If I do not find a husband soon, I shall be too old. No one will want me and I shall be the only spinster in Farrell history. Is it any wonder that I resorted to such desperate measures in an attempt to persuade …' – she slanted a humiliated look at the doctor – '*someone* to fall in love with me and wish to take me as their wife?'

As a fresh flood of tears began streaming down her hollow cheeks, the doctor shook his head.

'There is no shame in wishing to be loved, ma'am,' he remarked levelly. 'But I think it best that you do not divulge the name of the man towards whom your intentions were directed.'

Perdita did not reply, opting instead to disappear under the bedclothes in a shrivelled fit of mortification.

It was early evening when Charlotte and the doctor eventually took their leave of Wetherington Hall. Upon them announcing their departure, Perdita had briefly surfaced from beneath her covers and awkwardly thanked them both for their part in saving her life. Although now more convinced than ever that the girl was quite mad, Charlotte could not help but feel some pity for her. On the other hand, she was grateful that the day's events had provided her with several missing pieces of her puzzle. Firstly, as Perdita had been gallivanting all over the countryside, it would not have proved as difficult as Charlotte had first thought for the girl to travel to Hamilton Manor and carry out the spiteful acts there. Secondly, regarding the matter of the letter informing Lady Farrell of Charlotte's riding breeches, Charlotte recalled that she had seen the green, veiled figure the day she had been out riding and bumped into Kate Tomms. Perdita, evidently, must also have seen Charlotte – in her breeches. And finally, Charlotte now had the motive for Perdita's actions – her desperation not to be the only spinster in the family's history.

Walking down the steps outside Wetherington, Charlotte sneaked a look at the doctor. The entire way in which he had dealt with the embarrassing situation had deepened her respect for him. Doctor Leigh had, quite obviously, been the target of Perdita's intentions. In fact, so obsessed must Perdita have been in her quest for him, that, having gleaned some notion of the compliment the doctor had paid Charlotte at Lady Fisher's birthday party, the girl had been so racked with jealousy, that she had instigated Charlotte's fall. Yet, undoubtedly aware as he was that he had been the target of Perdita's affections, the doctor had not once made mention of it – in jest or otherwise. Edward had been absolutely right when he had remarked, however humorously, that Dr Leigh was both handsome and clever. But not only that, he was also, as he had demonstrated that afternoon, a man of integrity and professionalism. In fact, his meddlesome behaviour notwithstanding, it occurred to

Charlotte that it would be quite easy to fall in love with Daniel Leigh. Not, of course, that *she* was in love with him: her heart, along with her necklace, belonged to a mysterious highwayman. The doctor interrupted her musings.

'So,' he began, 'I understand from your little friends at Murphy's Mansion that you have been taking very good care of them since they arrived in the area.'

'They are a delightful family, sir,' explained Charlotte shyly, 'who have so far encountered nothing but hardship during their short lives. I am merely doing what anyone would do in the circumstances. I am attempting to ease their plight.'

The doctor nodded his head thoughtfully. 'Very admirable, my lady. But I fear it will do you little good to consider their plight above that of your own. May I beseech you once again, to reconsider your decision regarding this ridiculous marriage.'

Reaching the bottom of the steps, Charlotte swung around to face him. 'I confess, Dr Leigh, that I find your ability to cope with matters of a medical nature most impressive. But I can assure you that my future marriage, most definitely not being of a medical nature, has no need at all of your attention. I therefore consider your remarks extremely intrusive. Now, if you don't mind, I do not wish to hear another word on the matter.'

During the silence that subsequently stretched between them, Charlotte did not remove her eyes from the doctor's face. She was, though, forced to suppress a shiver at the frosty manner in which he was regarding her. She also noticed, for the first time that day, just how exhausted he looked. There were heavy bags under each of his eyes, worry lines etched upon his forehead and a shadow of black stubble covering his jaw.

Having prepared herself for his caustic reply, the longer the silence endured, the more confused Charlotte became. What she was not prepared for was the doctor peeling his eyes from hers and announcing, in a matter-of-fact fashion, 'I shall return your horse to Hamilton Manor, ma'am. You take the carriage. It is not safe for a young lady to be out on her own.'

And with that comment, Charlotte found herself alone outside Wetherington Hall, with only the gargoyles and monsters for company.

Chapter Twenty-one

RACKED with exhaustion and having no desire to pay yet another visit to Wetherington, Charlotte penned a note the following morning, expressing both her and her family's best wishes for Perdita's recovery. With regard to her own family, Charlotte thought it fitting to provide them with only a diluted account of the drama. This decision was prompted by an incomprehensible loyalty to Perdita. She was sure the girl would not be at all desirous of her secret being scattered all about the county should it come into the possession of such malicious gossips as Mirabelle McGregor. But, for all Charlotte derived no pleasure from the fact that Perdita had almost lost her life, her relief that the girl could no longer jeopardize the marriage, was increasing hourly. Having invested so much energy in maintaining the charade of her betrothal to Frederick, she could ill afford for anything to go wrong at this late stage.

Harbouring a strong suspicion that Becky and her family would be desperate to know the outcome of yesterday's happenings, Charlotte rode over to Murphy's Mansion after luncheon and provided her grateful audience with her adapted version of events. Afterwards, having no desire to return to Hamilton Manor, she and Victor headed off deep into the countryside.

It was not until the sky had turned slate-grey and spots of rain were stinging her face, that Charlotte realized exactly how far away from home they were. A seed of apprehension took root. In only her breeches, a cotton shirt and a light jacket, she was inadequately clothed for such inclement weather. She reined Victor around just as the first rumble of thunder sounded. Shivering, she scolded herself for being pathetic. It was only a storm after all. What harm could it do her? She kicked the horse on.

But Charlotte's positive thoughts did not last long. As the light dwindled still further, an uneasy feeling wormed its way under her skin. Try as she might, she could not shake the suspicion that she was being watched – a suspicion which, to her horror, was soon proved correct. She was mindful of horses' hoofs behind her – a group of horses' hoofs. Raw panic began pulsing through her. The realization that she was being chased washed over her like a bucket of icy water. Not daring to look behind her for fear of what she might see, she impelled Victor forward. And then her heart jammed in her throat. A horse's head, gaining on her, came into view. The horse overtook her and then another appeared, followed by a third. They were encircling her. She could not turn around; she could not overtake them: she was trapped. Her heart pounding, she pulled Victor to a stop just as a fourth horse drew up behind her. The rain was still lashing down but, consumed with terror, Charlotte no longer noticed it. Refusing to look at her captors, she held her head high, focusing on a spot between Victor's ears. Instinctively she knew that these men formed one of the many groups of itinerants who roamed the countryside, stealing whatever they could. But she also knew that such men, particularly when outnumbering their prey so heavily, were capable of much more than stealing. She had heard tales of their exploits which had shocked her to the core: vile, sordid tales, of ways in which these despicable characters derived their sport – particularly with women and, she realized with a racing heart, particularly when they were presented with the rare treat of one travelling alone. Determined not to cower, Charlotte's gaze remained fixed firmly in front as the rain grew steadily heavier. The men began circling her in an intimidating manner. From the corner of her eye she could make out a portly man dressed in dirty, brown knee-breeches and a grubby, yellow waistcoat. He reined his horse in close to Charlotte's. She wrinkled her nose as the strong smell of alcohol filled her nostrils.

'Now then. What do we have here?' he sneered.

Ignoring their grunts of approval, Charlotte remained silent, giving, she hoped, no indication of the fear roiling inside her.

'A pretty filly, no less. And one not adverse to a little sport, I'd wager.'

Charlotte threw him an icy glare.

'Now then, miss. Let's relieve you of your jewels before we start on any, er, other items.'

An insidious snigger reverberated through the group.

'I have no jewels on me,' declared Charlotte stoutly.

The man narrowed his porcine eyes. 'No jewels, eh? Well, I'd best take a thorough look myself.' He stretched out a filthy arm towards her.

In the blink of an eye, Charlotte whipped her little knife from the waistband of her breeches and jammed it into the man's hand. He shrieked in pain, alarming his horse. The animal reared on to its hind legs, casting its rider to the ground with a heavy thud. All sneering ceased as the men's alcohol-fuddled brains attempted to make sense of what had happened. But, not waiting for them to reach any conclusion, Charlotte clapped her heels into Victor's flanks and the horse shot off at a thunderous pace.

Her relief was short-lived. She had underestimated the men's reactions. In a flash, three of them were streaking alongside her again. This time, though, there was no laughter or jeering, but three pistols aimed at her and three sets of bloodshot eyes, glinting with anger. Charlotte now knew that whatever chance she had had to escape, tentative as it had been, had vanished. She was completely at the mercy of these men and her fate would be all the worse for riling them. She brought Victor to a stop once more, every hair on the back of her neck standing on end.

'So. You want to play dirty, do you?' bellowed a man in a stained blue tailcoat, much too large for him.

Charlotte said nothing.

'Think we've got a lively one, here. Soon whip that out of her, eh Joe?' he declared, waving his pistol at her.

'In a jiffy,' leered Joe, flashing two rows of broken, yellow teeth. 'Although whipping weren't the first thing on me mind.' The others snorted with laughter while Charlotte recoiled. 'Who's gonna go first, Lenny?'

'Well, now,' mused Lenny, tipping back the rim of his hat with the tip of the pistol. 'Seeing as though she's injured Mac, I reckon she's gotta bit of making up to do with him.' He gestured to the man in the yellow waistcoat who, some way behind, was in the process of hauling his podgy frame back into his saddle. 'Get off your horse, madam.'

'I will not,' replied Charlotte.

'You will do what I tell thee,' countered Lenny, raising his free arm as if to slap her.

Charlotte closed her eyes, awaiting the impact of his dirty calloused hand against her skin. Instead of the sting of his strike, however, she almost fell out of her saddle as the sound of a shot being fired vibrated through the air. They all turned their heads in unison to see a striking figure charging towards them. Dressed all in black, save for a blue kerchief about his face, his cloak streamed out behind him and he was holding his pistol high.

Charlotte's heart leaped as recognition pulsed through her. She quickly realized that she was not the only one who was aware of the man's identity. Her assailants' features, only seconds ago triumphant at the re-capture of their quarry, were now blanched and twisted with fear.

'Lord,' exclaimed Lenny. 'It's that Courteous Criminal, Joe. Don't fancy messing with him.'

'Me neither,' shuddered Joe, already in the process of turning his horse around. 'Come on. Let's get out of here. There's plenty more where she came from.'

The other two men followed suit. 'Aye, yer right there,' muttered Lenny, flashing Charlotte one last lear. 'Shame though. Not often we 'ave the chance of a prime article like 'er.' And with that parting comment, they were off.

As they disappeared, Charlotte did not move, her eyes glued to the lone figure riding towards her. The rain was hammering down but still she was oblivious to it. This time it was not through fear though. Now she was numb, devoid of all coherent thought. The entire situation felt surreal. As if to assure her that it wasn't, a flash of forked lightning lit up the sky directly above her, jolting her back to reality.

The man was almost upon her before he slowed his horse. There was little light remaining and that, combined with the shadow of his hat and the kerchief, meant that yet again she could discern nothing of his features. A conflicting mix of emotions began swirling around her. This man was a criminal, just like the others. He robbed and terrorized people just as they did. He had even robbed her and taken her mother's precious necklace. So why then did she not feel afraid? Why had the fear which had flooded her body only a few moments before, been replaced by something she could identify only as stirring excitement? He drew his horse nearer. Charlotte held her breath, waiting for him to speak. It felt like an eternity before he did, in the same muffled voice she had heard in her head dozens of times since their first encounter.

'If I may say so, ma'am,' he began, 'this is no night for a young lady to be out.'

Charlotte said nothing. He was right. Her behaviour was totally irresponsible. At the mere thought of what might have happened to her, of what could be happening to her at this very minute, bile rose in her throat. The man said nothing more but, in one swift movement, unfastened his cloak and tossed it about Charlotte's shoulders. As he leaned forward to fasten it about her neck, she held her breath once more.

'Follow me,' he commanded briskly.

Neither wanting nor daring to question him, Charlotte did as she was bid.

They did not stop riding until they reached the gates of Hamilton Manor. For all it had taken them over an hour, Charlotte could scarcely recall the journey. She had been lost in thoughts of the man she had been following, the man whose own cloak was so near to her skin that it caused her to tingle. Her heart was pounding with anticipation as they faced one another again. The power of speech apparently having deserted her, she found she could say nothing. Instead, she unfastened the cloak and handed it back to him. As she did so, he caught hold of her hand and pressed it to his lips. Despite the barrier of the kerchief and the pelting rain, their heat pierced her once again. Then, all at once, he whipped the cloak about his own shoulders and was out of her sight in seconds.

Just as with the drama involving Perdita, Charlotte concluded that it would be unwise of her to divulge all the details of the evening's events to her family. The less they knew of the dreadful ordeal she had come close to suffering, the better. Her explanation, whilst standing dripping wet before her father, had therefore consisted of nothing more than she had merely forgotten the time and had been too far from the house to turn back before the heavens opened. This having been accepted with much remonstration but very little questioning, she had been allowed to escape to her rooms without too much delay.

Lying in a steaming tub of soapy water, her thoughts had wandered to the feelings the man had once again stirred in her. It was some hours later, in the dead of the night, when it first occurred to Charlotte that she had made no mention to the highwayman of where she lived.

Doctor Leigh appeared equally as unimpressed as Lord Hamilton at her actions. Charlotte and her father were seated in the breakfast-room the following morning when the physician paid his call. Lord Hamilton, still in high dudgeon, insisted the doctor examine his daughter.

'But what in God's name were you doing out riding alone at such an hour and in such dreadful weather?' demanded the doctor.

'Exactly what I asked her, Leigh,' boomed Lord Hamilton, two grey horn-like curls protruding from either side of his head. 'It does not bear thinking about what could have happened to her.'

'It most certainly does not, sir,' concurred the doctor. He drew up a chair alongside Charlotte and placed his hand against her forehead. Charlotte felt a shiver pulse through her at his touch.

'Really, Father, I have told you, there is no need to make such a fuss,' she declared, brushing the doctor's hand away.

'We'll leave that to Dr Leigh to decide,' said Lord Hamilton, as he began pacing up and down the room.

Just then, a silent Adams appeared in the doorway, causing them all to start. 'Excuse me, Lord Hamilton,' he droned, 'but Master Edward has requested a word with you.'

'Hmph,' huffed the old man, directing his pacing to the door. 'Well, you check the girl over, Leigh and I'll go and see what young Edward wants. Between the two of them they are enough to drive a man to despair.'

The door swung shut behind him, leaving Charlotte and the doctor alone.

'Well, as far as I can see you are in perfect health, ma'am,' remarked the doctor, before standing up and following the route Lord Hamilton had taken just seconds before.

Chapter Twenty-two

GUILT riddled its way through Charlotte. Just as the mantua-maker had employed so much meticulous care with her wedding gown, cook had demonstrated exactly the same quality with the wedding cake – and with equally impressive results. Some thirty inches square, the cake bulged with plump, dried fruits concealed beneath a thick layer of expertly applied white icing. Harriet had launched into raptures at the unveiling. Charlotte, conversely, had had to summon every ounce of her energy to appear half as enthusiastic. She was only grateful that Albert, who had also been present, had managed to divert some of the attention away from herself, by awarding cook the ultimate compliment: 'Don't think even Mrs Tomms could have done a better job than that,' he had declared, before taking a large bite of his cheese sandwich.

'Oops!' exclaimed Dr Leigh, as Harriet, whirling about the hall, clattered directly into him.

'Oh, Doctor, I am sorry,' she giggled. 'Charlotte is always telling me not to be so excitable.'

'Is she indeed?' asked the doctor, throwing Charlotte a frosty look as she lagged behind her sister on their way back from the kitchens. 'And what, may I ask, is the cause of all this excitement?'

'Cook has just finished Charlotte's wedding cake, sir. And it is quite the most beautiful thing ever,' declared Harriet. 'Oh, the wedding is going to be so perfect that I can scarcely wait for it to arrive.'

'Well,' said Dr Leigh, accepting his hat and gloves from the footman, 'thank goodness then that the day is almost upon us.'

Harriet smiled dreamily. 'Oh, are not weddings the most delightful things, Doctor?'

'Delightful is indeed one word for them, my lady,' remarked the doctor archly.

Charlotte paid little regard to the sarcasm in his tone. The man had made his opinion perfectly clear – on several occasions. Charlotte's own thoughts were a million miles away from cakes and doctors. They were occupied with the one person who made her feel her life was worth living: the infamous Courteous Criminal.

'Miss McGregor is outside, my lady,' announced Adams wearily, as he pushed open the door to Edward's bedchamber. 'She says to inform you that she will only come in if you can assure her Dr Leigh is nowhere in the house.'

Edward gave a snort of laughter. 'Well, in that case, Adams, you may tell Miss McGregor that Dr Leigh has taken up permanent residence here.'

Adams's non-flinching expression demonstrated that he had failed to see the humour in this remark. So too, apparently, had Harriet.

'Edward,' she chided. 'Do not be so mean. You may tell Miss McGregor, Adams, that the doctor has already paid his visit today and that we are not expecting him again.'

'Very well, ma'am,' sighed the butler.

Mirabelle sailed into the room a few minutes later, wearing a maroon carriage gown and Angoulême bonnet. Bertie, surrounded by the aura of one still crippled with mortification from the scene of their last visit, trailed behind her.

'Are you absolutely sure that ghastly doctor will not be returning, Harriet?' demanded Mirabelle, as she stripped off her gloves. 'Not, I hasten to add, that I am the least bit intimidated by the man. I simply do not find his presence at all agreeable – particularly, for one who is, after all, little more than a servant.'

'Oh, I hardly think one could refer to Dr Leigh as a servant, Mirabelle,' countered Edward. 'The man is one of the finest physicians in our land and also one of the most pioneering.'

'In your opinion, Edward,' dismissed Mirabelle. 'I, however, find him nothing more than an arrogant chawbacon, who has obviously forgotten his station in life. Now, tell me, Harriet,' she said, settling herself on the edge of Edward's bed, 'is there anything of any note to report?'

'Why, yes there is, Mirabelle,' replied Harriet, her eyes shining brightly. 'Cook has just finished Charlotte's wedding cake today and it is the prettiest cake I have ever set eyes upon, is it not, Charlotte?'

'It is, Harriet,' concurred Charlotte, with a weak smile.

Mirabelle's eyes swivelled to Charlotte, but before she had a chance to speak, Bertie broke in.

'Oh, I do so love cake,' he declared, eyeing Charlotte as though she were a tasty morsel herself.

'Hmph,' snorted Mirabelle, her attention shifting to her brother. '*Love* is putting it mildly, Bertie. Do you know, Harriet, we were taking afternoon tea with Lady Farnsworthy yesterday and Bertie devoured no less than *four* queen cakes. I confess, I did not know where to look. The man has all the manners of a farm animal.'

'I was hungry,' protested Bertie.

'You were a pig,' countered Mirabelle. She followed this remark with a series of porcine-like grunts. Of all those present in the room, only she seemed to find these the least bit amusing.

'Goodness, miss, I can't believe you's gonna be wed in a few days,' gabbled Becky as she rooted through the basket of food Charlotte had just delivered.

'Me neither, Becky,' replied Charlotte, who was watching little Harry as he toddled across the floor.

'Then you'll be a real grand lady,' proclaimed Becky, covering the basket again with the muslin cloth.

'I shall be no such thing, Becky,' countered Charlotte, affecting a genial smile for the benefit of the child. 'I shall not change at all.'

The subject was not pursued further as Harry gave a loud sneeze and plopped down on his padded bottom.

Hamilton Manor was in uproar when Charlotte returned home several hours later.

'Oh, Charlotte,' gasped a distraught Harriet, rushing into the hall to meet her. 'Something absolutely dreadful has happened.'

Charlotte's heart sank to the floor. 'Whatever is it, Harriet?'

Harriet reached out and took both Charlotte's hands in hers, tears rolling down her face. 'It's your wedding cake. Someone has sneaked into the kitchens and trodden it to a pulp. Cook assures us she can make another in time, although not, of course, as ornate but ...'

As Harriet continued rambling, a chill swept through Charlotte. She had imagined, with Perdita Farrell safely ensconced at Wetherington, that it would have been the end of these incidents. Clearly it was not. But, if Perdita wasn't responsible – and in this case she certainly couldn't be – then who was? Who else felt so strongly about her marriage that they would resort to such drastic measures to prevent it? And who else had had the opportunity to carry out these deeds? There was only one other person Charlotte could think of: a picture of Dr Daniel Leigh flashed before her.

Lying in her bed that night, Charlotte did not even attempt to go to sleep. Instead, she examined her new disturbing theory in detail. Was it Daniel Leigh who had set out to sully her reputation with the Farrells and thereby her chances of marriage to Frederick? The more she pondered, the more it all made perfect sense. Daniel Leigh had certainly been at Hamilton Manor the evening of her betrothal ball when her gown had been ruined. Daniel Leigh had seen her in her riding breeches and had had the perfect opportunity to slip a note to the countess. Daniel Leigh had questioned her over her transport the evening of the dinner with the Duke of Sussex. And Daniel Leigh had been made all too aware of the wedding cake that morning. And, added to all of that, was the fact that the man had made no secret of his views on the union. The evidence was stacked up against the man in an incontrovertible fashion. Yet Charlotte's anger at him was tempered with disappointment. She had respected him. She had assumed that, with his impeccable reputation and professionalism, he would be way above such petty acts. Still, she pondered, as her mind flitted back down a well-worn track, one never really knew what a person was capable of. She, for instance, would never have imagined herself capable of falling in love with an elusive masked highwayman. Yet she most definitely had.

*

So despondent was Charlotte the next day, that the very thought of food made her nauseous. She could not even face going to breakfast. Instead, she remained in her bedchamber gazing out of the window, noticing nothing of the scene beyond. Her nausea increased tenfold the moment Harriet appeared in the doorway announcing that the wedding gown had been delivered.

Harriet's devastation at the ruined cake the previous day was completely usurped by the excitement of the dress's arrival. But, just as with the cake, Charlotte could not muster an ounce of genuine enthusiasm. Dragged from her chair by her sister, Harriet insisted they both watch the footman carry the article, wrapped in a number of white sheets, up the stairs. Charlotte was therefore reluctantly standing beside her sister on the landing when, to her dismay, Dr Leigh stepped out of Edward's bedchamber. Her emotions vacillated between shock and anger. For all she had thought of little else since forming her new theory about the man, she still had no idea how best to confront him.

'Oh, Dr Leigh,' enthused Harriet. 'Walters is just bringing up Charlotte's wedding gown. Is that not the most exciting thing?'

Charlotte observed how the man's features hardened. Clearly he did not share her sister's fervour.

'Well, it would certainly appear that you think it the most exciting thing, Lady Harriet,' he remarked.

'Of course, you are not allowed to see it,' informed Harriet earnestly. 'Not before the grand day. I shall not even permit Mirabelle to see it when she comes to call this morning – despite the fact that she will no doubt say I am most dreadfully rude. That way, everyone will have a great surprise when they see Charlotte in her finery in the church.'

The doctor's gaze moved to Charlotte, who was continuing to observe him closely. 'Well, then in that case I must agree that it is very exciting, Lady Harriet,' he declared coolly. 'I myself am very much in favour of surprises.'

Despite her sister having to employ all her restraint not to take a peep at the fastidiously wrapped-up gown, Charlotte had awarded the garment no more than a cursory glance as it hung over the door of her armoire. This was, after all, to be the dress in which she walked to her dismal fate and, therefore, no matter how beautiful it was, she had no desire at all to wear it. Besides, she had more important matters than dresses on her mind. What had Dr Leigh been insinuating when he had remarked that he was very much in favour of surprises? Was he referring to the surprises he had inflicted on her by cutting up her gown, ruining her coach and the destruction of her wedding cake, amongst others? If he was, then she had just presented the man with yet another opportunity to surprise her. And that opportunity was hanging over the door of her armoire shrouded in white sheets. A plan to catch the man began forming in her mind. She pulled the high-backed chair from the side of her bed, over to the corner of the room and crouched down behind it.

Her back was aching dreadfully and she had carried out a thorough inspection of her fingernails, before her patience was rewarded. Charlotte's blood froze as the bedchamber door clicked open. She held her breath as footsteps padded across the carpet towards the armoire. Anger speared her. How dare Daniel Leigh treat her so? How dare he continue to interfere in her life? Well, she was about to tell him exactly what she thought of him. But it was not Daniel Leigh who cried out in shock as Charlotte sprang out from behind the chair. Nor was it Daniel Leigh who dropped a large bottle of ink, obviously intended for the wedding gown, all over the floor. And it was most definitely not Daniel Leigh who burst into floods of tears and begged her forgiveness. With her head of tight red curls and milky skin, Charlotte was amazed to discover that it was Kate Tomms.

'But why, Kate?' asked Charlotte, as the two of them sat on the edge of her bed, tears still streaming down Kate's face. 'Why did you do all those dreadful things?'

'Oh, miss, I didn't know what else to do,' confessed Kate. 'I could see how unhappy you were and how you were trying to put on a brave face an' all. But I could tell you didn't want to marry that man. And so I started to think how I could get you out of your predicament and I thought, miss' – she accepted the lace handkerchief Charlotte offered her – 'I thought that if I couldn't come up with a way to talk you out of the marriage, which I didn't dare even try, me not being good with words and everything, well, I thought maybe it would be easier if that Farrell lot put an end to it.'

'I see,' mused Charlotte, still not quite being able to believe what she was hearing. 'But how did you know about the ball and the carriage and the cake and even the dress?'

'From my pa, miss. He filled me in every night with the latest happenings. And I made out I was keen to hear them all just because I love weddings. And I wrote that letter, miss – the one about the riding breeches. Took me an age 'cos I'm not very good at writing. But I did everything I could think of, miss.' She cast an imploring look at Charlotte. 'Please don't be angry with me. I don't want to see you miserable. You're one of the kindest people in the world, Miss Charlotte, and you deserve to be happy. I was only trying to help.'

'I know you were, Kate,' said Charlotte, taking hold of the girl's hand and squeezing it. 'But I'm afraid your efforts, as well meaning as they were, have all been in vain. I am to marry Frederick Farrell tomorrow and that is the end of the matter.'

'Oh, miss,' gasped Kate, throwing her arms around Charlotte and breaking into a fresh bout of tears and Charlotte, as much as she tried not to, found herself doing the same.

Chapter Twenty-three

THE day of the wedding dawned – in theory only. Long after the sun was due to rise, the sky remained as black as coal and the rain, which had clattered against the window panes all through the night, did not ease one iota as the household began to stir.

Harriet, as expected, was in raptures, hardly pausing for breath as she chattered merrily over the breakfast table. Charlotte, on the other hand, found she could string little more than two words together. Flooded with nausea yet again, even the two sips of coffee she had braved had, a short while later, made an unpleasant reappearance. As her sister and her maid fussed about her, executing a complicated series of preparations, Charlotte felt as though she was in a dream – playing no part at all in the proceedings, but merely standing on the periphery like an impassive observer. Her eyes were drawn constantly to the clock on the mantel as the minutes ticked by with terrifying inevitability. The ceremony was due to take place at eleven o'clock. These were, therefore, her last minutes of freedom, the final countdown to her new role as Lady Frederick Farrell, Countess of Wetherington – the beginning of her new and miserable life.

The arrangements, in which she had played no part, dictated that Charlotte was to travel to the church accompanied by her father. The countess having deemed none of the Hamilton conveyances suitable for a bride whose wedding was to be attended by a member of the royal family, had sent over one of the Farrell coaches to transport the pair. Harriet, meanwhile, was to go on ahead in the Hamilton coach, driven by Albert.

With all her preparations complete and her gown donned, Charlotte stood at the window of her bedchamber. The rain was still teaming down and showed no signs of abating. She watched as Harriet, protecting her pretty pink gown with a large hooded-cape, picked her way carefully down the steps to the carriage. Albert, swathed from head to toe in oilskins, held an umbrella over her. Harriet climbed into the carriage. The door was slammed shut. Albert jumped into his seat and the conveyance began rattling down the drive, battered by the elements. Charlotte's eyes swivelled once more to the clock. It was half past ten. Panic rolled inside her. She took a deep breath. It was not too late. She could still change her mind. At a rap on the door, she whirled around to find her father there. Observing the pride spreading over his face, Charlotte's last glimmer of hope extinguished. For the sake of her family she could not, and would not, change her mind. She would bind herself for life to a man she could scarcely bring herself to look at.

'Ready?' asked Lord Hamilton, beaming broadly.

Charlotte contorted her lips into some semblance of a smile. 'As I'll ever be, Father.' Her words were barely audible.

With her father holding the umbrella above her, Charlotte took her leave of Hamilton Manor for the very last time as Lady Charlotte Hamilton. The rain was still continuing to lash down, falling in sharp vertical rods. The coach provided by the Farrells was not one that Charlotte had seen before. Just like Albert, their driver was swathed in waterproofs with a broad-rimmed hat shielding his face. No footmen were present at the back of the coach but, given the appalling conditions, Charlotte thought little of it. The driver whipped open the carriage door and she and her father wasted no time in climbing inside. As soon as the carriage began trundling down the drive, the old man took his daughter's hand in his and squeezed it.

'Not too late to change your mind, you know.'

Charlotte's eyes shot to this face. Her glimmer of hope flickered faintly. Did he know? Was he offering her a way out? But the teasing look upon his countenance told her he was not. Her stomach plummeted. 'Don't be silly, Father,' she remonstrated lightly. 'Why on earth should I wish to change my mind?'

Lord Hamilton winked. 'Only joking, my dear. Can't imagine any girl wanting to give up the opportunity to become the next Countess of Wetherington.'

Charlotte could not reply. As her father launched into one of his amusing stories of a disastrous wedding he had attended many years before, she heard not one word. Her mind was closed to everything other than the movement of the carriage as it left the demesne of the manor and took a left turn in the direction of Wetherington Hall. The route thereon was relatively straight. But, much to her and her father's surprise, after some ten minutes, the carriage swung sharply to the right, making an unexpected detour from the main road. Lord Hamilton was less than impressed by this sudden diversion.

'What the devil's going on?' he expostulated, releasing his hold of Charlotte's hand and reaching for his cane. He banged it against the roof of the carriage. 'You're going in the wrong direction, coachman,' he boomed.

The coachman did not reply.

Lord Hamilton banged even harder. 'What on earth are you about? Enough of this larking around. We shall be late.'

Still there came no response.

Resorting to desperate measures, Lord Hamilton yanked open the window. Rain pelted into the carriage, causing a rash of dark circles to spring up all over Charlotte's ivory silk skirts. 'Stop!' roared Lord Hamilton, his face red with fury. 'Stop the carriage this instant.'

But their coachman appeared not to hear these commands. An exasperated Lord Hamilton slammed the window shut and flopped back on to the squabs.

'The man has gone completely mad!' he exclaimed, running a hand through the centre of his hair and causing it to stick up quite outrageously. 'What on earth are we to do?'

'I really don't know, Father,' professed Charlotte, whose feelings of dread were rapidly being surpassed by confused relief. She threw a disdainful look at the bouquet of lilac hydrangea lying on the seat opposite, tied with a white ribbon. How she hated hydrangea. But her choice of flowers now seemed of no import, for Charlotte had an increasingly strong premonition that even if she had been allowed her beloved roses, she would not be carrying a bouquet up the aisle today.

The carriage continued its erratic journey, making so many complicated twists and turns that it was impossible for Charlotte or her father to keep track of their whereabouts. Their predicament was further hampered by the weather, the dismal conditions limiting visibility to only a few yards. Inside the carriage, the windows were covered in pregnant beads of condensation, quivering precariously as the conveyance thundered along puddle-strewn roads and tracks, with scant regard for the comfort of its passengers.

Eventually, the carriage jerked to a halt. The wheels had not ceased to turn before Lord Hamilton had leaped from his seat and was wrenching open the door.

'Have you gone out of your mind, man?' he cried, jumping to the ground with a sprightliness that betrayed his years. 'What in God's name are you thinking of?'

Curious to learn how the coachman was to excuse his errant behaviour, Charlotte poked her head outside. The heavy rain battered her face but, so stunned was she at the sight before her, that she failed to even notice it. The man had his back to her as he pointed the pistol at her father, and there was little doubt now that the person who had been driving their carriage was not in the Farrells' employ.

'Go inside,' she heard him command Lord Hamilton. The barrel of the pistol briefly indicated the old barn outside which they were standing.

Lord Hamilton shook his head. 'Not without my daughter.'

'I can assure you, you have no need to worry on your daughter's behalf, sir,' replied the man in muffled tones. 'Go inside and I promise no harm shall come to her.'

With the rain lashing them all indiscriminately, Lord Hamilton remained where he was.

'Please do as he says, Father,' pleaded Charlotte, as she observed the old man opening his mouth to make more protests.

Lord Hamilton seemed to consider his daughter's request for several seconds before agreeing to it. 'You scream if he touches you and I shall be straight out,' he called to her. Then he glared wrathfully at the man. 'You harm a hair on her head and I shall hunt you down myself.' And on that threatening note, he whisked around and marched into the barn.

As the large wooden door crashed behind him, the impostor turned to face Charlotte. With the barrel of the pistol, he tipped back the rim of his hat, revealing a sodden blue silk kerchief around the lower part of his face.

'You!' gasped Charlotte. Her heart began thundering. After all her dreams, the Courteous Criminal had actually come to rescue her. Or had he? She had no idea how she should react; what she should say. What was the social etiquette when one was in love with a dashing criminal who, merely seconds before, had been waving a pistol in the face of one's father? As he approached her, she was conscious of nothing but the heat of his eyes upon her and the pounding of her heart.

He reached the carriage and pulled down the steps. 'Get out,' he ordered brusquely.

Charlotte did as she was bid. Only inches separated them as they stood facing one another. Wrought with nerves, her legs shaking, it was all Charlotte could do to keep herself upright.

'I would advise you to say nothing of my involvement today, ma'am,' pronounced the man at length. 'But I think you will find this of interest.' He produced a scroll of white paper from inside his cape and proffered it to her.

Bewildered, Charlotte made to accept. As she did so, he grabbed hold of her hand and, just as when she had returned his cape, planted a kiss on the back of it. Then, in a flash, he vaulted back into the driver's seat of the carriage and was gone.

Charlotte stood, transfixed, watching the conveyance as it disappeared into the murky distance. By the time she joined her father inside the barn, she was soaked through to the skin.

Chapter Twenty-four

IT was some three long, yet enlightening hours later before the rain eased to such an extent that Charlotte and her father could consider leaving the barn. As they did so, they refused to acknowledge the heavy drizzle that persisted, or the fact that they were cold and hungry. They also had not the first clue as to where they were or which direction they should take. But, in light of their new knowledge – obtained from the document which had been thrust upon them – and their ensuing frank discussion, their eagerness to return to Hamilton Manor remained paramount. It did not, unfortunately, make their journey any easier. Charlotte slipped and skidded about the mud in her thin silk slippers while Lord Hamilton lost his footing on more than one occasion.

It was some hours before they came upon a farmhouse. Exhausted, they staggered to the door. The young woman who opened it to them, made little disguise of her surprise at the extraordinary sight before her: the bedraggled bride in her beautiful, mud-splattered gown and the dripping wet old man, with his mop of disarrayed hair. Wasting no time on explanations, and much to the bewilderment of her brood of children, the woman ushered the pair inside. As they sat by the fire, she provided them with steaming mugs of beef stew and a plate of bread and dripping. Upon her husband's return, the woman requested that he transport their unexpected guests to the neighbouring farm, where, she had no doubt, they would prove equally as obliging.

And so it was, via such unconditional generosity, that Charlotte and her father reached Hamilton Manor ten hours after they had left it.

Adams released a sigh of despair as he opened the door to them. 'If I may take the liberty of saying so, sir, it does not appear that all has gone quite as planned today.'

'Indeed it has not, Adams,' confirmed Lord Hamilton wearily, as he handed over his dirty, damp hat to the servant. 'There has been quite an unexpected turn of events of which you shall all be duly informed when we have had a little time to come to terms with it ourselves.' He then ran two hands through his wet hair causing both sides to jut out at sharp angles.

Adams demonstrated his understanding with an inclination of his grey head. 'In your absence, sir, I was forced to admit two visitors to the drawing-room. They appeared extremely … *desirous* to await your return.'

'Lady Farrell?' asked Lord Hamilton, a wave of anger darkening his fatigued features.

Adams nodded. 'I am afraid so, sir. And not in the best of humours, if I might be so bold as to add.'

'Well, you need not worry, Adams,' declared Lord Hamilton, striding across the hall with a new surge of energy. 'This will be the last time any Farrell will set foot inside this house, bad humour or not.'

Lord Hamilton burst into the drawing-room to find an anxious Harriet curled up in a chair in the corner. The poor girl was obviously making an attempt to distance herself from two of the other occupants, who had assumed their seats in the armchairs either side of the fire. Doctor Leigh was also present, standing before the rain-drenched window, staring out into the darkness beyond. He whisked around to face them as Lord Hamilton bowled in, a wet and dishevelled Charlotte scuttling behind him. They both came to a halt a little way inside the door, awaiting the reaction to their arrival.

'Well,' huffed the countess, shooting them a look overflowing with contempt, 'I see you have had the good grace to turn up … *at last.*'

'Indeed we have, ma'am,' concurred Lord Hamilton. 'And I would appreciate it if you would remove yourself from my chair.'

The countess's thin lips narrowed to two straight lines.

'As you wish,' she announced, rising to her feet and moving to the sofa opposite the fire. 'Although one would have thought we had matters of much more import to discuss than chairs. The small matter, for example, of you and your daughter making myself and my son a laughing stock in front of our entire family. And the Duke of Sussex.'

'Oh my, what a great pity,' retorted Lord Hamilton, marching over to the fireplace from where he faced her directly. 'I do apologize, Lady Farrell. How very selfish of me not to have permitted my daughter to walk up the aisle today in order that you, once she had provided you with an heir, could discard her as though she were no more than a used slipper.'

Lady Farrell's face grew pale. She lifted her chin to the old man. 'I believe you must be all about in your head, sir. I have not the first idea what you are talking about.' The tremor in her voice did not go unnoticed by Charlotte.

'Oh really,' remarked Lord Hamilton, with feigned surprise. 'Then please do permit me a moment to check my facts.' He withdrew the scroll of paper from inside his jacket and rolled it out.

'Now then, we shall see if I am all about in the head or not.' He ran his eye down the paper. 'Hmm. No. I do believe I have already mentioned Clause One of this contract you had your solicitors draw up – duly signed, I should add, by all those Farrells concerned. Now, this clause states that, upon the immediate birth of an heir, my daughter is to be committed to a mental asylum far away from here and all association with the Farrells is to be completely erased.' He lifted his brows sardonically as his eyes shifted to the countess.

Frederick began to emit an extraordinary strangled sound, but no one paid him the slightest heed, all attention being focused on the exchange between the countess and Lord Hamilton.

'That contract!' exclaimed Lady Farrell. 'How in God's name did you get that?'

Lord Hamilton shot her a satirical smile. 'It came to my person this morning, ma'am. Although I must say, quite why you committed your evil intentions to paper is beyond me.'

'Because one can never be too careful regarding matters of such importance, Lord Hamilton,' she blurted out. 'One never knows when one may lose the use of one's faculties. And we Farrells are of such a weak disposition that absolutely anything could strike any one of us at any moment. Why, if I were to have a stroke tomorrow, I might well lose my power of speech.'

'Oh, and how upset we would all be were that to happen,' remarked Lord Hamilton sarcastically. 'But, unfortunately for us, it is not your speech which has already deserted you, ma'am, but your sense of right and wrong.'

The countess bristled. 'We Farrells have a stronger sense of right and wrong than most, sir.'

'Oh, I beg to differ, ma'am,' retorted Lord Hamilton. 'Let us, for example, consider Clause Two of the contract where, with my daughter duly disposed of, Frederick is to marry his cousin Felicia-Sophia who, one can assume from this, is not able to produce children of her own.'

'The poor girl suffered a dreadful illness in childhood,' she muttered, shifting awkwardly in her seat. 'It is not her fault, sir, if she is unable to provide us with an heir.'

'Indeed it is not her fault, ma'am. Nor is it any fault of the Hamiltons. That small fact, however, does not appear to have affected your plans at all, given that Clause Three of the contract states' – he turned his attention back to the piece of paper, holding it up to eye-level once again – 'ah – yes – that once Frederick has married Charlotte, he is to do everything in his power – including permitting no financial assistance at all – to force us Hamiltons from our home in order that Perdita – and whichever poor wet goose she weds – may remove here.'

'She was very taken with the house, sir,' chipped in Frederick with misplaced adroitness.

Lord Hamilton flashed him a look dripping with incredulity. 'Oh, I see. Then please do forgive me, my lord. Had I known that Perdita was very taken with our home, then we should have volunteered to remove from it immediately. After all, it appears that the wishes of the Farrells must be adhered to at whatever cost to us.'

The countess heaved a breathy sigh. 'You seem to forget, sir, that the Farrells are one of England's most distinguished families. You have not the first idea of the burden one feels belonging to such an esteemed lineage; the pressures it places upon us. Our plans, as ruthless as you appear to consider them, were purely for the benefit of our heritage.

There are times, sir, when sacrifices must be made for the sake of one's family.'

'And the Hamiltons were to be that sacrifice,' spat Lord Hamilton.

'The truth is,' she continued, 'that were Frederick not to produce an heir, then our entire fortune would end up in the hands of my late husband's brother and the whore he chose to marry. Together they have produced a child who is little better than a gutter urchin. I am sure even you can understand that we simply could not allow that to happen. I had little choice but to take it upon myself to safeguard our interests.'

'But wh-why me?' asked Charlotte, unable to take in all she was hearing.

The countess turned her head to her. 'You are not, on the whole, a disagreeable-looking chit, Charlotte, and, as you are aware, good looks have always prevailed amongst the Farrells. We also considered the fact that, as you had played quite an insignificant role in Society up until our association, your eventual disappearance from our circles would not cause a great deal of concern.'

Lord Hamilton emitted a snort of anger.

'I can assure you, sir, that I had only my family's best interests at heart,' she professed.

'Oh really?' proclaimed Lord Hamilton, now visibly seething. 'Well then, I can assure you that I have only my family's best interests at heart, Lady Farrell, when I order you and your pathetic, whinging son, out of my house this instant. And if you ever come within a mile of me or any member of my family, I can also assure you that I shall take matters into my own hands and that will most definitely put an end to your particular branch of Farrells.'

Frederick gasped loudly, clasping an emaciated hand to his throat. 'Why, I have never been spoken to so in all my—'

'Out!' roared Lord Hamilton, so ferociously that Harriet emitted a terrified whimper.

'Come along, Frederick,' ushered the countess, rising majestically to her feet. 'I refuse to stay here a minute longer with this man and his … his … *hair*. How we could, for one moment, have considered his daughter as a possible—'

'Enough!' bellowed Lord Hamilton, yanking Frederick's bony form from its chair. Grasping both him and his mother by their puny arms, the old man proceeded to drag them from the room. Charlotte, who had been standing all the while just inside the door, whipped it open. With the unwelcome visitors being thus removed from the premises, she all but staggered around to the fireside chair Frederick had so recently vacated and flopped into it. Harriet, clearly astounded by the revelations, gaped open-mouthed. It was left to Dr Leigh, still occupying his spot in front of the window, to break the silence. He addressed his words to Charlotte.

'May I suggest, ma'am, that you change out of that wet dress immediately, before you catch your death of cold.'

Charlotte met his eyes. 'Oh, believe me, Doctor,' she replied evenly, 'you do not have to threaten me with death to persuade me to change out of *this* dress.'

As Charlotte lay in bed that night, her mind awhirl with the day's events, she could scarce believe that her fantasy had come true – almost. The Courteous Criminal had rescued her from a fate the equivalent of life imprisonment – albeit in more salubrious surroundings. Yet, although she would never be able to thank the man enough for permitting her escape, only half of her fantasy had been realized. He had not taken her away with him. He had left her to wind her weary way back to Hamilton Manor where she and her family were now faced with the same problems which had hung over them before Frederick Farrell's proposal.

Although she had followed the wishes of the Courteous Criminal and said nothing to her father about his identity, Charlotte had confessed her knowledge to the old man of their financial situation during their discussion in the barn. Tears had streamed down his face when he had discovered that his daughter had been prepared to throw away her entire future for the sake of her family. He had spent a great deal of time remonstrating with himself about how he had failed to discern her true feelings. But Charlotte had assured him it was no fault of his own. She had been committed to her fate and determined to allow no one a hint of her sentiments. Lord Hamilton had gone on to assure his daughter that they would find another solution to their money problems.

Charlotte had appeared to accept this assurance, but, deep within her, the worry of what was going to happen to them all now, continued to fester like a gangrenous wound.

Chapter Twenty-five

PREDICTING a stream of curious visitors to the house the following day, Charlotte escaped as soon as she could, riding out in the direction of Murphy's Mansion. Here, too, she knew she would be faced with a barrage of questions – particularly from the ever-inquisitive Becky – but these, at least, would revolve around a genuine concern for her welfare rather than providing new fodder for the gossip-grabbing tabbies.

Although still grey and cool, the rain, which had continued well into the night, had at last stopped. In its wake was a trail of sodden evidence, the roads littered with murky puddles and the pulp of battered autumn leaves. As Charlotte drew nearer to the house, she was amazed to see no trace of the children outside. They were not in the main living area either, she discovered, as she pushed open the door to the cottage. The sound of low mumbling, caused a pang of apprehension to pulse through her. Nervously, she made her way towards the room at the back of the property from whence it had come. The sight there did nothing to ease her anxiety. All five children were huddled around Harry's makeshift crib, tears streaming down their faces.

'Whatever is amiss?' she asked, as all five grave little faces turned towards her.

'It's Harry, miss,' sniffed Emmy. 'He's not well and we don't know what to do.'

Panic swept over Charlotte. 'Let me see him,' she asserted, much more confidently than she was feeling.

She walked over to the crib with shaking legs. Harry was lying atop a white sheet, wearing nothing but a clean white vest and nappy. His eyes were closed; the rise and fall of his little ribcage providing the only clue that he was alive. Charlotte laid her hand upon his brow. In spite of the fact that the child was deathly pale, she found his skin to be burning hot.

'It's serious, isn't it, miss?' said Emmy, desperation filling her eyes. 'He's going to die, isn't he?'

'Not if I can help it,' replied Charlotte, sprinting from the room.

If ever Charlotte had needed a sign that there was a God, it was presented to her on a silver salver the moment she clattered up the drive to Hamilton Manor and found Dr Leigh on the verge of leaving. He was untying his gig from the post at the side of the house. Hearing her approach, he stopped and turned towards her. His countenance shifted seamlessly from surprise to concern as he sensed Charlotte's panic.

'Good lord, woman, whatever is it now?' he demanded.

'There is another emergency, Doctor,' she panted, bringing Victor to a halt in front of him. 'The baby at the cottage.'

The doctor's brows snapped together. 'Little Harry?'

Unable to catch her breath, Charlotte nodded her head. 'He has a fever.'

Re-tying the gig, the doctor began running towards the stables. 'Go back to the cottage and tell them I am on my way,' he shouted over his shoulder.

Back at Murphy's Mansion, Charlotte found that the sobbing had not subsided. In her already fragile state, she felt more than a little inclined to join in. But she could not. For the children's sake, she had to be strong.

'The doctor is on his way,' she informed them.

Becky sniffed and swiped the tears from her cheeks with the back of her tiny hand. 'I think he might be too late, miss.'

Steeling herself, Charlotte peeped into the crib. Harry's chest was barely moving. Fear clawed at her as she realized Becky could be right. No longer having the strength to fight them, tears began rolling down her face at the same moment as the door crashed open and in stormed Dr Leigh. Without saying a word, he marched over to Harry. The other children scuttled out of the way to allow him access. Upon reaching the tot, he placed his hand over the child's chest.

'He's hanging on, but we must act quickly,' he announced. They all watched in amazement as then he strode over to one of the beds and whipped off a brown blanket. Scooping up Harry he pressed both the child and the blanket to his chest. 'Tie this tightly around my back,' he ordered Charlotte. 'I'm taking him with me.'

Shaking, Charlotte did as he requested. No sooner had she tied off the knot than the doctor was heading towards the door.

'I'm coming with you,' she cried.

The doctor did not reply, but swung himself and Harry into the saddle of his borrowed horse and spurred the animal on.

They rode for twenty minutes before the doctor steered his mount off the main road. Charlotte followed him closely, just as she had done the entire journey. Her anxiety for Harry was mixed with a growing curiosity as to where they were going. They entered the drive of an old manor house. Charlotte noticed that the once grand gates of the property were covered in rust and the lawns either side of the drive were overgrown and peppered with weeds. Even the house, although it too had obviously been stately in its day, had now sunk into a state of disrepair. A horrific image of Hamilton Manor in just such an abandoned state in a few years' time, flashed through her mind. She swiftly banished the picture. For the moment, at least, there was something of much more import to consider: little Harry's life.

Halting at the bottom of the steps which led up to the shabby porticoed entrance, the doctor leaped down from his saddle, taking care all the while to support his unsuspecting load. In a flash, Charlotte too had dismounted and was bounding up the steps after him, filled with apprehension about what she was to discover inside. She could not have been more surprised.

Contrary to the neglected aura the building emitted from the outside, inside it was sparkling clean and full of ordered hustle and bustle. The entrance, with its gleaming black-and-white chequered floor, had several corridors leading off it and a large branching staircase in the middle.

'Wait here,' ordered the doctor. Still clutching Harry to his chest, he darted towards one of the corridors.

Her head spinning with questions, there was no time for Charlotte to voice a single one before he disappeared. Regaining a little of her composure, she decided to seek her answers elsewhere. A stout woman, dressed in a plain grey gown and white apron was marching purposefully across the hall. Charlotte caught her attention.

'Excuse me, ma'am. This may sound rather, er, odd, but do you mind telling me where I am?'

The woman flashed her an ingenuous smile. 'Why, you're at Ranleigh Hospital, ma'am.'

Charlotte furrowed her brow. 'Ranleigh Hospital? And is this where a Dr Daniel Leigh works?'

The woman's smile stretched into a broad grin. 'Oh, he does more than work here, miss: it's his hospital. Set it up from nothing, so he has. A veritable saint – that's what that man is.'

Charlotte's eyes grew wide.

'That's not to say, mind,' continued the woman, shaking her head, 'that it's not sometimes mayhem here. But, even though we complain, none of us would change it for the world. Why, whatever would happen to the sick around here if it weren't for Dr Leigh? It does not bear thinking about.'

'No,' whispered an awe-struck Charlotte. 'It certainly does not.'

Charlotte had no idea how long she had been sitting on one of the wooden chairs scattered around the walls of the entrance hall. She knew only that it must have been several hours because of the fading light outside. The constant stream of activity had at least served to provide her with some distraction while she waited. It had also made her wonder at the obvious efficiency of the hospital. For all the never-ending bustle, it was apparent that everyone knew exactly where they were going and for what purpose. She had watched in admiration as the same woman she had spoken to earlier appeared with a scruffy, smiling toddler in her arms. The child's mother, some years younger than Charlotte and caked in dirt had sobbed with gratitude as she reclaimed the infant. Then there had been the appearance on the doorstep of a scrawny, ragged boy, on the verge of collapse. In his arms he was carrying a frail, wizened old woman with a racking cough. No sooner had the pair entered the building, than they were whisked away by another member of the caring staff.

Charlotte observed all of this in amazement. Her only experience of doctors thus far had been within the comfort of her own home. Of course she had known places like this existed, but, until she had walked through the doors, she had not fully appreciated their need. Were it not for places like Ranleigh Hospital, then these people, and hundreds more like them, would lie suffering in the streets or dying in the gutter.

She caught sight of Dr Leigh coming towards her. He looked both exhausted and earnest. With growing trepidation, Charlotte raised her eyes to his as he stopped in front of her.

'How is he, Doctor?' she ventured, in a wavering voice.

'Much improved,' replied the physician, peering down at her. 'He is definitely over the worst, but I think it best he remains here for a few days, until he is completely recovered.'

Flooded with relief, Charlotte experienced a crushing urge to jump out of her seat and fling her arms around the man. In view of his brusque tone, however, she quelled it. 'I shall never be able to thank you enough for what you have done, Doctor. And I know the child's family will feel the same.'

The doctor said nothing, but continued to stare at her.

'Please do allow me to pay for Harry's treatment,' she added. 'It is the very least I can do.'

Still he said nothing.

Charlotte was beginning to feel extremely discomfited by his cool manner. 'Er, well,' she muttered, rising to her feet, 'I am sure the family will be desperate for news. I shall go to them at once.'

He nodded his head briefly. Eager now to escape his strange manner, Charlotte flashed him a grateful smile before taking her leave of him. She was halfway across the hall when he called her name. She turned to face him.

'I would be grateful, Lady Charlotte,' he said levelly, 'if you would refrain from mentioning this hospital to anyone of your acquaintance.'

Charlotte gazed at him, astounded. How could he fail to be proud of such an achievement? Surely he should want the whole world to know about it. But then she recalled Dr Reuss. Had he not mentioned that the successful Daniel Leigh was noted for his modesty?

'If that is your wish, Doctor,' she rejoined, with an understanding smile.

'It is,' he replied, with no smile at all.

Even with Victor almost flying through the air, it seemed to take Charlotte an eternity to reach Murphy's Mansion. When she did at last arrive, it was to find the family exactly where she had left them several hours earlier. Emmy was clutching one of Harry's blankets. All five little faces were white with anxiety.

'He is out of danger,' announced Charlotte. 'He is going to be fine.'

Their tears began again but this time, for a quite different reason.

Observing Dr Leigh's request, Charlotte had not mentioned Ranleigh Hospital to anyone at Hamilton Manor. The man's competent dealings with Harry and the revelation of his thriving medical venture had served only to deepen her esteem for him. All her previous anger at his meddling in her personal affairs had long melted and she could not now help but feel a little flattered by the concern he had shown her. Now that her father had informed him of her motives for wishing to marry Frederick Farrell, she had hoped that the doctor would understand; that he would not think her callous and that he would forgive her discourteous behaviour towards him. She had even hoped that the two of them could become friends – although quite how one handled having such an attractive male friend she had not the first idea. But the physician had evidently neither understood nor forgiven her. His continuing cool and distant behaviour towards her left Charlotte feeling both dejected and hurt. And she had no idea what to do about it.

Charlotte was sitting with Edward the following day when the doctor paid a call. Her heart fluttered upon seeing him. She attempted a cheery 'Good afternoon, sir.' But the doctor did nothing more than incline his head to her. Charlotte's disappointment was quickly overtaken by irritation. Why was she allowing the man to make her feel like this? What did it matter what his opinion was of her? After all, had she not coped perfectly well without the friendship of Daniel Leigh for the last one-and-twenty years? She could cope just as well for the next one-and-twenty. But, to her growing frustration, she realized that she had no wish to.

At the doctor's arrival, she was conscious of the easy, relaxed atmosphere in Edward's bedchamber shifting to one of intense awkwardness. Fortunately, her brother did not appear to notice. No longer cognisant of how to act around the physician, Charlotte was grateful when he disappeared into the bathroom, mumbling something about rinsing out some bottles. Mere seconds later, a breathless Harriet bowled into the room. Still wearing her pelisse and bonnet, her cheeks were flushed with excitement and her eyes bright.

'Good lord, Harriet, whatever has happened?' asked Charlotte.

'Oh, you will never guess, Charlotte. Not even if we sat here for weeks,' gushed the younger girl. She plumped down on the end of Edward's bed and began fiddling with the ribbons of her bonnet.

'Well, if we shall never guess, then hurry up and tell us,' ordered Edward.

'Very well then,' said Harriet. 'It is to do with … Mirabelle.'

'Mirabelle?' echoed Edward. 'What of her?'

Harriet took a deep breath before announcing, on a long exhalation, 'Her carriage was held up yesterday evening, by … the Courteous Criminal.'

From the bathroom came the sound of breaking glass. All eyes swivelled around, but they could see nothing of the doctor. Charlotte's stomach, meanwhile, was lurching. She had had no news of the Courteous Criminal since her fateful wedding day, although that fact had not prevented the man from occupying her thoughts both day and night. A million questions sprang into her mind but she found she could voice none of them. It was left to her brother to pursue the matter.

'The Courteous Criminal?' repeated Edward. 'But whatever did he do to Mirabelle?'

Harriet tugged off her bonnet. 'It is too ghastly for words, Edward,' she declared, shaking out her curls. 'Poor Mirabelle was travelling home alone from a visit to her Aunt Mabel, when, all at once, the Courteous Criminal, dressed in his usual black, with his blue cravat, appeared before her driver and ordered the coach to a halt.' She paused for breath, her brother and sister eyeing her impatiently. Charlotte was aware of the increasing pounding of her heart.

'Well,' continued Harriet, 'the man then demanded that Mirabelle step out of the carriage and ordered her driver and her footman to drive on. He said that if either of them breathed a word of what was happening, then he would not think twice about killing Mirabelle.'

Charlotte's eyes grew wide.

'But what did he do with her?' demanded Edward. 'Did he take her jewels?'

Harriet nodded her head. 'But not only that, Edward. He was perfectly horrid to her.'

'Horrid?' gasped Charlotte. 'But I–I cannot believe that he—'

'Oh, I know you found him perfectly charming, Charlotte,' interjected Harriet, 'but he was not at all charming to Mirabelle. Do you have any idea what he did?'

Edward and Charlotte shook their heads.

Harriet's already grave countenance grew more earnest still. 'He ordered her to remove her pelisse and her boots and stockings, then he made her wade waist-deep into the river – which, of course, was perfectly freezing – and told her to put her head under the water and count to ten.'

Charlotte's mouth dropped open while Edward released a snort of laughter. 'Is that all?'

Harriet shook her head. 'Indeed it is not, Brother. He then ordered the poor girl out of the water – Mirabelle, of course, was both dripping wet and shivering with cold – and do you know what he then did?'

Her audience shook their heads again.

Harriet clasped a hand to her chest. 'He produced a bag of garden worms and emptied them down her chemise.'

Charlotte gawped in amazement. She could scarce believe what she was hearing. As much as she disliked Mirabelle, she could imagine having a load of garden worms wriggling about in one's dripping wet undergarments would not be at all pleasant. But Harriet had not yet finished.

'And then,' she ploughed on, 'he produced a pair of scissors and cut off all of Mirabelle's hair.'

Charlotte's hands flew to her mouth. 'He didn't!'

'He did.'

'Hah!' roared Edward, tears of laughter rolling down his face. 'That is the funniest thing I have heard for an age. Mirabelle McGregor, dripping wet, with no hair, no shoes and a chemise full of wriggling worms.'

Despite her initial horror at the tale, Charlotte's lips began tugging upwards.

Harriet, however, was not in the least amused. 'It is not funny in the slightest, Edward. Mirabelle is in such shock that she can scarcely speak. It was left to her poor mother to relate the tale to me. You can imagine how upset she was when she saw her daughter standing at the door in such a pitiful state.'

'You don't mean to say that Mirabelle had then to walk all the way home like that?' guffawed Edward.

Harriet nodded. 'Indeed she did, Edward.'

'Hah!' roared Edward, collapsing into fits of laughter, just as Dr Leigh came out of the bathroom.

With this latest shocking tale of her hero spreading through the county, Charlotte could still not find it within herself to believe that the man who had stolen her heart, had treated Mirabelle McGregor in such an appalling fashion. She could only surmise that, whoever he was, Mirabelle must, in her own inimitable fashion, have offended him in some way. She did not have long to ponder the mystery.

Two days later, Charlotte, Harriet and her father were sitting around the breakfast-table when Adams brought in a copy of *The Times*.

'Good God!' exclaimed Lord Hamilton, spluttering steaming hot coffee all over the white tablecloth as his eyes fell upon the headline.

'What is it, Father?' asked Harriet, smearing a knob of butter over her toast.

Holding the paper up before him, the old man shook his head in disbelief as he scanned the front page. 'The Runners have only gone and caught the Courteous Criminal,' he announced.

No sooner had the words left his mouth, than Charlotte's head began to swim.

Harriet set down her knife and picked up her slice of toast. 'Oh, do tell us who it is, Father?'

Lord Hamilton put down the paper and turned to face his youngest daughter. 'I think you will find, Harriet,' he declared, looking more than a little stunned, 'that it is someone with whom our family is very well acquainted.'

Harriet's toast stopped mid-way to her mouth. Charlotte, meanwhile, who had never before experienced a fit of the vapours, felt seriously close to doing so now.

'Who, Father?' demanded the younger girl.

'I can hardly believe it,' intoned the old man. 'And nor will you, I am sure. You will never guess if we were to sit here for an entire week.'

'Then tell us, Father,' urged Harriet, in an uncharacteristically assertive tone.

'Very well, then,' said Lord Hamilton. 'The Courteous Criminal is the man known to us all as … Bertie McGregor.'

Harriet's slice of toast fell to the floor, accompanied, a moment later, by her elder sister.

Charlotte had been lying on her bed for over five hours. As soon as she had recovered from her fainting fit, she escaped to her room, threw herself on the bed and cried until she was drained of tears. She could scarce believe that the man who aroused such feelings of passion within her and who occupied her thoughts for so many hours, was the odious Bertie McGregor. Of course, having given the matter much thought, it all now made perfect sense. Had Bertie not always harboured a *tendre* for her; had he not admitted to them all that he would like to be remembered for some feat; and was it not his father's law firm who acted on behalf of the Farrells, allowing the man easy access to the countess's legal documents? With the revelation of his identity, Charlotte now knew that the highwayman she dreamed of was nothing more than a fantasy figure. But that realization was of little consolation; the news that it was Bertie McGregor left her completely and utterly devastated.

Daniel was exhausted. It was five days now since he had received the letter and it had taken him precisely that length of time to absorb the news.

He slowed his horse to a trot as he approached the castle. It looked exactly as he remembered it when he had last seen it almost ten years ago. Perched on the end of a rugged cliff, it reigned over the surrounding area with an air of grace and superiority. At the entrance, he slid down from the saddle and handed the reins to the waiting groom.

The door was thrust open by another familiar sight: Carstairs, the family butler. He too had changed little since Daniel had seen him last. His frame was as rotund as ever and his thick dark hair in the same style in which he had always worn it – albeit a little greyer around the temples.

As the servant greeted him, Daniel's eyes darted about the enormous, wood-panelled entrance hall. Nothing at all appeared to have changed; the place even smelt the same with its distinctive mixture of polished wood and centuries of dust.

The butler informed him that his meeting was to take place in the yellow drawing-room. As Daniel marched along the maze of corridors, he noted the wall of family portraits, the hanging tapestries, the wooden chests and the Persian rugs – all a little more worn and faded than he remembered, but all in their usual places.

He reached the drawing-room and pushed open the door, ready to learn his fate.

Chapter Twenty-six

CHARLOTTE was alone in the library at Hamilton Manor. So absorbed was she in her melancholy, that she did not at first hear the knocking at the door. Upon bidding the person enter, her heart skipped a beat when she saw who it was.

'Oh,' she gasped. 'Doctor Leigh.'

To her great chagrin, however, the doctor did not appear the least bit pleased to see her. He offered her a bow as he came to stand before her.

'May I sit down, ma'am?' he asked, in a completely neutral tone.

'Oh. Of, er, course,' spluttered Charlotte. 'Please do.' Her heart began pounding as he lowered himself into the wing chair opposite hers. What on earth did he wish to speak to her about? Given the steely look on his face, she had the distinct impression that he was about to chastise her for something. But what? She had, just as he had bid, made no mention of Ranleigh Hospital to anyone, and if he was to accuse her of doing so, she would—

'May I enquire as to your health, ma'am?'

So that was it. Her father, concerned about how low her spirits were of late, had sent the physician to examine her.

'My health is very well, thank you, Doctor,' she replied, matter-of-factly.

She met his gaze. A swarm of butterflies began fluttering inside her. Yet, at precisely the same time, a tide of disappointment washed over her – disappointment that he had not come because he wished to see her, but purely at the request of her father. Well, she would not allow him to affect her so. She lifted her chin to him. 'You may tell my father, Doctor, that there is no need for him to worry about me. I own I have not been in the best of spirits lately, but I am certainly not in need of any medical attention.'

He regarded her levelly. 'I am not here at your father's request, ma'am,' he professed.

Taken aback, Charlotte raised her brows. 'Oh,' she muttered, wondering then, why he was there.

Several seconds' silence stretched between them.

'I, er, imagine the news regarding Bertie McGregor must have come as a great shock to you,' he suddenly announced.

Charlotte nodded, as tears pricked at her eyes. 'You could say that,' she murmured.

'I have heard that, due to his father's connections, the man is to be sent abroad rather than face trial.'

'So, I believe,' replied Charlotte. Her eyes moved to the flames of the fire and her thoughts, yet again, to the fanciful highwayman. A sudden image of Bertie McGregor pushed them aside. How could she ever have—

'I have been to see little Harry,' piped up the doctor. 'He is doing very well indeed.'

Grateful for the change of subject, Charlotte turned her head to the physician. 'None of us can ever thank you enough for what you did for Harry, Doctor,' she said, with a genial smile.

'I was merely doing my job, ma'am,' he replied, with noticeable diffidence.

Looking at him, Charlotte's heart swelled with something she did not at first identify. 'Then may I say how well you do it, sir,' she rejoined, as colour flooded her cheeks.

Their eyes met again. The butterflies in her stomach increased their fluttering. She had almost forgotten just how handsome Dr Leigh was. With a pang of embarrassment, she recalled how badly she had treated him before her inauspicious wedding day. Little wonder he had not forgiven her.

'I would, er, like to apologize to you, Doctor,' she began, the colour in her cheeks deepening.

'Whatever for?' he asked, raising his brows to her.

Charlotte diverted her eyes back to the fire. 'For the, er, appalling way I treated you when you were attempting to persuade me to change my mind regarding my marriage to Frederick Farrell. It was very ungracious of me.'

'I can assure you, no apology is necessary, ma'am,' he replied.

'Oh, but it is,' countered Charlotte, turning to him once more. 'My behaviour was quite unforgivable. I do hope, however, that having learned of my reasons, you do not think me heartless in any way.'

Her eyes moved from his and down to his lips, which were smiling at her in such a seductive manner, that it was all she could do not to reach across and kiss him.

'I do not think you the least bit heartless, Lady Charlotte,' he affirmed. 'Your reasons were highly commendable.'

'Do you really think so?' she asked, as relief began seeping through her. 'It's just that your behaviour towards me since the wedding day has been—'

'Has been what?'

'I thought that you— That is, I had hoped we could be—'

The doctor leaned towards her, his expression once again grave. 'I received a letter just after your wedding day, Charlotte,' he informed her. 'Since then, I have had a great deal on my mind – not least of all, you.'

'Me?' gasped Charlotte. 'But why should I—'

'I have to confess that I have not been completely honest with you,' he continued.

Charlotte wrinkled her forehead. 'Not completely honest? But whatever do you—'

'My name is not Daniel Leigh; it is Daniel Brandon.'

Charlotte looked completely nonplussed. 'Daniel Brandon?'

'Daniel Brandon, Duke of Ranleigh.'

Charlotte's jaw dropped. 'You are a *duke*? But I don't understand.'

The doctor shook his head. 'I can scarcely understand it all myself, Charlotte. I inherited the title the day of my father's death – the day after you were due to be married.'

This revelation did little to aid Charlotte's comprehension of what he was attempting to tell her.

'But-but if you are a member of the aristocracy, why ever are you practising medicine?' she asked.

'I'm afraid it is rather a long story, ma'am.' He turned his eyes to the fire. 'It all happened ten years ago when I informed my father that I should like to follow a career in medicine. I should explain, Lady Charlotte, that my father was a very clever man, an exceptionally clever man, in fact. Up until that point in my life, I had always accepted his decisions without question. For the most part, they were quite brilliant – with the exception of his decision to throw out his one and only son.'

Charlotte emitted an audible gasp, but the doctor did not look at her. He appeared to be lost in thought as he stared into the flames.

'As a young man, I had felt increasingly stifled by my father's strict control. I yearned to follow a career I believed in with a passion. But, in my father's eyes, I had only two roles in life – to run the family estate and to secure the Brandon succession.'

Although he now seemed oblivious to her presence, Charlotte nodded her head to indicate she was still listening.

'Once I had summoned the courage to inform my father of my decision, he was furious. In fact, even now, I have never seen a man so angry. He could not comprehend why, as he put it, I should wish to devote myself to saving the lives of sick, thankless peasants—'

He broke off, obviously picturing the scene.

'We argued constantly for two weeks before he offered me an ultimatum: I either forgot, what he called, my fanciful notions of medicine, or I forgot about my title and fortune.'

His gaze moved to Charlotte. 'You know, of course, which one I chose.'

Charlotte felt her eyes brimming with tears and her heart swelling once again – with what she now knew was love. She had first thought this man remarkable several weeks ago, but the more she learned of him, the more she not only admired him, but the more she loved him. It occurred to her that she had been fighting this love throughout most of their acquaintance. Refused to even acknowledge it. Convinced that it was the highwayman who had stolen her heart, she had not allowed herself to recognize her feelings for Daniel Leigh. But she no longer wished to fight them or ignore them. She loved this man with all her heart. But a bolt of sudden panic lanced through her. Why was he telling her all of this? There could be only one reason: he was going away, away to his estate, and she would never see him again. Now completely focused on this heartbreaking thought, what he said next, threw her into complete turmoil.

'I had thought, Charlotte, that upon my banishment from my home, my father would subsequently disown me. I was fully prepared for this, having little interest in titles and money. But, to my immense surprise, he did not. When he died I learned that he has not only bequeathed me his title, but the entire estate.'

As he broke out into a smile, a lone tear trickled down Charlotte's cheek. 'And you are come to tell me that you are now going to Ranleigh – to assume your new role?' she asked, steeling herself for his answer.

'No,' he replied, taking both of her hands in his. 'I am come to ask you to marry me, Charlotte.'

Charlotte's heart skipped several beats. Another tear escaped her. 'To-to marry you?' Now her lips curled upwards.

'I love you, Charlotte. I believe I have loved you from the moment I saw you in your riding breeches. Please say you'll marry me. I promise you I will take care of all your family. They will never have to worry about money ever again.'

Charlotte's head began to swim. He loved her and he wanted to marry her. This brilliant, handsome – and now rich – man, wanted to marry her. Her acceptance was on her lips. She opened her mouth to speak but no words came out. Instead, a picture of a masked highwayman, dressed all in black, with a blue silk kerchief about his face, flashed before her eyes. How could she possibly marry this extraordinary man when she was still harbouring such a fantasy; when it was unlikely that, as much as she loved him, even Daniel Leigh would be able to instil such passionate feelings within her?

He was looking at her now with an intensity which burned through to her core. Overcome with suffocation, Charlotte pulled her hands from his and rose to her feet.

'I am sorry, Dr Leigh,' she announced. 'But I cannot marry you.' And on that note, she flew from the room as fast as her legs would carry her.

Chapter Twenty-seven

WITH the exception of her brief acquaintance with the Farrells, Charlotte had never felt so miserable in her entire life. Three days had passed now since Daniel's proposal and she had seen nothing of him since. Edward's injuries were much improved and he was now allowed out of his room to hobble about on crutches.

Yesterday she had paid a visit to little Harry who was thriving. She had even taken along Kate Tomms, who had instantly taken a shine to the family and they to her – particularly when Kate had promised to visit again the following day with two of Mrs Tomms's meat 'n' potato pies.

Harriet informed her that Mirabelle and her family were to remove to Ireland. Following the incident with Bertie, they were understandably keen to distance themselves from the scandal which looked unlikely to die down for some time.

The marriage of Frederick Farrell to Felicia-Sophia Farrell was announced in *The Morning Post* that day. The wedding, so the paper informed, was likely to take place at Spa, where the family were taking the waters. They were, so it went on, unlikely to return to England for quite some time. Charlotte felt nothing but relief when her father read the announcement to her: she had no desire to set eyes on any Farrells again for as long as she lived.

The same, however, could not be said with regard to Daniel. She was, in fact, consumed with yearning for the man. She had no idea how used she had become to his presence in the house. And she was not the only one – her father, sister and, particularly Edward, all commented on how much they were missing his company.

Charlotte said nothing of the marriage proposal to her father and nor, evidently, had the doctor. He had, however, sent word that he had been called away on a family matter and did not know when he would return. To this end, Lord Hamilton employed a stout little nurse to attend to Edward. For all Charlotte had seen little of the woman, she had noticed that, since her arrival, there was a remarkable change in Adams, the butler. Yesterday, she even caught him humming to himself – on two separate occasions.

But while Adams's mood was taking a noticeable upward shift, Charlotte's was on the decline. As her father read out the contents of the doctor's note, she felt as though a knife were twisting inside her. Why had she not pushed aside the thoughts of the fantasy highwayman and accepted the doctor's proposal? Not only would she be marrying the man she loved, but, as the doctor himself had observed, the marriage would solve all her family's financial problems. But she loved him too much not to give him all of herself and, as much as she knew it was ridiculous, part of her heart still belonged to the fictitious character she had created in her mind.

So low were Charlotte's spirits that even a ride on Victor that morning failed to raise them. She was trotting miserably down a country lane, flanked on either side by thick gorse bushes, when she became aware of a figure riding towards her. Her blood froze in her veins when she saw that the man was dressed all in black, with a blue silk kerchief covering the lower part of his face. She drew Victor to a stop as her mind began racing. How on earth had Bertie McGregor—?

He drew his horse alongside hers.

Charlotte gaped at him. 'Wh-what on-on earth are you doing here, Bertie? We heard that you had been sent—'

She stopped as the man reached inside his cape and held out something to her. Her eyes grew wide as saucers when she saw what it was.

'My mother's necklace,' she gasped, accepting it from him. 'But how did you—?' Her eyes shifted from the pearls to the man at the very moment he removed his mask and hat.

'Doctor Leigh!' she exclaimed, as a million emotions began surging through her. 'But I–I don't understand.'

'I'm not surprised,' said the doctor, with a shy smile. 'Will you permit me to explain?'

Stunned, it was all Charlotte could do to nod her head.

'During my time away from Ranleigh Castle, Charlotte,' he began, 'my father denied me so much as a penny. I was desperate to set up the hospital but did not have the means to do so. I tried to obtain the money legitimately, but every avenue I pursued was closed to me – my father had seen to that. And so I turned to the only method available: crime. I robbed the rich to aid the poor. I took their jewels, sold them and used the proceeds to fund the hospital.'

'But you-you didn't sell my necklace,' stammered Charlotte.

'How could I when I knew how much it meant to you?' said the doctor, his smile widening into a broad beam. 'But, given my reputation, it would have looked a little odd if I had not taken it. Don't you agree?'

'I do, sir,' concurred Charlotte, her own lips now curving upwards. But the smile soon disappeared from her face as another thought struck her. 'But what of Bertie McGregor, Doctor? Has the man been wrongly arrested?' She pressed a hand to her chest. 'Pray, do not tell me that you have allowed an innocent man to take the blame for your actions.'

'You should know me better than that, Charlotte,' he intoned. 'Poor Bertie McGregor in desperation to achieve some kind of status – however notorious – took it upon himself to impersonate the Courteous Criminal. He carried out several attacks under my alias – including the one on his sister. You can imagine my surprise when I heard that there had been more hold-ups by the infamous highwayman, when I had been safely tucked up in my bed at Wetherington.'

Another shocking thought occurred to her as she recalled the intimacy between them during the incident with the band of outlaws. 'Was it you who rescued me from the ruffians, sir?'

'It was,' he said, beaming at her again as he jumped down from his horse. 'Although it took me a great deal of restraint not to tell you off for your irresponsible behaviour that evening.'

Charlotte blushed.

'And, if you are in any doubt, it was also I who sabotaged your wedding day. I overheard the countess and Frederick speaking of their plan the night before. As you know, I was against the marriage from the very start but, discovering what I did, I decided there was absolutely no way I could allow you to marry the damned popinjay. And so I searched the house the entire night looking for some proof of their intentions.'

Charlotte took a second to digest all this information before saying, 'I shall never be able to thank you enough for what you did for me, Dr Leigh. But I want you to have this necklace. My mother would have wanted you to have it – for such an admirable cause.'

'Oh, Charlotte. I don't need it now,' he laughed, as she slipped down from her saddle and into his waiting arms. 'With the money my father has left me, I have more than enough to improve the hospital. Perhaps even set up one or two more – with you to help me, as my wife. Will you marry me, Charlotte?'

Charlotte wrapped her arms around his waist and pressed her head to his chest. 'It would be my greatest honour to accept, sir,' she declared, delighting in the faint smell of his cologne. 'As long as you promise me not to carry out any more hold-ups.'

'You have my word,' he promised. 'I shall push aside all my criminal tendencies and concentrate on being a good and dutiful husband.'

'And I shall do my best to be a good and dutiful wife, sir,' she professed. 'Although I am afraid I know nothing of medicine or—'

'No, my love,' he said, raising his hand to her chin and tilting it upwards. 'But you know a great deal about flat fish and who knows when that may come in useful?'